Daithidh

Daithidh MacEochaidh — [obscured] the tongue as easily as cold cement — is a self-proclaimed master of Dirty Surrealism and an illiterary phenomenon of his own deconstruction: short story hack, plagiarising poet, novelist of nonsense and a tidy man at the bar skittles. This Tourettic Troubadour's greatest ambition is to write a *Mills and Boom* best seller, but will settle for a tall, handsome stranger and a box of Milk Tray. He is not married, but is working on it assiduously. He has no children, but once kept tropical fish. His psychiatrist hopes that this will be his last publication. She is not alone. Please see inside for details.

First Published in 2000 by route
School Lane, Glasshoughton, West Yorks, WF10 4QH
e-mail: books@route-online.com

ISBN: 1 901927 07 5

Copyright © Daithidh MacEochaidh

Editor: Kath Murphy
Cover Design: Andy Campbell and Dean Smith
Cover Image: Kevin Reynolds

Support::Big thanks, *go rabh mile maith agat*, to Kath Murphy, who has sweated copious blood, ink and correction fluid on this text. A muckle load of thanks is due also to Ian Daley who, despite the odds and the oddities of the novel, has persisted in publishing the unpublishable. Thanks to everyone at *route* for all the hard graft incurred in slapping my novel between a tasty cover and into the current catalogue, in particular, Dean Smith, Nicole Devlin, Andy Campbell and Kevin Reynolds.

Printed by Cox and Wyman, Reading

A catalogue for this book is available from the British Library

Events and characters in this book are imaginary. Similarity to real persons and events is coincidental.

Full details of the route programme of books
and live events can be found on our website
www.route-online.com

route is the fiction imprint of YAC, a registered charity No 1007443

YAC is supported by

Wakefield MDC, West Yorkshire Grants, Yorkshire Arts

Dedicated to the memory of my Great Uncle Salty Joe
who teld me mi fust rude rhyme
giving me the thirst fe mirth –
grasta De air do anam, a Chroidh

Because you'd already mind-whipped
yourself repeatedly
for what you'd done
out there in the streets,
whatever misfit thing
of rage or bleakness or stupendous
aberration,
and maybe,
you'd reached
an early
maturity.
(DeLillo, D. (1997) Underworld. London, Picador. p. 502)

Part One

The Shirt Box

The Forewarned[1]

My Uncle Salty died and bequeathed to me, not exactly his life's work, for that was trying to work out a system on how to beat the pools, and two bedrooms of t'auld hus were full of papers with the football results in, and of course t'auld Salty didn't win. That was his life's work and it took forty black bin-liners from Aldi to get rid of it. No, Salty left me this thing, and thing is believe you me the right word for the old shirt box of clippings, jottings, scribbling, scrawlings and one old black and white Swedish wank mag, curling at the edges, going by the name of my inheritance. Well, I waded through and tried to make sense of it and finally ended up scanning it in and trying to put it in some sort of order. It was then that I realised the error that I had blundered into. There had been an order. There had been a book, even Throbber's Weekly was part of it, but in my eagerness to arrange, re-arrange and make sense I had ballsed up the flow of narrative big styl-e and make no mistake.

When I kent what I had done I was all for throwing it in the bin and trying my hand at a proper job: paper-round, civil servant or selling the Big Issue. But I wouldn't give in and, for my sins, I persisted and re-read and re-ordered and made a worse job than afore. Just as I was about to set fire to the manuscript, times were hard and I couldn't afford coal, I discovered another software programme on my computer – Microsoft Binder. The binder was the dog's bollox and the wife's too. You just got all the old crap and bunged it in, pressed a couple of keys to supply consecutive page numbering and Tom's the name of my other uncle. I'd done it. It wasn't a novel, it wasn't what Salty would have wanted, but job's a good 'un and the cheque is in the post, so tha

---

[1] *The only thing I'm damn certain sure on is the ending, that is not up or open for renegotiation: an end is an end and let that be the end of it, so help me God, amen.*

can lump it. I just thought to warn you that was all, in case you wanted to buy a proper book instead, talking of which, is there any market at all for old Swedish porn, as I still owe the Co-op a couple of quid for Salty's funeral like?

Chapter One - Brown Dog Day

It was a brown dog day when the suicides cede just another twenty-four hours and the kids next door jig school, playing hopscotch on the sidewalk, chalked lines, voodoo circles, predeterminism just a stone's throw away - stand on a line you marry a swine - stand on a crack you marry a twat. It's a game running short of a future, bit like yon lass, Christine, who might come into this yarn if naught better turns up; yon lass living in the room of the cupboard under the stairs waiting for the day she'll buy a cheap DIY pregnancy kit and find herself with child. A day full of zeros all amounting to nothing like the hero of this story who any moment is waking up to sign on. Sleep squatting in the sills of his eyes, he takes a finger, dressed up in grime to rub last night from his eyes. A somnolent yawn staggers from his lips, half-drunk and still more than a half little crazy. A body slack with disuse slips from beneath fetid bedclothes and wanders at a threshold below operative will to the water closet and bathroom, pig iron, if you please. The plumbing like the house is late Victorian. The water in the sink is cold and slightly ferruginous. The wash is over - a couple of backhands thrown over face, neck and back. Water gurgles noisily down the plughole to flow in endless pipes and loops to the restless sewer below. The rest of the house is sleeping or waking or merely waiting for the day when its many rooms will be gutted and re-furnished.

Lazily, the hero dresses, changing into faded dungarees and an old sombrero given to him as a present from a retreating girlfriend many heartaches ago. He locks his door behind him, but wonders why. The room is empty save for lower life running a riot of metempsychosis. Spiders sit in the hearts of webs to prey upon stray flies – one spider might have been a famous surgeon and this fly newly caught was for sure a ballerina that had danced briefly with the *Ballet Ruis*, but as flies and spiders, none of this nonsense matters a bugger. In a far corner behind a hole in the wainscoting lives an old brown mouse who was once a

Sioux Brave, Lacota, who had given that Neo-Nazi Custer a reet fuck-in at the battle of Little Big Horn and now lives on the leavings of the room's lone friable rust-rotten rug. The room teemed with forgotten humanity and household dust of shed skin. It was a room of unredeemed dross and dreams held in check by lock and key and that was only some distant maybe.

The red bus ran on misery: from the disgruntled driver with his double-barreled hernia and unfulfilled sexual fantasies, to the one-parent mother with five bawling bairns taking up the back seat. Our hero played at rolling and unrolling his bus-ticket into tiny cigarettes and he did not think. He had long ceased to believe in thinking. Thinking was worth less than a good hearty fart after breakfast; it led nowhere save more thinking - an all consuming end in itself for itself. Thinking was something that he would return to when he was finally tired of life and could no longer trust his instincts. The bus pulled into a station foisty with memories of better days when fewer people had cars and even occasionally the upper classes condescended to use public transport and were thought none the worse for it, provided they looked suitably disdainful and patronising. Fucking hell – the good auld days – ration coupons and frigid sex and frozen peas just about to be invented. I say, old cove, ding-ding, last stop please!

Our hero had missed his stop, but naught to cry over, perhaps he had been dreaming again. Ron was worried about his dreaming, but was determined not to lose sleep over it. His waking hours were being slowly drained by vampiric living dreams supping and slurping the very gumption out of him. It was becoming so that only a veneer of vividness in terms of sensation divided the world from the dreamt world, a distinction too that seemed to be slowly fading with each sleeping hour.

Through a crowded street bulging with shopping eyes and tourists bowed down by snappy-happy cameras our hero threaded his way like a slim-eyed needle at the running stitch. The street set in York stone or faked glazed cobbles, shops brash with enterprise and cut-price smiles, became rendered interesting as a glossy picture on a fucked up fudge box after the sweets were gone. In that street authentically set as a period costume drama for the American market only our hero was misplaced, knitting together purpose and distance whilst thanking God for his dreams: such dismal streets, bargained beauty going summer sale cheap - what a nightmare waiting for the camera's click.

Despite the expense, the Department of Unemployment had had a new consignment of 98% pollution free air fresh from the F layer and was all fired up for an efficiency drive. The queue of disappointed people passed quickly, smoothly and almost elegantly from door to table to exit.

'Ah, Mr Smith, Mr Ron Smith, your six months rehabilitation interview is now due today I'm afraid, so could you step this way. The clerk will take your normal signature, your benefit will not be affected,' assisted the assistant and so our hero has been named Ron Smith, an unsurprising name that proffers nothing. A name sated with mediocrity and aspirations confined to the mundane. A name you can trust or better still pass over in silence. But today Ron is not passed over as he is called to interview to see what steps he has undertaken in the last six months to work.

Interview sodden with perfunctory questions and muted responses as the civil servant explains the Opt Out Scheme recently introduced by Her Majesty's Government. On a squeaky white board armed only with a large felt tip and a short fescue the civil servant carefully explains the new scheme: prosopopoeiaing the pros and conning the cons. He had a grand voice and greased back hair parted at the sides and Ron Smith felt sorry for him.

'Mr Smith, this scheme is tailor-made for you. Face it, as a long term unemployable all you have to look forward to is signing on every fortnight till you reach retirement age, with the indignity of every six months coming in here and explaining how it is that you haven't found yourself gainful employment. Whereas, if you accept this lump sum, that is it, you are off the books for life: no more signing on, no more accounting for yourself, no more lying about the odd day's undeclared labour. With this lump sum with which thou shalt be endowed, you can start a new life, invest in a little business, gamble on the stock exchange, or buy a council flat that nobody wants. Your own income! You'd be your own man. What do you say?'

'No.'

'But why? Can't you see what an opportunity lies before you?'

'Too cheap. What's ten years money for the rest of my life? No pension, no health care, no housing benefits and, if I fail, no other option but a work-farm somewhere in the sticks picking oakum till I can work no more - no thanks! And besides, I feel sorry for you.'

'You what?'

'Without me signing on where would you be? Sorry but I couldn't do that to you.'

'That's all very kind of you, but the only thing I'm working for is early retirement and enforced redundancy. I have my eye on a little place in the middle of Middle England where I can settle down and grow alpines and manufacture homemade garden gnomes. So you're doing me no favours, matey-boy, whatsoever.... Go on, what do you say? I'll sign you up for the Opt Out Scheme?'

'No,' said Smith standing up. 'Coming in here every fortnight and fucking off you bastards is the only thing that gives my life meaning. I'm not forsaking it for you. That's why I feel sorry for you.' With that Ron Smith left, leaving the civil servant mumchanced though still searching for the relevant form.

Midday was all bright sunlight and screwed up eyes. On legs constrained by gravity and other archaisms of Newtonian physics, Ron Smith wended his way through a maze of back streets, snickets and snickleways to The Albert. Before the developers moved in, the back room of The Albert was the resort of hip homosexuals, young girls tired of building-site chat-up lines and sad losers marooned from some other pop era with too much time and bitterness on their hands, either the Punk Revolution had let them down or the Sixties when just not quite enough people believed in free love and drugs and bullshit, either way it didn't matter a rehabilitation interview, because Ron Smith drank in the front bar. The front bar of what later became Tio's Tapa Bar was the meeting point for the lowest rung of the minor criminality and sad lonely old men with bloodshot Weltschmerz eyes. The Albert was that sort of boozer and Sundays weren't bad either, when Stan would set out titbits on the bar for the regulars: dripping butties, bacon bits and various cheeses. Sundays were popular. Rumour has it that it was this popularity that gave the developers the idea of what Tio's Tapa Bar could be if tastelessly over furnished: bring out ye olde flock wallpaper, clusters of copper kettles and coachloads of tourists sharing several lonely brain cells.

Panicking through the fluff of his pockets Ron fished out a pound coin craving better days and ordered half a pint of chilled stout. As chance would have it and fate not otherwise an old friend of Ron's entered The Albert too, ordered a beer and a packet of pork scratchings whilst drawing up a barstool alongside.

'Now then, charvo, how goes it?'

'Not bad, chiver,' replied Ron, moistening the crack of his lips with just the froth. 'And your good self, my fine fellow?'

'Middling to nothing... Hold on to my seat while I check the back room a minute.'

Ron nodded, sipped at his lips whilst groping, furiously fossicking through his pockets one more time, hoping to find some other pound forsaken to the fluff. An old geezer with a car CD player tucked beneath a crow black overcoat approached Ron. The old geezer reckoned he knew Arturo. Old man said that he knew that Arturo was something of a choring mushe. The old man wondered if Ron knew of Arturo's whereabouts. But Ron was having none of it. It would not be the first time that Arturo had been set up. Arturo was travelling and that was that. The old man tucked the CD player back beneath his crow wing then followed his shadow to the door.

The friend was back with a forehead full of worry puckered up like a series of recidivistic lobotomy scars.

'Didn't figure you for a back-room man,' said Ron. Though it was not a question, he hoped the explanation was lengthy enough to eke out his half-pint for just a few minutes longer. There was nothing in Ron's room but dust, this Sioux Brave mouse and a couple of distinctly nasty pieces of work in the spider line. Ron was not disappointed. The man fell to talking, confessional low down dirty talking, just man to man, chauvinist to chauvinist talking, all about how last weekend, strung out on whiskey rye where the friend picks up a young drunk thing round the other side of the bar, a pretty young thing with pale egg-yolk hair and hard little bitch tits poking holes through her tee-shirt, so they go back to her flat, this one room thing with single bed and cooking hob affair, all cockroaches in the corners and green mould on the wall, and how without any begging this girl bent down low and gave the best head he'd ever had in his meek miserable life her throat taking it all down to the balls and back again in a rhythm of pleasure close to a pain you could grow to love; it got so good he could not take any more practically ripped her trousers and pants off, she bent over real cute, hands on the bed, the twin moons of her arse arched high in the air, the friend is digging round with a burning bell-end when chancing to glance down he sees this pair of golden balls swinging there...

'What you reckon to that, mate?'

'You are not my mate. And I've heard it all before,' snorted Ron, who probably had. 'I'll give you another version of the same yarn. There was this lad and it was his stag do and all his mates had clubbed together for a stripper and on the night, there he is getting a rock on as the stripper does her stuff. There is a half-time break. The stripper does turns for the brass. The stripper goes to the loo, passing the lad's table and giving him the come on. The lad goes to the loo and makes a drunken pass. He comes back with a big cheesy grin on his chops bragging about how he just got a blowjob and all the lads cheer. Back comes the stripper to finish the act. She goes topless, big cheers, she swings her tits, big cheers, she goes bottomless showing what a cute behind she has, big cheers and then she turns round flaunting her cock and balls to even bigger cheers, except yon man whose stag do it is. That gaje is diving for cover, dying of shame, hoping to holy hell that his betrothed doesn't find out. And in case you haven't guessed all his mates were in on the deal, chipping in a bit extra for the blowjob...As I say, I've heard it all afore, pal.'

'No, Ron, you don't understand. I poked her, to the hilt, man, and ever since I've been haunted. I want to find her again. I want another go.'

Ron took a swift dig of his glass, banged the glass down: 'I wash my hands of you. You always were nothing but a great sackless bairn. We're finished.'

The friend makes like a Gioconda grimace, putting his best face on the verbal slap in the kisser, shuffles down the bar and opens his pork scratchings. Ron gave several saccadic squints between his half-pint and the clock on the wall. Time was deliquescently slow, seconds dripped by like gobbits of molten steel, glowing briefly in the mind before chilling to cold past. There was no way the glass of stout would survive the afternoon. Ron Smith was thirsty as silence. He looked across to where his friend wistfully munched on a particularly fine piece of pork scratching – bit of nipple with hair.

'It'll cost you a pint of stout.'

'What will?'

'Information on the chalrawney.'

Ron slipped off his stool like a shade. Purposefully like a sheriff in a western, he sauntered through to the scene in the backroom. As he approached, his sombrero cast a malignant shadow over the worn, cool green pool table.

'Which of you faggots knows a blond shemale with a dick? Very cute jailbait, probably with a flat and none too choosy, in here last weekend?'

A quadroon with quiffed yellow hair and a ring through his nose said he knew the score, but wasn't going to talk till Ron apologised for his downright derogatory language: 'You ought to be ashamed, 'faggot'? That is no way to talk about people! We are human beings, made as we are just as you have been also formed. What do you want to do, herd and us and gas us in concentration camps – camps for camps?'

This was quite some rhetoric for the back room and way over Ron's head this early into half a pint, but he tried not to show it, just ducked and dived a bit. He instinctively knew that he had been in the wrong and the manful thing to do was to admit as much. Ron took a knife from his dungaree pocket and stroked it against the bum hairs on the lad's throat. Ron naturally was not a violent man, but at times this sure took some believing. Ron was not a violent man, but then again in all fairness, he needed another hour's drink – this takes no believing at all. Ron got the girl's address, where she was working, where she could be found most nights. Ron put his old trusty persuader back in his back pocket, took off his sombrero and addressed the back room, 'I humbly apologise for my use of pejorative language. I have nothing against homosexuality and in future, I shall endeavour to ensure that my terminology is in keeping with my overall liberalism. But when I ask a question whether civilly or its contrary, don't fuck with me!' This was an even more amazing rhetoric from Ron and the backroom boys were moved. They moved a little bit more out of arms' way. It was obvious to them that they were dealing with some kind of dangerous sociopath.

What the hell! Ron had his info and Ron got his drink and a couple of pork scratchings thrown in for good will. The friend quaffed his drink with a single sacerdotal swig, just like Father Clarke did at St George's early, mid and late mass afore they took him away to be dried out. The drink burned all the way down. Suddenly, the friend's dark eyes flickered with a pantagruelian fire – he had an address, a name and a number and he sure as hell was going to use 'em.

Ron tucked into another pork scratching, ingurgitated the remainder of the half of stout which seemed too long a word for too little stout, as he steeled himself to rationing his thirst despite his all round appreciation and full contemplation of the rotund fullness of the unforeseen second pint. The next drink is necessarily inferior to the one prior, but Ron sipped the stout slowly attempting to glean the utmost utility from each sip, savouring his increasing diminishing returns. Time was discoloured froth clinging to his glass. Ron felt his life slipping slowly from him: each sip a slip – it was that slick. The muddied face captured in the well of the empty glass advised him to move on.

Carefully, with unhurried grace, he dashed the glass to the floor and walked out of The Albert to outface with consummate audacity the lambent afternoon. The petty vandalism of the glass breaking was an infrangible ritual inaugurated from the time when Ron had broken a glass by throwing a barman through it. The barman had been new, full of swank and harmless ideas like what a good job Hitler had made on the Gypsies and the Jews, puffs and pinkoes and the idle mouths of the handicapped and the insane. Ron had had to hand over half of his dole cheque that fortnight, but looking back on the window breaking incident Ron felt that he had had his money's worth and just to make sure he broke a fresh jar every time he imbibed there just to remind the bar-staff to watch their politics around him (boring but true, it was in all the local papers, both free ones full of advertising and that right wing penny dreadful with the extra absorbent Saturday edition).

Blinking like a sun-struck mole, Ron crossed the hot, sudatory street to where a footpath subfusc in half-shade led down to the riverbank.

This river was slate grey stirred with brown. It flowed deep and silent and cared not for the passing of the man armed with a scowl and a sombrero as he fought his way home, harling his ass through restlessness and the sombre knowledge that nothing awaited him upon his return, but the shape in the bed left by his own body that morn, that, and so much excess stale air.

It was an afternoon of iguana shade and strained sounds of town drifting down to the river's side to die. A drake called to his mate with all the rage that a deranged Daffy Duck struck with lust could muster. A seagull fought with a crow over a ditched half-eaten pizza left hanging out of a dustbin like the tumourous tongue of an oversized dog. A pair of lovers held hands and argued heatedly over the deposit for a terraced house that they had seen late last week. They still believed in each other and the constancy of the future. It was a big decision. It was some argument. No doubt divorce, separation, regrets and remorse would kick in soon. A barge hung low in the guts of the river, splitting the water into mutually flowing moieties that slyly re-entered each other before the swirl of a bend in the mid-distance, re-establishing ever changeable oneness. Perhaps these were the questions, change and permanence, but more likely not. It was an afternoon of substantive hopes and little else and Ron Smith was the little else, walking in rhythm to his breathing that never demanded aught else save the next lowering of his diaphragm. Water flowed under the bridge. Ron took some steps that led up to the street that would bring him home after traversing a creeping crescent of once magnificent nineteenth century houses. As usual, the workmen were in. This time converting a large attic studio flat into four rat-pits for the almost homeless who were duly grateful for any kind of roof over their heads. It was the gratitude that sickened Ron badly but he tried not to let it bother him, like the murder he found on the stairs that day. It was Mr Jenkins. And Mrs Jenkins was no longer ironing that day.

Mrs Jenkins cut her face on a smile right after slitting her husband's balls off with a lady-shave razor. Hell no she wasn't doing any washing-up that day or dusting, ironing or pecking specks of dried shit off the toilet bowl with a brush and a bottle of bleach. Hell no, especially the ironing (whoever heard of anyone ironing string vests and underpants) but that was the way

Mr Jenkins, master of the house, liked it. If he could find a crease there was hell to pay and a slap in the mouth. But, Mrs Jenkins wasn't ironing that day. She pulled up a seat and plonked her arse down on it and thereafter proceeded to roll one helluva kind-size, king-size, no-holds-barred, jolly-giant joint. The grass was acrid, but strangely sweet and thereafter she proceeded to file her nails for the first time in years. She made a one helluva shit-kicking pint-size Barcardi and boke and thereafter proceeded to paint her toes: rose pink or Day-Glo blue. It was then that she really got going, nipple piercing, constant uninhibited masturbation and most disturbing of all as far as the neighbours were concerned listening to Charles Mingus, possibly the *Black Saint and the Sinner Lady* or maybe *Cumbia & Jazz Fusion*. Truth be told now and wait while I tell ye, Mrs Jenkins could never abide Trad jazz. It all seemed too much of a Coon Show for her – *Well hello, Golly?*

Anyway, back to the main event of this digression, after the blood had congealed and stopped, she read a short story by Raymond Carver and refused to identify with the people portrayed there: such mean lives with not enough hope to go round and too little luck. If she wanted depressing lives she had her own already or any one of her neighbours or immediate acquaintances. So she knocked the bollox out of a couple of Mills and Boon Publications till she was in danger of bursting her stitches with laughing; stitches that had put her back together from the last attack of her husband putting the boot in. Finally, she sought refuge in channel hopping around the pointless parameters of daytime television. Anything to take away the worry in her mind, and this is her mind now, so listen up all you last-post and post-modern Freudians. In that dream of a day in court her defence spared nobody, everyone had their fifteen minutes of courted glory from old timers like Freud & Jung (one mentioned already, but that was a slip-up) to the newly solemnised high priests of menstrual tension. It was going swell till she dismissed her attorney, dabbled in a little plea-bargaining and addressed the jury. She just, Lord God of Israel help her, after twenty-five years, wanted to murder the dastard. It was simple as that. Summing up, the judge commended her on her concision (after all it was no skin off his nose) then gave her ten years of mucking out slops and making with the mop and this new psychological profile that a Quaker would have killed for. As it was parole wised up, giving her remission for good behaviour, thereafter, she took real pride in her work: no pissers gleamed like her johns, you could see your face in the shine on the taps, and they all missed her when she went, clubbed together and bought her a duster, cleaner and a pair of initialled rubber gloves. Continuing with these vain, vague day-dreamings following upon the murder of her most hated husband, she got out of Porridgeville, wrote a book, made the odd guest appearance on a couple of day-time chat shows, hosted an agony column once on American TV, but late at night she still tries to figure all the parameters, the angles, ironing out all those nagging little creases that folded and dove-tailed into her life.

Ron Smith found her, still daydreaming, returning to the ironing board to flatten out a pair of threadbare y-fronts with blood stains up the back. He stepped over Mr Jenkins, belly up, turned off the telly, the gramophone and disconnected the iron hot with overwork and raw burnt flesh.

'I'm sorry, Mrs Jenkins,' Ron had started, taking off his sombrero and holding the hat forlornly in his hands. 'But I shall have to phone the police; you know that don't you? Can't keep this quiet...Here, I'll make a cup of tea first.'

The tea was poor quality, My Auntie's Tea Bags, tasting of stale leaves ripe in the heavy glut of autumnal decayed days sliding into the slush of wet winter – but that was just the hard sell. The tea quenched Ron's thirst for doing the right thing. Mrs Jenkins had given him a mug of tea, what had the police ever given him but a couple of kick-ins and a burnt out caravan when he was on the drom, before the asocial life was outlawed under laws made for civil protection and purple-rinsed crones rotting in rotten boroughs of the Home Counties and other self-regarding residencies of the self-righteous. The new laws, the Glorious Revolution, had done for him and no longer was it possible to play the 'good citizen'. To cement his resolve at not informing the police of Mrs Jenkins' misbeseeming misdemeanour Ron helped himself to a chocolate-coated biscuit.

He was still seated on the kitchen chair helping to demolish the packet when Mrs Jenkins returned from e-mailing the police. Mrs Jenkins was pleased that Ron was comfortable and asked if he would like a warm-up. Whilst on his second mug of tea and fifth chocolate-coated biscuit Mrs Jenkins volunteered to do his ironing any time he needed to dress up and make a good impression. Ron was touched and promised to bring round a packet of biscuits when his dole came through on Wednesday. It was all so civilised, even the police behaved themselves, desisting arrest and refraining from their usual show of misfeasance. Sergeant Spado the Sado quickly concocted a cost benefit analysis of charging Mrs Jenkins and once all the options were taken into consternation: judging possible judgements to a sound-bite-ometer of tabloid opinion, cost of trial, imprisonment, putting the bairns into the care of fully-paid up professional paedophiles and such like, it was immediately realised that it was in nobody's interest to bring Mrs Jenkins to trial. The Sergeant had a cup of tea and tucked into the last of the chocolate biscuits whilst his men kicked the corpse downstairs and filed a report of death by misadventure. With no chance at all of any further biscuits being forthcoming Ron took his leave of Mrs Jenkins and dragged himself across the hallway to his room.

Coming in from the pub and back from his reveries Ron found that nothing much had happened to his room since he last looked upon it. He had the vague notion that when he did not perceive it the room ceased to be, that it flashed in and out of being as he opened or shut his eyes. Once closed to the senses his room became relegated to a vague sense datum of memory diminished with past. This was all a load of auld bollox of course. Ron was well in the wrong. Whilst signing on and imbibing, several flies had demised in the dust-strung threads of the spiders' webs. Their chain of being passed on unnoticed into a lotus flower seed in far off Cathay, a sour fruit of a tamarind tree on the outskirts of Mumbay and the last ended up as a louse egg fastened to the fibres of a tallith owned by a red-haired fair-skinned Sabra who lived in an Arab confiscated home not fifty yards past the Wailing Wall.

Of course, Ron was not to be knowing any of this. He wouldn't even attempt to know this. He was content with ignorance. Okay it was far from bliss but he was happy with his lot for even nothingness was too much for him as he lay back and listened to the afternoon schedule on Radio Four. The wireless was one of his few pleasures left and he appreciated such quality time as, hungry and mildly intoxicated with eyes shut and ears open harkening to the flow of sounds he could no longer relate to, he pissed his life away. Thus to his chagrin and all round vexation did sounds from the room above spoil his sprawled slumber on his old sweat-sodden mattress.

In the room above, Una stamped. Her dictionary of Mediaeval Occitan hugged idly to her crumpled breasts as she took it in turns to thrust her feet in a downward direction. She was built on finer lines than a frost withered vine, with lank hair like wet sand and an inverted chest that made her feel inferior to other women – there's peer pressure for you. She was completing a PhD on the languages of the Langue D'oc: Provencal, Occitan, and Catalan as it is spoken in and near Rousillon. Una studied on borrowed money and rationed time and was building up to a breakdown she couldn't afford. Lacinating self-doubts kept her awake at night and the day was spent brooding over the night to come. As her body languished her mind became keener, her prose more self assured, written with an adamant nib and a controlled concise hand, but all to no avail, as she neared completion of the thesis her mental preoccupations became more acute, limited only by the paucity of her nervous energy; for two days she had not eaten, for a week she had not slept, at times she heard voices telling her to shed her blood as a last sacrifice to herself in imitation of Christ on the cross: deicide - God's sacrifice of God to God. She held onto her rosary beads and the semblance of sanity all morning, but as afternoon rolled her into evening, as the long night made an entrance her psychosis assumed control. In deep anguish and agitation, she paced throughout her room in mixed beats of a manic logaoedic. She was having a hard time of it all right.

Below, Ron watched illuminated scintilla of plaster flake from the ceiling in descending spirals as Una thudded above. Ron felt sorry for the student. She seemed vulnerable as glass and as far as Ron went that was very vulnerable indeed. Ron could tell without trying that Una was indulging in some kind of sciamachy, but he didn't trouble himself with wondering what could he do about it though his eyebrows puckered up like cavorting caterpillars, till he remembered that he'd given up introspection ever since he had been diagnosed with schizothymia - physician heal thyself, amen. After all, he was naught but a schnorrering schlemiel living in a schlock-house with no time for schmucks or schmaltz. Then again all these Ss he kept ascribing to himself it were becoming too slick maugre his love of alliterative verse and he couldn't remember if Ss counted or not. He thought of getting out his battered copy of the *Seafarer*. He did not think longly, which wasn't an adverb, but Ron thought that it ought to be, after all, there is widely, though again not smally. Perhaps, he would get around to having a think about this, but then again not. After all, apparently the adverb was on the decline in spoken and to a lesser extent written English. And besides when all's said and done he had given up with the thinking malarkey and what have you. As far as debates of language were concerned he was on parole, all that fucked up fragmentation between signifiers and signifieds, what was that to him, when he couldn't master a basic adverb placed in just the right place, finally.

He turned the wireless up.

The clangour of the upper room failed to diminish, but assumed greater intensity by the way of the foot-stompings being accompanied by high-pitched ululation, whether of joy or woe it was not possible to ascertain, and neither did Ron seek to find out as in a peek of pusillanimity he buried his head beneath his obdurate pillow and there would have remained if Una's legs had not shot through the diaphanous skin of plaster of his bay window's ceiling. In a mental state verging upon the disinterested, Ron surveyed the thin, white shanks of the student as they poked through his roof. He noticed that Una only wore one red sock, hand-knitted with a personalised hole where the big toe stole through like the blunt snout of some foraging animal. A streak of blood slid like viscous slime down one side of her left leg to fall in gobs of dark crimson to a little pool below. No doubt, Una had suffered some sort of hurt in her short fall. The legs struggled briefly for a few seconds but to no avail. It was no use, Ron felt sorry for her.

'I say, how're diddling?'

'I wouldn't like to say. I believe I have suffered some contusions to my yoni, but that's okay: I wasn't using it anyway except for urination and the odd time the plumbers are in.'

'Oh that's quite all right then, for a minute I thought thou had hurt yourself.'

'Arrah, mi Boy, trust God I'll be quite fine enough, just so long as you gives me a hand pushing my feet back to my side of your ceiling.'

'Nay bother, no trouble at all,' said Ron, standing on a stool, having taken a soothfast hold of Una's ankles, then pushing upwards with all his might. It was done. Una was back on the top of the bay window and maugre and despite himself, Ron asked what it was she thought she was doing.

'I was having a go at self-slaughter,' replied Una in a maundering low undertone, deeply aware of her own state of sin.

'Oh aye, and how were you doing that?' asked Ron, just to

make conversation.

'Throwing myself off your bay window, but then the roof gave in, so.'

'Bloody typical, shoddy work the whole lot from top to bottom, someday someone will—'

'Quite,' Una demurred.

Ron scratched his pate with a thick thumbnail. His sombrero was resting by the bed like a hard working bit-part actor in search of an equity card. He couldn't help wondering if he was wearing a bit thin. Oh well, the afternoon and evening were certainly not lacking in drama today and he hoped it would not interfere with his constitution. Ever since rescuing some obscure tract on Taoism from a house clearance one sad day, he had a vague idea that excitement wasn't conducive to his state of well being That said his first suicide presented him with a possible solution to his own unease with continual existence. It would be as well to take notes and besides it was no bad way to spend a mauvaise d'heure. In a distinctly pellucid manner, he stroked his mazzard thoroughly before venturing what could be construed as an impolite question.

'Would you mind if I came up?'

'You wouldn't be talking me out of it now would you, because it would be no use, mi mind's made up and that's the truth of it, so.'

'Fair enough, I only want to watch... Hang on a minute, I tell you what, some of my floorboards are loose at yon end of the room, yon side where the rug runs out. I'll bring a couple of short bits up to lay across the hole, if you like? That should make things a bit safer.'

'Oh thanks, that would be a good idea and no mistake. Just you don't try to talk me out of it and we can get along grand,' beamed Una. It was a pleasant change to come across someone a bit more practicable rather than the figments of men and pishrogues that flitted through her head from time to time.

Suspiring slightly from unsought exhaustion Ron made it to

Una's room, several floorboards snucked a touch surreptitiously under the crock of his oxter and without trying to talk the lass out of it once. Of the room itself he was greatly impressed: a seemingly antediluvian horologe miskept temporality by a walnut veneer wardrobe which might be worth a few bob, maugre woodworm, and books thick with learning were disseminated about the room in what might have amounted to almost restless abandon if gravity had not afforded them some stability at their point of rest. As for Una he felt sorry for her. Indeed a pitiable sight, standing with clotted blood streaking one chalk-white leg, and her sinewy thighs creeping from her worn off-white pants showed every sign of progressive horripilation. In a tired tie-dyed tee-shirt two sizes too large she shivered by the open window. Thanks be to God it was a warm evening.

'Nice books,' said Ron, who though he maintained that he could barely read, maintained a high regard for those that could and even more esteemed those who actually did read. That was some maintenance all right.

'Arrah! There's a woman on the market who bees selling them a pound a pound. She would sell them five pounds a yard, but she didn't make enough money that way. Would you like a present of them when I'm after going?'

Ron did a quick calculation, even re-selling at a discount rate of seventy-five per cent, there were more than a couple of drinks in the collection. 'Ooh aye, love, that's right good of thee.'

The worm-riddled floorboards sufficed to make a secure platform over Ron's bay window. Grabbing two stools with worn foam seats Una and Ron contemplated the onset of night. The gloaming came with a promise of a hint of the omnium gatherum to come. The two lesbians from the first basement flat vacillated up the garden path, weighed down by shopping and stopping to chat on how their garden patch was growing, when one bag split, spilling an intestinal collection of hard bought and fought for merchandise to scatter amongst a mixed bed of rosebay willowherb and opium poppy. A domestic fracas of the venial kind ensued as Jo chastised Terry for her wanton extravagance and greed. (For the benefit of passers by this was an old argument, so old in fact that it was probably auld: Terry would sneak in little luxury purchases and on finding them Jo would give her a right kick-in and earful at least, mainly about how they had to economise and all the rest of it – worse was when Manchester United lost, Jo would come in steaming and beat the shit out of Terry if she so much as put one look out of place.) Terry just broke down and cried over a burst whinberry and truffle yoghurt leaking its extravagantly purple fluid to the brown baked earth. A jar of best pesto had also broken, as had other divers goods; goods it is to be remembered that were hardly necessary, but made Terry's recently incurred lowlife status worth living.

It was tiresome, the wait, the petty argument and the pity he couldn't help feeling for the scrawny student seated by his side who had been sickened by life of life. He'd come upstairs to see off fifteen minutes and to maybe try and learn something much against his better instincts and there he was still just killing time. He would risk a question lest peradventure he fell to dozing.

'I say, Jo, what's the meaning of life?' he bawled down.

'Eating good pussy, smoking a little dope,' assured Jo, at the top of her voice whilst showing not a jot of dubitation, although Terry had finished rescuing remnants from her wayward shopping and looked distinctly less convinced.

Sad to say Una was not convinced at all and she did not need being talked out of it. She knew her why of life but because of it, she was dying. Seated by the strange man who smelled of the musk of unwashed dishcloths and wore a reassuringly wide moth-eaten sombrero she explained her fixation with the dead. The dead: all her best friends, the only folk she knew. It had started long before her birth in Gleann Bharr, the slow persistent decline of the Gaelic language and culture. In the far North of Tir Chonaill she had been born to a swiftly ageing Gaedhealtacht. In the whole of Gleann Bharr only a handful of houses still spoke

Gaelic to any great extent, her parents' house included. Her father, a local fiddler, poitin maker and acknowledged master of doing the double (claiming the Bru and what have you at the same time as doing a bit and a pint of plain is better than a nod and a wink to the local Garda) played the Highlands of Donegal and cried in dialect when he drank too much of his own brew. Locked in the thought-sphere of a dying offshoot of a dying tongue most of the world had a compelling and overwhelming alienness and disquieting otherness that defied ready assimilation. At least that is what it said in this book she bought in her first year away at the university there: *Critical Theory, Constructing Deconstructions & Talking Bollox For Beginners*. She was necessarily estranged from a world that she sieved and understood through an antiquated language breathing its last, crippled by disregard and poisonous regret. Only place she ever felt at home was home and the five other houses that still spoke the Gaedhilg. Then one by one the old friends, the old speakers that still carried the correct *blas* of well-worn words began to die out. At every new funeral there were fewer and fewer mourners. When they came to bury her father, apart from the officiating priest only her mother and herself came to pay their respects and the Irish Government officially declared Gleann Bharr Gaedhealtacht dead. At the time, she had been studying for her Master's Degree at Queens in Belfast. Her thesis was much admired: *Terms and References for Oestrus in Livestock Garnered from the Gaelic Dialect of Gleann Bharr, County Donegal*. She passed with flying colours, but her heart was no longer in her work, despite being offered a grant to find a Gaelic speaker alive and still speaking in Kilcar, the postmaster's family not included, a great speaker and local poet would you know? No, it was no good. She turned away from Gaelic studies, finding a new lease of life in the French dialects of Provencal. Yet this new found enthusiasm was tainted with the first omen of the tragedy to come: she had become drawn into the world of Occitan that had been consigned to history. All her heroes, all her sources of more than academic joy, had long since perished, their tongue all but forgotten: unhearable and unsung. Last summer she had toured the Langue Doc and met those who still claimed to speak remnants of Occitan. It was all mapped, a fine linguistic treatise was forthcoming, but it was not enough. The great flowering of poets and Cathar priests had withered to cast only barren seed. Her work was finished. All that could be said had been written. She had typed up (in an approved MLA handbook style) her own death certificate. She was going to greet the dead. Today was a good day to die. Simply nothing could unsay the truth of that.

To Ron the girl seemed to drop like a knackered old clotheshorse. It was over too quickly to really peruse the matter in an objective manner. Her last words still resonated inside his head as his eyes took in the crushed form scattered below in a twisted displacement of life. He no longer had to feel sorry for her, which was some relief, but he did and hence no relief at all, all said. Something like tears made his eyes itch with salt-water and he felt a sudden hunger to go to the girl and hold her in his hands. He was spared the expense of real emotions as a crowd gathered below and crowded his vision of spilt humanity.

An ambulance came but she didn't have insurance. They managed to save her eyes and one kidney. It was just enough to cover the cost of incineration, call out charge and a little on top to keep the Hospital's Trust Fund off the paramedics' backs.

Ron took in his floorboards, found the student's key and locked the flat after him. He'd have a word with Calo, Arturo and Rawnee's eldest, soon enough about these bits and bobs and what-have-yous. If the books weren't worth anything, there was always the wardrobe. Downstairs, back in the room where the brown mouse remembered the time Sitting Bull had spent the day staring at the sun and slicing flesh off his arms as he sought a vision, Ron curled up by the still-playing wireless and fell asleep. It had not been a brown dog day after all.

Chapter Two - Late Bulletin

Ron has been suffering recently with broken nights. His sleep has become increasingly erratic. As a result, his dreaming is now imbued with almost psychotic attributes, elements or otherwise discrepant phantasmagorias. It is often the case that, not only does Ron experience lucid dreaming, but that on occasions he is unable to tell whether or not he is dreaming. A typical example of this is when he dreams that he is dreaming, not only seeing himself dreaming, but dreaming of the dreaming of his self that he sees dreaming.

Overall, Ron's mental and physical health is suffering as his sleep continues to deteriorate. One of Ron's greatest difficulties is linked somewhat tenuously to the flow of time. Time no longer seems to be moving in a forward direction nor seeming even linear for that matter, but rather time is the moment surrounded by other temporal aspects. Time is not only the now, but the now with perhaps a dash of past and hint of future or, for what it is worth, of possible time. There are occasions where grammar is used symbolically in order to better reflect the hypostasis of Ron's mental outlook. Thus, do not be alarmed to see verbs unmarked for tense or the jumping between tenses. This is not the world. This is Ron's world uniquely shaped by his idiosyncratic spatial and temporal projections.

'A low front is moving in from the Atlantic bringing rain to Northern Ireland in the early part of the morning, reaching Cumbria and Lancashire by mid-morning and the Pennines sometime around lunchtime. The outlook then, is more wet weather to come but possibly breaking up slightly by the weekend…'

Chapter Two & A Wee Bit More

Deep purple night, a shramming wind blew through the twin holes of Ron's bay window to haunt with cold, making yon lad shiver and shake and keep awake till a Dookerin Dook came to steal his consciousness away. They took a walk by the moon above by the way of several scintillating stars that hopped in the sky as lively as blowflies. The Dook had a lot to shew Ron, not least the intricate machinations of a stochastic universe set against the stultifying emptiness of an expanding space/time continuum. Having dropped into the sill of a black hole, Ron came over a touch bilious watching so much time flowing backwards and nothing to be done about it, except a quick spit and holding onto the seat of his dungarees. He was there when Jesus pleaded on the cross for a little more time and mankind sprang from a swollen ape's womb in the heat of the African plains. He thought to see himself reduced back in upon himself till he was only so much shot sperm and glossy egg bound by the promise of time, so that when the Bildungsroman was over Ron would be none the wiser. He had hoped to see his soul slipped into the soup of things, and thereafter stew for eternity. The Black Hole was poor dookerin: it only shewed the past and left the future curved like a cobra's contoured question mark. By the time it came for Siva's dance, Ron had left to seek solace in the frank dissembling vastness of space, seemingly so nakedly empty yet gravid with promise. He and the Dook searched the unribboning gloom for a hiding place for God and Captain James T Kirkegaard. The sinuosity of Space and Time brought them back to themselves. The Dook was done in, sought some place to rest its weary subsistence.

Resting by Caer Eabrac's Gothic Minster, they sought consolation in the keening of a lone gargoyle with a face rotten with acid rain who moaned that the bones of God were weeping to a little sand, leaving his house reft and open to the emptied heavens; and no one came except to stare where God once came

in transmogrified blood and bread, and all is empty now save the tourist shop by the knave though that probably was the wrong word, but they sold souvenirs by the score except on Sunday when they brought in the carcass of an abiotic cypher to feed plumed, perfumed crows with maws heavied by ritualised conceit and consumer cannibalism, but what the hell - shit goes down...
In truth, the gargoyle wept mostly for himself. The world had grown too knowing for evil and, thus forsaking evil for some other consumer commodity, murder had become a mass produced affair held in sway by supply and demand or fluctuations in currency. Sin or rather its adjective *sinful* was only drawn upon to sell anything from lingerie to cream cakes – *naughty but nice* – man it would take a Jerry Archer to write a line like that. In utter abnegation, this rain-rotten gargoyle had resigned himself to transience and to demurred decay.

Meanwhile back with Ron and his flyer... Ron was disappointed with the Dook, in place of crystal balls and poring over hands whilst tutting knowingly, they had walked the vaults of an empty universe and nothing further was known. He wouldn't have believed the Dook even if it decided to tell him about his future after all; not only that but had got it right as well – disbelief ran like a rampant rat. Getting it right had nothing to do with a good dookerin service for a Gajo, a punter. No, the point was always to give the customer reassuring, top quality, and what they want to hear, bullshit. The giving of comfort and assurance or in other words hornswoggling Gorgios was what was required – to hell with truth. He was about to pay the Dook off, clipped coin at that and some stray token from a fruit-machine, when who should be turning up on some Seventies set of a planet where strangely they all speak American, but Captain James T Kirkegaard with a Scouse accent.

'Eh up, you bastard, seen any birds yet?' asked Captain Kirkegaard. Ron was too surprised to speak. This was not how he had imagined the Universe's leading frontiersman speaking. Disappointedly, Ron shook his head and sighed.

'Don't worry, kiddah, there's bound to be a few birds soon. There always is. I beamed down with a couple of wankers in red uniforms who got wasted straight away. Now, that's a signal for me to get all emotional, give some fucker a twat-in and get laid. It never fails.'

Ron had heard enough and he dibbed auld Kirkegaard one. He started to walk away. He wanted out from this, but there was no sign of the Dook. Like a terrier yapping at his heels, Captain Kirkegaard tailed along behind still bragging of his sex-ploits. 'Eh, whac, should have seen me two light years away yesterday. I beamed down and there was this bird just gagging for it. Smelt a bit like cabbage and had one foot growing in the soil. Should have seen her, bright green with three nipples and more holes in her than a Swiss cheese - can't beat a bit of green, whac! '

Ron had had really enough of enough and that was enough by anyone's standard of tautology. He took off his sombrero. He looked down at the small fat sweating bastard, trussed up in a corset and a glued-down wig and couldn't help dibbing him another right hook. Captain Kirkegaard sank like a sack of spuds – mash gets smashed.

'This day and age it is no way to talk about the alien other, exotic other, you ought to be ashamed of yourself, Captain.'

Captain James T Kirkegaard was far from ashamed. He was up, dukes raised, and jumping in with an ankle-high jump-kick. Ron stepped aside and batted him a sharp left jab. Captain flew through the air. His glued wig finally giving up the fight, sending a special props sandy brown DA up into the stratosphere to boldly go where no other periwig had split an infinitive before. Captain T Kirkegaard was really miffed now. He started tumbling all over the set. Ron was not impressed and when by chance the Captain ventured near, Ron dug a low uppercut into his guts. The Captain was well fucked. He lay on the ground moaning and warning Ron not to chance his luck one more time.

'Don't mess with me, you bastard! You just wait till my mate Spocky takes a pop at you. You won't mess with old Spocky. He's a handy lad. Once he gets his Fulcrum grip on you, you've bleeding had it, whac!'

Ron had tears in his eyes. The Captain had been a sort of hero of his. There he would be rigging up a television, running off an old generator, and himself, Arturo's wife, Rawnee, and Arturo's children, Calo the eldest, beautiful Tchai and the simpleton, Manush, all gathered round watching the fat fucker sorting out the universe. It had been fun time, something to escape to, leaving the hard life of the drom behind for a while.

'That's enough, Captain!' a stern voice warned. A beautiful deep-purple Black lady walked across the set. She wore a light silver dress that shimmered like stars. She was tall and powerful, at least eight foot tall. A beautiful Goddess thought Ron, but kept the thought to himself in case he was falling into old sexist habits of thought that he was so arduously trying to break. Captain Kirkegaard had no such inhibitions, 'Wow! Look at the tits on that. I bet she's a hot fuck and a half!'

'Enough,' the lady ordered. She swiftly clicked her fingers and Captain Kirkegaard found himself fighting for his life with a huge inflatable doll – model 234B with real hair and vibrating lips. Ron was going to give a hand, but the Captain warned him off. 'Leave her to me, whac! I told you, din I? A bit of rough stuff and a shag: it's the same every week.'

Ron hoped that the inflatable would win. The lady disturbed his brown study and guided him to a dais where birds sang and the air was filled with strange delicate lute music – Dowlands fourth collection or again possibly not. Ron began to cry. The lady stroked his hand. Ron said he was so sorry. He saw the Dook and Ron knew that soon it would all be over. The lady leant over and slowly washed his eyes with her scarlet tongue. Ron sobbed like a child.

Morning was nearing. Many in the house were sleeping. Terry and Jo snuggled into a kiss that embraced every orifice. Christine, the runaway, moaned laconic groans of deep unease in her bed in the room below the stairs. Mrs Jenkins hadn't as yet been to bed, as there was still the ironing to be doing for the funeral. She was to wear a black skirt replete with many pleats requiring much of the ironist's art. Others who border unnamed in this story as yet, in rooms both above and below stairs, slept as dawn slid rose grey into a new day, as methodically, devoid of lust, merely dependent upon friction, Ron stroked his lingam though not to onanistic release. Ron gave his old man a couple of strokes whilst coming round from sleep, but thankfully waking up in time to put an end to such an unseemly habit. It was habit and a poor habit at that.

It was getting to the stage when he only indulged himself once a week, finding it enough of a disappointment to stop him regretting his solitary existence. With mounting perplexity he remembered the excess of former days when he'd burned to fuck: lied, cheated, drunk or dragged his way into any pants that were available whilst in the process picking up crabs, clap and a poor opinion of himself. At last, he could reflect with disinterest that none of it had been worth it, that sex had been something else misplaced in his life. Ron wasn't a prude, hung-up, puritanical or captivated by ascetic aspirations, far from it. He just refused to be fooled by sex's apparent importance. Films, music, fashion all jerked sex off, not with Dionysian abandonment, but like a tired whore just turning tricks and pricks – business only. Hell, his hand wasn't much, but it was his own and no one in their right mind could make a fashion accessory out of that. Ron turned the wireless up and listened to the farmers' news on Radio Four.

By the time Woman's Hour had finished Ron thought about making a move. A quick wash and dump, and he was almost ready to face the world. He poked around the kitchen searching for something to scrounge and scran, set his heart on a demitasse of stolen coffee and soggy bowl of muesli. He smuggled the dirty dish and chipped cup in a pile of unwashed pots put into seep in the sink – he had to nash. It was Tuesday. Tuesday was visiting Gran day.

Gunnarsgate was snided with school-parties on their way to

view the walls. Staggered along the route, beggars, street musicians, artists, entertainers and hippie lookalikes offering to bead and thread hair. The sun shone uncertainty, still undetermined as to whether or not it would rise on the morrow. Nonsense: a bicycle bell intoned a two-toned Te Deum, a windscreen washer with one leg soaped a car by a traffic light red, as a misanthrope with a runny nose walked down the middle of the white lines, avoiding touching the sides pleading for alms or directions to the next town. Beneath the notched shade of a sombrero, a hero crossed town with a heartfelt smile and dominoes on his mind. Taking a turning off Gunnarsgate, he entered a cul-de-sac of sectioned homes for the blind, the deaf or just any fucker waiting to die. Outside, deadheading roses, an octogenarian in a Norfolk jacket with cataracts like fish-scales cluttering up his eyes complained about the smell of drains and lost litter. Inside the first flat a retired Calabrian in his birthday suit played a tarantella on an impoverished pub piano as the old woman upstairs yelled obscenities on the phone to the man from the council, whilst Norfolk Jacket picked up the cornered litter as unconcerned Ron let himself in to his Grandma's home.

As he thought, Gran still hadn't replied to his drop of last month: double six. It was a fresh game, but already there was a decidedly generous coating of dust slowly burying the dominoes. Gran did not even talk much these days, but mused on her wish that before she died she'd like to taste one more mouthful of aichi.

'Afternoon, Bebee, it's Ron here. I say, are thou knocking or what? It's your turn tha knows.'

The Gran didn't move, remained aloof contemplating the taste of aichi straight from the fire. Ron bagged up the junkmail thrown through the door and made a cup of tea. Last week's milk had gone off, so they had it black, but it wasn't good enough for Gran, remaining in her chair maintaining the same stiff posture she had assumed since that late cold snap the other month before May. It had been a long miserable winter, not to say miserly, especially for Gran who had had her gas cut off for non-payment and answering back. Thankfully, the electricity was still on. Not even Gran could afford to mess those guys around: it was pay up or we'll repossess your flat or worse, the debt sold to a collecting agency and they didn't care a fuck for anybody. It saddened Ron deeply. He loved his Gran, but he knew deep down that she was a nobody. Ron drank his tea and wondered if the mice had left any biscuits. The cupboard was bare save for a tin of horsemeat given by the EU for free to all old age pensioners over seventy-three, still claiming Income Support and getting away with it. It was nay use, if Gran wasn't playing, then he may as well go for her pension. As usual, Ron had to forge her name. Gran had never been able to write even before the little stroke that had taken away the use of her right arm. It was doubtful if she even could remember the name given to her, when she was dropped unawares in the back of beyond of yon kirkyard t'other side of the border, not that Puro Deya Sbanck minded as she cut her own umbilical cord, wrapped bairn to her breast and collected a bit of firewood whilst she was at it. It had been bad times back then and no mistake, too hard possibly for names just to be given out willy-nilly and why don't you. Still she was his Bebee and Ron loved her. He just wished she would drop six-five so they could get on with it, not that he minded dominoes, but he did prefer fives and threes or even windmill, come to think of it, not that Ron would be thinking of it, since that be against some of the principles that he does be trying to abide by, now that he has acquired them at long last when all's said and done – still, on with the show.

In the post office, the girl gave him a cellophane smile and a demure eye. He didn't know what the fuck that meant and anyway he wasn't interested. He just wanted Gran's pension. As usual, he called for one or two messages on his way back from the post office: a small loaf of white sliced, shortcake biscuits and a collapsible carton of long life milk. So much for shopping.

The fresh cup of tea, spot of milk and a biscuit was better

than the first, but Gran still wasn't having any, caught up as she was in mental reveries about what to be doing about double-six some fine yesterday. Ron stashed the cash in an old cake tin by the glass with the hunting motif that had been promised to him by his granddad, not that that counted for anything for the very same glass had been promised to Peter and Paul and all, so you see Ron wasn't holding his breath for one day possessing that glass, the hunting glass that stood in the pantry in which Gran kept her best false teeth whose use was steadfastly prescribed for emergencies, photography or Sunday best only. There was a fair stash in the tin and when he asked to borrow a tenner Gran didn't say a word agin it. He would give Gran another hour and if she hadn't made a move he'd go back home for something other pointless to do with his three score and ten.

When he got home, Tracy on the second floor had a message for him: someone had called round earlier for him; didn't leave a name, but looked like a bit of a Paki. It meant nothing or something and Ron just gave a shrug, but he thought he had to take exception to the pejorative noun. 'Tracy, I really think that it is time that you stopped referring to anyone from or immediately descended from persons of the Asian subcontinent as Pakis. For two reasons, pray hearken: firstly, they may or may not be from Pakistan; secondly, and this settles the matter, whether or not the person referred to is from Pakistan the name is still highly derogatory.'

Tracy blew a super-dooper bubble-gum bubble and scratched her arse lazily, before pointing out that the term was derivative, given that it is a shortened form of 'Pakistani'. Ron didn't need this, all this debate about language, no way. Ron needed a pint. He knew he'd find Calo down The Albert. There was a tenner in his pocket, so he invited the lass along too if she fancied. She didn't fancy it just at the minute as she had her child to feed, but if her friend could manage a bit of baby-sitting after tea she would love to pop along later for a Babyslam and Tequila with a small cocktail pickled onion it. True this was not everyone's cup of tea and Ron was strictly a Guinness or real ale wallah, but *Dog's Breath,* as a Babyslam Tequila with a pickled egg or onion in it was called, was copping quite a wallop with some of the young trade down at The Albert these days. Perhaps this was another reason why the new owners would in time to come decide upon the construction of the tapa bar, then again, maybe not.

'Aye, all right then,' said Ron.

The river was still there though a weak sun above was definitely dipping below the horizon and to hell with Copernicus. The breeze was cool with the promise of rain and the ferryman hung his head low, paddle lamely held in his hand, as he listened to the slow lugubrious voice of the river, its mudded drone. For forty years, the ferryman had plied his trade, taking tourists across the River Dhobi and none the bloody wiser. A German writer had once visited Caer Eabrac and had been ferried over the river every day that he had stayed. Oft times, they would chat. At other times, they had been content to let silence suffice. When the German left he promised that one day, he would a book about the river's song and his friend the ferryman write[1]. The ferryman thought that the 'Kraut' was no friend of his and how about a tip instead you tight-arsed bastard and that is no place to dump a verb when all's said and done. The ferryman was not only ungrateful and ungracious, but he was also superfluous to requirements. There were plenty of bridges over the River Dhobi linking both banks of Caer Eabrac. There was no reason for his existence except as a curiosity for visitors and the occasional exposure on foreign travel shows. The boatman's head was grizzled and grey. The boat leaked and he rowed more unsteadily from day to day, but still he listened to the voice of the river, making a meagre living, satisfied to hear the river's song and to go his own way.

Some folk are easily pleased.

Ron passed him by still entertaining that first thought of the man when they had met all those years ago: what a prat. Nose

[1] Obvious that the person thinking in German is.

curved, hooked into his chin, Ron got into top gear as he passed the ferryman. He couldn't bear the smell of self-centred saintliness and do-it-yourself sanctity. To Ron he was an arsehole with a paddle and a leaky boat, but that is not what was written in the town's tourist guide.

Further ahead, just beneath his turn off for The Albert some lads and lasses were layking, teaching a dog new tricks. They'd throw the dog into the river and as it paddled back in they'd pelt it with cheggars. Strangely, despite being slowly brained by the fruit of the chestnut, the dog still came back. Ron paid the ferryman his fare, one and six and a threepenny bit tip, and directed the man's craft to where the dog struggled. <u>Swift</u>, Ron knocked in its head, tied a brick around its neck, and said good luck as the dog dove beneath the indifferent brown of the Dhobi. Ron never could bide wanton cruelty. As the skip drew near to the bank, the bairns sent showers of stones to skim and crash against the craft. A stone chipped a tiny bark of skin from Ron's forehead as if to mark him out as a sinner – the mark of Cain or canine killer perhaps, it was hard to say. A trickle of ruby rich blood clotted to a miniature solid mandala.

The boatman was pished about the lack of the adverb – 'swiftly' for Christ's fucking sake.

Some folk are easily miffed.

The alley was rich with river mist and the smell of dog piss. Ron hirpled slightly from a stone that had slipped beneath his sole and sandal. It could wait till he saw Calo. Discomfort became a minor sore and then something of a nagging pain. Ron tried to add it all up. He wondered when suffering could be enough to prove the argument one way or t'other: a blister, a childhood taunt, torture, rape and slow murder - all illusively lacking quantification, but since when was sums the answer to the problem of evil? He stopped, instinctively kicking the pebble loose. It couldn't wait till he saw Calo. Besides, this was no way to disprove that God exists.

Calo was propping up the bar. The back room was quiet save

for two camp catamites shooting pool and snorting coke. They were part and parcel of Britain's New Entrepreneurial Pride – a Nation of Shop Soiled Shoddy Goods again, wrapped up neat and packaged for the massaged masses. The complete cessation of benefit for the unemployable under twenty-fives and the rather generous grants and tax-breaks for enterprise schemes provided you never had the cojones to come scrounging back again had initiated, got the ball rolling of, the greatest sex industry in the world: no longer have businessmen the need to invent bogus meetings in the East, they could clock off at five, have an aperitif, little bite to eat perhaps, before committing bestiality, statutory-rape or the wilder diversions of S & M, sex shows or go to a budget-price bordello such as MacPheckit where a tasteless hamburger and chips is served free with every whore. Nay, no longer were the Brits the greatest imperialist bastards the world had ever known, no longer were the Brits the greatest slave trading nation that history had ever known – nay, the Brits were the greatest cheap fucks with their sexy, cool slogan, *Make a Buck and Fuck and not War – Sign Up and be a Whore, Your Country Needs You!* printed free on the government's start up package *Don't Sit on Your Best asset – Sell It*, available whether wanted or not to all idle mouths whatever their age. The two young lads shooting up were in luck: so far they had only superficial syphilis and one tax demand – captains of industry with their very own lavatory. On the other hand, away from the prey of pederasts, the rhetoric and lefty ramblings, in the front parlour a man with nine fingers and a dated trilby played a selection of Old Irish bullshit, struggling to change key on a piano tuned by a blind Schoenberg enthusiast. Elsewhere, in the huddled shadows of cornered tables, deals were made over fives and threes, and pride hung by one throw by the dart-board smuggled into the gap by the Gents' door and the lamed one-arm-bandit. Behind the bar, a fat man with bugger-straps and a badly patched string vest polished glasses with fetid breath and a ragged cloth of linen with a faded design assuring any casual reader that it's so bracing at Torridmororless – another part of Spain that the Spaniards wanted returning and bloody sharp mind, too. The Spanish ambassador was demanding urgent action at any EU summit where there was free booze going, insisting that since China could have Hong Kong back could Spain have the Costas and Gibralter; in return Spain would hand over all old aged pensioners, gangsters and lottery winners to Blighty, providing the fuckers were never to be smuggled back on package tours to spoil Spanish soil. However, so far the Union was strong: No Surrender, rang the official party hot-line. The Spanish did not insist over much, cowered slightly in case the Brits if pressed would play various wild cards: Ceuta, The Basque Country and Catalonia. But, anyway, Calo was propping up the bar and it's about time the author progressed the story.

'Now, Uncle, and how goes it? I thought thee were lost; what took thou so long?'

'Out at Gran's most of the day,' Ron replied, taking his sombrero in his hands.

'How's the Bebee?' inquired Calo. 'I haven't seen her since I got back.'

'Well hearken, charvo, for she is not good. Sits in her chair all day and night, stumped on double-six, thinking about a last taste of aichi,' Ron said, edges of his lips twitching grim. 'Anyway, charvo, what thou having?'

'Nought for me, sticking with water,' said Calo, miserably swirling a glass crammed with ice around. 'Just got back from Spain, paid mi respects to Camaron and had a little holiday – not bad.'

'Aye! I heard thee were travelling, no one ever said Spain. I thought thee had gone down to the Wesh.'

'No. I had myself a touch of sun, sex and sangria and a dicky stomach in Cadiz,' said Calo, his nose hooking downward following the corners of his lips into a passable scowl. 'By the way, there's one in for thee,' continued Calo, stabbing the air in the direction of the beer-pump with a long thick forefinger.

Quickly, the fat barman pulled a pint of black stout. Ron

sipped his pint suspiciously. Calo was generous, almost well off, and he liked to play the Raya just like his father, old Arturo, but you couldn't always trust him. The stout slid into his belly like a sly sigh. Ron cracked dirty, 'Business good?'

Calo smiled. Bits of gold shot between his teeth glimmered ostentation.

'Well, I took the government up on its offer: ten years' worth. I have had enough of scratting a living, ducking and diving for fuck all - as of today I am a fully qualified businessman - entrepreneur if you will.'

'Thou shall rue it or if not thee, then close kin shall suffer for it.'

'I didn't know thou had taken up dookerin, Uncle,' said Calo, not trying to disguise the scorn in his voice. Ron grabbed Calo by the throat, but Calo wouldn't back down. 'Listen, Uncle, our problem is that we never get enough for a pot to piss in. The only way to get ahead is business, without that we're just so much chaff to be blown about in the wind. Only way to stop us getting our arse kicked is to pack a fat wallet in it. I am a businessman... So put me down, Uncle, and barman another pint for mi pal.'

Ron knocked the froth off his second pint. He wasn't a happy womble. Calo was too much like Arturo for comfort and that hurt. Ron glanced up through a hole in his hat at the cracked ceiling above and wondered if he'd catch an aichi in the wooded banks by the far bend of the river yon side of town.

'By the way, Nuncle, there's a hole that wants graving at St Olaf's, pick you up at eight sharp, ten pound cash in hand, no questions asked and anyway I'm paying thy tax - what do you say?'

It had come at last, the reason for Calo's calling, but two pints of stout and a tidy little job weren't all bad news. Ron touched his hat, signalling an agreeable 'Aye.'

'Sound, I shan't pay you now, in case thou sups it, but I shall see thee at eight sharp, so don't let me down, Nuncle. Time to nash, for I mun see a man about a dog.'

'Calo,' Ron called out, tersely. 'There's some stuff that might be worth taking a deek at back at the gaff.'

'I'll give it the once over when I pick you up or drop you off,' said Calo, stroking his tash thoughtfully – he was thinking of shaving his tash off, going in for a more clean-cut image now that he was an official businessman.

Ron nodded goodbye, gazed stoutly at his porter. He was in a brown study: the pitch-black pint, nicotine stained walls, the worn creaking floorboards, and the rime of grime beneath his thumbnail – all seemed to add up to so very little in the end. Suddenly, a fluttering hand pecked at his shoulder, a hand not to be ignored, and Ron turned to find the slime green eyes of his housemate, her pale face betraying thin starved bone and a hungry mouth clamped in a smeared smile that slid over a buttercup yellow snaggletooth. Ron was in lust. Old pains self-equipped with longings stirred his loins and his blood beat thick. He ordered a babyslam tequila surprise, before escorting the short, bleached blond to an unstable table by the shove a pound coin board.

Tracy slammed and a stream of effervescence streamed from her nose like over-stimulated effluence which was dabbed to a nicety by an over worked foulard which she kept in her handbag by her purse of light change, tampon and emergency packet of condoms anxious of reaching their sell-by date. Tracy laughed, her rosebud lips efflorescing around the yellow centre of her snaggletooth. Ron laughed too and hoped that he was not due another dose of unsought love forwearied as he was of such a substantiated emotion.

The lass was gawky, unsure of herself, as she drank she talked about her little boy that had learnt to crawl and cost her fourteen stitches several on the tail end. It was painful, everything was laid bare: the fierce beatings of the little heart beneath her breast and fashion vest. The worry she at times couldn't contain, like not getting his wind up, meningitis, would he grow up rough and take crack-cocaine and the social worker that was coming round sometime any indefinite week for a ten month assessment. Tracy was worried, but she'd go through it all again. Perhaps.

Ron relayed the past through his mind and couldn't do a thing with it. They'd have another drink, make small moves, like stroking her hand as he passed her another bottle, letting his knee slide against hers under the table, boisterous play when he cracked a joke and if all augured well he'd make a move, move in close, nibble a little kiss, he could see it now before his eyes, her small eager face and her sweet deep sighs, the taste of her cunt pungent and animal, her breath warm down his neck, the embrace of legs urgent and tremulous, and the raw disappointment of cold early morning. Ron looked at the lass munching happily on a packet of Salt and Sod All Potato crisps. Ron squeezed her hand and decided to leave.

'Would you care to share a bag of one of each?' Ron asked, swilling the dregs of his pint around his glass like a poor excuse for a merry-go-round.

'Aye, can do,' smiled Tracy, spraying fragments of crisps in cloud of spittle.

'Time for bed said Zebadee,' said Ron, finishing off his ride on the merry-go-round and showing his age and unreasonable ambition. Ron had always wanted that spare horse on the Magic Roundabout, but this had nothing to do with this sudden desire to take the girl to bed: *Time for bed, said Zebadee*, but what did that fuck with a tash and spring up his ass know about women?

They skipped walking the alley, leaving it to the soft falling rain and stalking stalkoes or late-night interlopers out walking their dogs, but headed instead across town to Barry Heinz's Fish 'Ole which sold a very superior 'one of each' where Ron ordered a take-away haddock and chips with everything on it. Huddled against the rain seeking hot slivers of fish or fat fried chips Ron and Tracy made it home to wide-awake baby and slumbering babysitter. Through a hardly stifled yawn, Clare from upstairs mouthed, 'Good night' and disappeared around the bend of one of the old servants' stairs, up to her rabbit hutch recently reclaimed from a neglected part of the attic and two squatting hamsters, whilst Tracy changed Samuel's nappy, as Ron tried to leave, but was conned into making gurgles and goos thus keeping the mother sunny-side up. The child too was happy, unreasonably happy, surprisingly fat with cherry red cheeks and striking blue eyes that closed silently into untroubled sleep that outlasted the night.

When the baby was safely lain in its makeshift cot of a bottom drawer of a chest of drawers made, Tracy bad Ron to take a seat, patting a place by her side. Ron watched with unexplainable interest as clouds of dead skin-dust bled into the air before taking his seat as baden. When Tracy came close, Ron moved away, not from any sudden coyness, but distancing himself from images that came to his head like unbidden melodramas, underwritten by the past that started in bed and ended in love despite every effort to the contrary.

'Is it me?' she said, doubt a question mark held tightly in her eyes.

'Nay, it is me,' he said, shifting slightly further away.

'The bairn then?' she said to him, a wobble troubling the skin of her chin.

'Nay, it's me not him,' he said.

'Then what's the matter then?' she said, a smile fragile about her lips. 'Don't ye want it, don't ye like me, don't I turn ye on then - ye're not queer?'

'Nay,' he said with a slight shake of his head. 'I just can't be bothered going through the same old rigma-hole,' said Ron resisting the merging of I and thou, into the psychic twinned identity of I-thou and the bairn too, the subtle shift of personhood into an internalised conglomerate based on need and mutual misunderstanding, the frictional infighting of any relationship as the different members pull and strain, vainly trying to assert dominance, an antagonistic dialectic that fights for self and then retreats to the self that is safely subsumed by the other, so when the break comes the depersonalisation takes its toll, a self no longer able to define itself except as the I-thou that no longer is, a self alienated, at home with nothing but the scars of dependent love, a necessarily impossible love born out of the struggle of being and the subjugation of being. All of this fluttered through Ron's head as he turned to Tracy and assured that, 'Sorry, love, but I can't be arsed with relationships.' Ron pulled on his bottom lip.

'Who the hell said aught about the autonomy of the self? What's wrong with having a shag? You've got some bloody nerve, Ron!' shouted Tracy, angrily, who had been following the internal monologue by a simply stunning feat of subaudition. 'Who the hell said anything about love? I fancy a night of no-holds-barred, deep-down-dirty monkey-fucking. It's been over a year since I had one. If I'm not bloody careful mi twat's gonna heal over!' This was more information that Ron cared for, but at least for a moment the release of invective cooled Tracy's temper, though doing nothing for the subduing of her ardour. 'Come on, pet, don't you fancy me? Don't you fancy a bit of the other?'

Ron wouldn't lie to himself, not for anyone. He stood up.

'So you are going, thank you oh so very much!' snorted Tracy, her arms fiercely folded beneath her Pseudo-Bra re-stylised breasts.

'Got a sink in here? This one of those rooms with a small sink and a kitchen?'

'Aye,' affirmed Tracy, slightly puzzled. 'Through them there curtains,' said Tracy, pointing out a discoloured maroon curtain hanging dejectedly from an improvised washing line.

Ron passed through, parting the curtains, taking off his sombrero, kicking off his sandals, dropping his dungarees in a crumpled heap by his ankles and with unexpected delicacy he stepped away from his clothes and on finding a spelk of soap he carefully washed himself. Amused, from the mattress thrown on the floor, Tracy watched and started to undress, after first procuring a couple of condoms from her bag. Ron sauntered back whilst trying to dry himself on a beer towel hung from a disconnected gas fire with real glowing coals.

The first thing she noticed was the smell of man beneath the smell of soap. Next the surprising softness of his sallow skin, felt then her pudendum churn hot honey, felt his prick stiffen from playful licks, felt the hardening of his nipples as she brushed each with lips. His tongue spilled into her, sending spasms in waves to shake her frail birdlike frame. She came once, it was fast and sweet and ended too swiftly. She came, drawing a moan from deep within. Wasting no time, she sheathed his pumped-up cock and drew him in, arching her back and digging in her hips. She bore down on him again and again, feeling him spurt sperm tight inside her and came again, coming till his penis slumped slack and she grinded him down for a final moan that sent her whole body into quakes of shivers.

'Thanks, pet, not bad,' said Tracy.

Ron withdrew his wilted cock from the condom, the neck of which he tied with a knot not taught by the Scouting movement. Tracy rose and turned off the light. They crept beneath the covers, uncomfortable but holding each other tightly, and listened to the night traffic outside slowing to sleep. The thud of blood slowly subsided in his head. Ron ceased to feel the melting sensation that had fused him to the girl. Her hand cupped gently his John Thomas and Ron felt betrayed by sex again and how good it was. A car drove into the night, the sound of its engine diminishing to nothing but an echo within his head.

Tracy slept on, snoring softly.
* Some folk sleep easy in their bed.

Chapter Three
Enter a Tadge of Domestic Strife

Baby and mother were still heavily sleeping when Ron awoke struggling with indolence and sleep as he reclaimed his clothes. Checking on the time, he pulled back a chink of curtain to greet the day. A sepulchral sun was scaring the shit out of grey-arsed clouds scudding by doing their best to get the hell away from this slate-grey day. He was in danger of running late, swiftly he kicked open the door to his own room, kicked off his sandals and forced on his big boots - a present he had acquired when he once did a little work on a siding for some railway or other. He hurried downstairs, passing the door to Christine's box-room below the stairs where he heard her moan out from the shell of sleep, startlingly erotic in the sombre quiet of early morning. His John Thomas was starting to fill out a bit, but he fought the good fight and pulled away from Christine's door in time. Ron hoped he had no time for opportunist sensuality, but not too much.

Outside, leaning against the gate, a dwarf with delirium tremens searched through a formal photo album for a past life with a sepia finish. The lad was getting there.

'Look, she my mother,' pointed the dwarf with a broken finger to a lady beautiful and dark, seated in an alcove of antiquated design, but possibly due to be back in vogue any Sunday supplement day soon. The lady was striking a pose with a frill-trimmed parasol. It looked corny, but genuine and authentic at the same time – genuinely corny. 'The big man, he my father,' pointed the same wounded finger to an upright man, distinguished by his late forties and little else. 'He was Armenian, a very clever businessman, and my mother a Sephardi who married out of the family and was cursed by her own father. We had a big house not far from the river.' The snapped finger sped onto a picture of a big house in its pristine prime: horse and carriage, servants, butler and everyone knowing their place, though the odd one was looking just a smidgen out of focus. It took some recognising, but the dwarf had come home, crouched over his own front step. 'And these are my brothers and sisters and over here the servants.' This time he pointed with his eyes only, his fingers were apprehended by a violent tremble. And the girls were pretty and dark and the boys healthy and slender. The dwarf had pain, hallucinations and a story.

Calo pulled up in a three-tonne lorry.

'Jump in, Prazla, we're running a little late,' said Calo, not waiting, reversing over a pile of rat-ravaged bin-liners dumped on the sidewalk. Some bags split and tatty newspapers spilled hither and thither till Calo jammed on the brakes and took a deek. Sizing up the situation he loaded up the bags and later that day got a tenner or so for the job lot from the re-cycling place yon side of Priorsgate. Suffice to say the pick-up was turned round and Calo was raring to go, glancing at his pocket watch as once worn by a stationmaster for the Derwent Valley Line – the subtle transience of history, held on a chain, kept in a pocket.

'He's with me,' said Ron.

'Who?' asked Calo, staring across the seat out of the side window.

'This wee man,' said Ron, swinging open the door. The dwarf struggled in and up, braving it all with a sequacious smile and photo album. Ron banged the door home. Calo drove.

St Wilfred's stood a little way out of town, in a hamlet converted to commuter-ville, but, despite its size, at once upon a time or two only the most important people had been buried there. The poor of that parish had been buried in the next village in a sodden field good for rough grazing and little else. A rowan and a yew tree graced the neatly laid out cemetery. The dwarf wandered freely, visiting headstones or taking his rest beneath the trees as Ron delved and graved a fresh hole for the expected dead and Calo promised to be back at twelve, and with that he sped leaving a trail of cold purple hydro-benzines and other smuts to hang condemned in the air.

Coming up the narrow snicket by the roadside, a portly

Punchinello hailed the morning in sexton garb. He addressed Ron, ignoring the sleeping person of the dwarf. Ron wiped his face, gave a perfunctory nod before carrying on digging. The sexton wanted to speak to Mr Herne, apparently there were several old graves to be moved. Ron offered a price, but the sexton gave a pre-emptive smile and said he'd wait till he spoke to Mr Herne. Ron shed an indifferent shrug from off his bowed shoulders and informed the flaty that Calo would be back at twelve. This sexton sauntered away, whistling some tastefully set psalm as the dwarf, sat on the edge of the grave, began to tell something more of his story.

A talesome flow of words wept unconditionally from swelled breast to pulverulent mouth, beginning enfolded within heart of family, proud anxious father, grateful protective mother and a series of siblings overjoyed at the arrival of the 'wee fellow' - a name breached into birth by the lone ageing Irish cook. If he fell he picked himself up, if he couldn't reach, he dragged a chair or seat so as to reach, if gamins from poor streets teased him in his garden, he grabbed a stick and would get a beating, if repulsed at a dance, he took a chance and asked another yet another, if unsure what to do with his life, he took a boat and travelled Europe, speaking French, antiquated Spanish and ancient Haik - he was strong and had become a man thankful to no one. Poverty and pity one time brought him back. Seeking release he joined a circus, he had to humble his carefully cultivated dignity, a clown, a dwarf, a figment of fun to make the tall people laugh - a hungry heart held in abeyance by a laugh. In the circus he found money, found fame, but suffered his wealth with regret and shame, till he saved sufficient to start his own circus that travelled the East, became the darling of the liberated proletariat: his bright red and white striped circus became a felicific temple undertaking tours of the Soviet Republic. All was well till he began to hear suppressed cries haunting the laughter spat out in cathartic roars beneath his dripping red and white rent tent. Pity came back and taunted him again. His heart was too big for his frame, till the day they came and gave him a one man tour of Siberia...It was over, a social experiment, his banished life, he was old, very old, a hundred years or more, but he had returned, inside his guts a cancer burns to which he treats raw vodka and morphia, but he has returned to find a house, a scrapbook of memories and a languishing inheritance, but chiefly he has returned to die, though scared of the omnipresent pain contained in the present and would pray to a disclaimed God to take his final sigh in sleep, civilised and on the sly.

There was more, much more but how much faluting fabulation can one dwarf manage seated by the side of a grave as a man with a spade sets about his business? Not much, seemingly.

The talking was done, the dwarf was dry and in pain, from beneath his jacket he drew forth a half bottle of pure white spirit. Ron banked up the gravesides, when he'd finished he glanced up to find the dwarf soundly sleeping, his breath light and faint as mistle thrush's fart. Ron sighed. He couldn't help himself. He dug the grave deeper, then stood on his spade to get out. The dwarf was still lost in the arms of Morpheus. Grabbing his feet, with one swing, Ron dashed the dwarf's head against the highly ornate tombstone of Mrs Ethel Brown, beloved wife of Henry and darling mother of Harold and Eva, born 1834 died 1892, sadly missed, rest in peace. Ron checked that the dwarf was truly dead afore throwing the corpse and album into the grave and covering the body with a scattering of ruddy earth. Ron was meticulous about death. He was himself somewhat sceptical about it all and he nursed a great fear of being buried alive. But the small traveller had died indeed. A quick prayer to Saint Antony, the patron saint of gravers, and Ron could sit back in the mortified shade, sink a mouthful or two from the orphaned bottle and await the return of Calo. Somewhere a wren sang, but Ron didn't notice.

Eleven came with the threat of rain and Ron slept on beneath the shade of an untrammelled tree that had been a Brahmin, beneath six psychotic daisies who had played no mean part in the battle of the beginning of the world, held back petalled scimitars and talked of the time when they had been great amongst the kshastriya ignoring as best they could the sleeping chandala. Distant days of great slaughter when the car of the Juggernaut had ravaged the plains of Indus, a time for jackals, a time for vultures and hearts that shrank not from triumphalist jugulation. Quiet amongst quieter neighbours the daisy chain wept tears of impotency as the sweat of the chandala fell amongst them, seeping to the roots poisoning everything unclean. Cloud thinned and the burning wheel of the sun bore down upon the sleeping and the dead alike. At home, the brown mouse remembered the time when Kicking Bear returned from the Paiute having learnt a new dance and no stealer of buffalo fat could touch him. The mouse hopped from leg to leg in the centre of the plain carpet whilst above, spiders fed upon the juice of clumsy flies. The chandala slept on amongst impassioned flowers and outraged leaf-spreading halidom.

Back in the flat, fetid with baby shit and overworked air, a social worker sipped piss-willy tea from a chipped cup with faded roses trained up the handle. Her face was framed by steel spectacles that she didn't need, but which afforded her a more officious air or so she hoped. A ladder staggered unevenly up the purple stocking of her right shaved calf. Her report was already made. It was time merely for its presentation. Tracy chewed the skin off her knuckles, her face white and tight and brittle as china. In the makeshift cot, by the makeshift bed, Samuel out-stared the sky's hues of oblivious blue. The social worker had finished wetting her unfurled lips with tepid tea and tried to furnish her voice with a decidedly delicate funebrial tone culled from the mortician's school of elocution - turn left, just by Netto as one is going to Bargain Basement.

A Nazi officer encased another famous Jewish composer with gut-spun hate-thread – a web of spite shook slightly. Out of breath, heart more fleet than friendship, the brown mouse keened for the treachery of Little Big Man: of all the Sioux to betray Crazy Horse it had to be him. Crazy Horse entered the real world, his horse always dancing, his father foretold that he would never be slain in battle, and upon his return to earth he saw everything clothed in shadows. By Wounded Knee Creek a red heart beats, beating out time when the Black Hills will be returned: a horse dancing. Brown Mouse chewed his tail to shreds, gazed up above at the unlit light bulb and danced and danced, entering a trance where Crazy Horse sees clearly and the great medicine man of the Hunkpapa Lacota awaits his reclaimed land and reborn children.

The day sliced in half, gentle falling of summer rain, Ron awoke refreshed to witness the prism-plashed semi-curve of refracted light. The earth was alive with possibilities, the world had been opened, the horizon spanned by: gestating embrace of divers lights and Ron was awake to life. A three tonne pick-up growled up the road at spluttered speed. Ron rose, straightened his sombrero and walked down to meet Calo quickly.

'Eh up, how goes it?' Calo bawled out the open window, lurching to a halt.

'Not so bad, but by the way, yon vicar wants a word: there's some graves to be shifted or summat,' Ron said, leaning against the cab.

'Should've made him an offer.'

'I did, but yon man wanted to speak to Mr Herne,' said Ron and Calo's eyes lit up though he managed to hold back a guffaw. Calo backed up a bit and tore away up the village.

Ron wasn't going anywhere. The day was clearing. A swift with sickle wings sliced seconds from the sky. Calo was back, rubbing his hands.

'A nice little bootsi for some mushe,' beamed Calo.

Ron looked less impressed with the phrase 'some mushe'. Ron threw his spade in the back of the pick-up and clambered up into the cab.

'Now as for thee, I've something on a bit more lucrative.'

'Oh, aye,' said Ron.

'Just bought the street rights on Gunnarsgate. I want you to manage it for us. It's a steady nine to five number: that's when the folk are allowed to pester passers-by, City Council by-law 26; after that time, they'll be banged up for the night, so ensure our people are off the streets by then, we haven't bought the mugging franchise. Now, each of our clients pays ten pound per shift, that's either a morning or afternoon, or they can pay a discount rate of fifteen pounds a day, a bargain, eh?'

'Oh, aye,' said Ron.

'As for yourself, for every fiver you take a pound, that's no small change at the end of the day. On top of that, I'll pay thy tax and whatnot and I've never met thee afore if anyone asks. I can't say fairer than that. So, what do you say?'

'Done.'

'Let's shake on it,' Calo's hand left the wheel and lined with a gob of spit the deal was sealed.

They were nearing town. The traffic was sluggish and slow, every inch gained became somehow precious. Calo was smoking a poisonous roll-up mix of dark shag and last year's beech leaves.

'By the way,' Calo said, from a smoke curling corner of his mouth, 'Behind thy seat, there's a bit of a present for thee I bought in Spain.'

From behind the seat Ron pulled out a brand new blue sombrero. Ron's eyes clouded slightly as he held the hat gingerly by the brim.

'Don't take on,' said Calo seeing the look in Ron's eyes.

Ron said nowt.

Calo spat out of the window. The traffic was still slow, but the turn into Ron's street neared. Ron wound down his window and sat the new sombrero on a pile of rubbish slouched by the kerb. Calo turned into Ron's street, pulled up outside the house.

'So then, where's this gear?'

'Inside,' Ron said, an Airfix model of taciturnity.

At the yon end of the street, a house rampant with run-away rot and insipid dilapidation was having its guts torn out by a team of imported Micks and Blacks and Dogs working on the cheap. Calo briefly gazed on, scratched his thick mustachio with the side of his thumbnail 'fore following Ron inside. Seated on the stairs between Terry and Jo, Tracy wept, the remains of her soul splattered like sick on her face. They had taken her child away.

It hadn't been easy. At least three different forms had to be filled in by the social worker. All that data, all those figures, by heck it took some working out. Thankfully, the figures had all been on the state's side. On the simple scale of happiness, there had been no question that the child would stand a better chance of happiness and social advantage when adopted by a couple of the barren upper middle class. Still Samuel was not lost without a fight. But today's newly privatised social worker is fully equipped to deal with most commonly found forms of obcordate illogicality, she merely pointed out that it was within her capabilities to write a report stressing the squalor of the home environment and thus advising in no uncertain terms that the child be forcibly removed and taken into care, whereby the child would be auctioned to the highest bidder, worse, to keep a child in such conditions was a heinous crime, a crime that the state and the crusading moral majority of the Frustrated Mothers' Union took a very dim light on indeed, so why risk imprisonment? Far better to accept the rather lucrative terms and conditions of voluntary adoption: three thousand pounds tax-free. Samuel was signed away immediately, leaving in the arms of creative officialdom, the officer well satisfied that her commission had been fairly won.

The Social Security came round without a moment's notice and fined the mother for undeclared income: three thousand pounds or six months hard labour or become a voluntary victim of human experimentation. Tracy paid up in full. Tracy sat on the stairs nurturing despair.

Ron took her hand, stroked the cool clammy flesh - something had died quietly inside. Terry and Jo shooed him away; it took a woman's touch. It took more than that, but Ron left.

Calo had seen it all before, long before the Democratic Revolution and the Glorious Enabling Act – the Glorious Revolution. And though only a bairn he had watched social workers and the police when they came for the Smiths and had never forgotten. There had been seven kids in that family, who didn't go to school enough and shewed every sign of poverty but not neglect, and were taken into care. As far as he, Calo, knew the Smiths were still trying to get their kids back. Nothing was new, but the walnut wardrobe was a tidy piece of work and the second hand typewriter could come in handy for some kind of folk technology village. He paid Ron up front and slipped him a twenty pound bill over and above the ten for the morning. Tracy moved towards her memories and back into her room making way for Ron and Calo to shift the gear from Una's room. It was all in a day's work.

First Discrepancy of Salty's Shirt Box

Tracy couldn't believe that it could be so easy to lose her child. She had the social worker go over the figures one more time and still she could not believe the result. Okay, the figures, the net balances and all the rest of it were not in dispute, but she couldn't believe it was the right decision, that somehow seemed something else. Still, you couldn't argue with maths, not unless you were dead brainy, which Tracy knew she was not, still…such a small word, 'still' and it still kept coming back as if she was stuck and couldn't think anything else. It was more than a mental pause, it was like hitting a point of balance and being scared or unwilling to move one way or the other.

'Could I hold t' bairn one last time?'

'Well, strictly speaking, it is no longer your child, once you have signed on the dotted line agreeing to the assessment and it would be deeply unprofessional for me to-'

'Fuck you then,' Tracy grabbed this estranged child of her own, ran to the window and didn't stop.

The social worker began to punch in other sums. Her bonus was no longer looking so certain; still, there was always the next client.

Terry and Jo ambled up the garden path. There spread before them like burst whinberry and truffle yoghurt was one of the single mothers of an upstairs flat. They were about to walk on as it was becoming a bit of a bloody habit, this folk diving out of windows, when they heard a cry. Miracle, oh sweet Lord Jesus and Lord God of Israel be praised, the bairn was all right. It had landed softly on the spread belly of its mother.

Terry picked up the bairn. Jo muttered, 'More expense,' but no one took her on and she was only half-serious. Terry and Jo adopted and Jo earned enough to fuck off the social services and so every cloud has a positive aspect.

Calo skirted round the mess. Ron paused for thought. He couldn't help it. He thought and thought then felt and his head felt ready to burst. His hands gripped tightly into fists. The veins stood out on his hands. He was itching to hurt, to hit back, when Calo said, 'Are you going to shew me this stuff or not? I haven't got all night.'

Suddenly, Ron remembered he'd given up the thinking business and guided Calo to Una's flat. Calo gave it all the once over and was pretty damn chuffed. Nothing was new, but the walnut wardrobe was a tidy piece of work and the second-hand typewriter could come in handy for some kind of folk technology village. He paid Ron up front and slipped him a twenty pound bill over and above the ten for the morning. Terry, Jo and Samuel moved aside allowing Ron and Calo to shift the gear from Una's room. It was all in a day's work.

Here Endeth the First Discrepancy

Calo said goodbye to Ron, advising him to be up nice and early for the street didn't sleep. Ron needed a drink.

The Albert was shaded in second-hand smoke. A joker in a tinselled two-piece suit and a superficial smile told jaded gags about mother-in-laws, the cruder niceties of sex, tempered by a bit of bitching about Blacks and fags, but no one bothered to laugh, except when Ron sat him down with a mouthful of microphone - it had been a josh too far, offensive to his sensibilities of being a fully paid up card-carrying member of a long sidelined minority. It had been the lad's big break: one incisor and half a canine - bum! bum! hey now ladies and gentlemen. Ron briefly forgot his hate in the smile of a half-pint mug and a party of Coopers and Scamps who had arrived in town with the remains of a fun-fair. Mostly they wanted news of Arturo and if not Arturo, then that young scamp Calo, as it was well known he was on the up, on his way to becoming quite a Pharaoh, which pissed Ron off no end though he stayed for another pint of chat.

By the time Ron had arrived back, the house was alive with new-found residents with buckled arms heavy with collapsible cardboard cop-outs who had wandered up from the far end of the street where their former house was being worked over by a property developer; lucky for them that part of the attic had recently been made into extra squats. Ron climbed up to Tracy's room, cut her down from the electric light flex; there was another room free after all: it was someone's lucky day and there was no helping that. Ron was tired, blood sluggish with alcohol and orphaned regret slurring words of sleep in the arteries of his head, lulling him into a false sense of security: the unwritten night of deep sleep, where a nicely placed period becomes a full stop in the grammar of God; where sin and syntax meet and do a little dance, despite a full beery bladder and an unbidden semi-erection.

Chapter Four – And Why Not?

Gunnarsgate was littered with hawkers, musicians and erubescent beggars baking in the sun. A couple of raggy-heads sold threading hair, others slaughtered music with homemade tin whistles or instruments picked up here and there and over yonder that they couldn't play, whilst a small-time entrepreneur had a sign strapped to his back, 'Tonsoral Parlour – the Senator's Choice,' and clipped scalps two pound a throw, by his side an out of work poet who'd recite an ode for two quid, a sonnet Petrarchian, Elizabethan, or otherwise for a pound up-front and right down at the bottom of his hit-list a hastily constructed haiku or lightly rhymed limerick for fifty pence, notwithstanding a preacher in a born-again suit yet to be rumbled, who at first eschewed paying till he had his butt kicked by Ron, sold salvation on a first come first serviced basis about a God for the good and the damned who'd separate the sheep from the shepherd, and when it came to gays, the men from the boys, and damnation too for dykes, Blacks and other buggers, whom he called the devil spawn of Ham, and Reds and Holy Joes and the Jews who had first persecuted the Nazarene or anybody who had sex before he did or did drugs, that included those he didn't sell, or anyone at all that disagreed. And others too stood in line, staggered along the street, others that had no skill to sell, but begged people their daily bread with a gaunt look and a battered hat of misspent coppers. Ron went back to the preacher, who was talking of the Rapture and people sure were falling for it, he was selling Nazi Bibles bound from human skin faster than it took to blink or think and people did neither but froze salvation-bound, all open-mouthed, satisfied by a cut-throat messiah. Even some misguided mestizo with not the quite right shade of skin was cheering an apoplectic amen for an Anglo-Saxon, fair-skinned, blue-eyed Aryan, heaven help us. Ron came back and kicked the preacher's teeth in, once, twice, and thrice for the Third Reich and another to be going on with while waiting for the rapture to set in. Ron was making money, but it was no good he knew, though he also knew that the money would do to be going on with. Ron patrolled Gunnarsgate, an indolent shepherd of lost sheep, searching for a slaughter-house.

A tangerine girl, all river of ribs and unripe body, begged to turn tricks on the corner by the bridge. Ron wasn't too sure about how that stood with by-law 26, she pleaded, she even offered to suck his dick, but Ron slapped her face with a five pound note and told her to be gone from his street. It was a fast disappearing morning, all tam-tam sun and meagre, mediocre miseries waiting for the rest of their life to happen. It was a day like yesterday and all the rest of tomorrows. Ron crouched down on his hunkers and practised sending spitballs as far as he could, some to the other side of the street. Boy could Ron spit.

Dinner-time and Ron regulated the shift. Dinner-time and Ron invested in a portable clockwork radio to while away the hours with Radio Three interlaced with Four. Afternoon was much the same, save a preacher with a severed head beneath his oxter, walking along the middle of the road for gratis, proclaiming the second coming of Christ; a Christ bound by poverty and for the poor who though lowly born would be king of all, restoring the kingdom of heaven on earth, installing a new found multi-million dollar pleasure park, Disnee-Eden, where mankind can dwell and be made whole again. This was more the God that Ron didn't believe in, a poor man's socialist nailed to the cross, a big bearded God above with white hair and a couple of doves up his sleeves, whilst Holy Joe is out putting some virgin up the duff, probably via her ear or one of the other less carnal orifices and so Ron left him to it not even asking for a nominal sum and besides he weren't, as far as he could tell, selling anything, in fact no one took him on at all except Ron who didn't believe in him, still it whiled away the afternoon, pleasantly soaking up the sun and being forewarned of the world to come. If he wasn't careful Ron could wind up happy. A pit-bull with a scarred muzzle cocked his leg up a solitary lamp-post, fore wandering off for a fight - just killing time. Not a bad sort of a day to be out and about, thought Ron, going against his better principles and having a wee mental notion of a motion on the sly like.

Calo came to escort Ron for a pint down The Albert and to take over the takings. With precipitous care Calo explained how he would like the takings banked. Ron was not so sure. He didn't trust banks; it spoke too much of officialdom. But Calo was insistent; he was a big businessman now. Calo had just squared another deal with the town's licensing authority. Apparently there was a corner of Haarkongate for rent that the Masons had been trying to keep under wraps, but Calo had managed to sniff the lease out and a contract had been made. Haarkongate was prime crime space. Since the regulation of crime and its confining into certain recognised districts there had been a resultant rise in the cost of pavement space - it was nearly going through the roof.

'I'm not so much dealing myself, pal,' Calo confessed, still only quaffing iced water. 'Nay, I ain't having aught to do with that game, a right game of soldiers. One can wind up seriously dead for a patch of pavement floor nay bigger than thy shirt. I'm just renting out the pitch. I've had a good measure up. There's just enough space for two. Now you don't have to worry. I've got the lads lined up: Junior and Winston.'

'Don't tell me, a couple of white guys looking for their first break since leaving public school,' Ron said, searching the bottom of his glass for another drink in a pique of rare sarcasm.

'Course they're Black. You don't think I would be so daft as to flout the Stereotype Laws when I'm just starting out. By the way, another bitter please, barman, for mi pal.'

The Stereotype Laws had been introduced to secure the employment rights of specified recognised minorities, such as Micks who could only work on buildings sites, be quaint media front men provided that they had their leaving certificate in Stage Irishism or drunken tramps tied to an officially recognised park bench, as for their mots they were confined to nannies and nurses or if particularly talentless banished to the country and western circuit This group was in clear contradistinction to Blacks who were afforded a slightly wider choice, for example, dancers, musicians, top athletes willing to wear the butcher's apron, muggers, petty gangsters and drug dealers, as for the Chinese they were still deemed inscrutable and therefore tied to traditional restaurants and take-aways. Maybe Asians from the Indian sub-continent fared the best: take-aways, restaurants, lawyers, medics, corner-store owners, any petty business up to quite moderate providing they didn't mind fleeing again if the natives cut up rough. Certain other minorities were yet to be defined by supplements to the law, some were sidelined and forgotten whilst others were considered too powerful, for example like the Jews, though there had been an amendment suggesting that they might be confined to commerce, banking and classical music, but that was just another stereotype waiting upon political will – and anyway, the Glorious Revolution of Charles the Fifth that established the dictatorship of the silenced majority was not some kind of narrow minded proto-nazi state, lessons had been learnt from history, gradual solutions were the answer, finally.

'Now, take two hundred per person per night and there's fifty quid in it for thee. They report to you at the beginning of every shift, eight thirty, but remind them that they must be off the streets by four thirty a.m. - what do tha say?'

Ron nodded. It was all money in the bank. Money didn't make any sense to Ron, but he kent the distinction between poor and miserable, and rich and miserable. In any event, Ron had never felt that there had been much point to the pursuit of happiness, but he'd have another pint of bitter though.

Two suave Blacks introduced themselves. Their smiles were bright and their knife work efficient. They made a token haggle over price, but Calo wasn't budging, it was foolish to try and browbeat a former grychor, but these up and coming entrepreneurs weren't to know and besides they were just going through the motions, it was the cheapest pitch that they'd ever come across, but Calo wasn't to know. They swapped a round of drinks and agreed to take on the lease starting next week and it was time that Calo was expected home, Fenella[1] was waiting. 'Shom nash' Calo said and left, but the Blacks stopped for one more with Ron, they felt sorry for him with his drunk dog look and second-rate sombrero. Winston was the muscle and Junior the accountant, though on the face of it the roles ought to have been reversed, Winston had won a scholarship to the School of Oriental & African Studies, Mallet Street, and Junior was strictly ex-Golden Gloves imported in from New York by some foot-loose Yardies with distinctly international motivations. Ron sank like a paranoid penny into the hole of a wishing well, Ron sank into his cups like a collapsed sigh, Ron ran with his mind speeding away to some distinct infinity where parallel lines intersect just to say one last hello, goodbye, and he was feeling paranoid as hell. He didn't trust himself, the Blacks, barmen and the skull moon above, and wandering home by the cold bone river bank, where death had called today saddling his black horse by the ferry and taking rowers for a ride across the River Styx, two gamins stole the pennies from his eyelids, but death had called today and he was searching for another, rumour had it that Ron had been assassinated, they searched the synagogues, mosques and the crematorium, they raided supermarkets on the edge of town and opened a few tins of baked beans and discounted spaghetti, and they plundered thirty shilling skeletons for glue, but they never found Ron, no they never found him not at the end...

Ron fell upstairs, holding onto the dado rail with fumbling finger-tips, holding onto his head and a faith temporally returned from a teleological suspension of the unthinkable - crashing into his room like Zeus maiden-hunting on his day off to find

---

[1] Fenella is not mentioned again, speculation has it that given her low status, an embarrassment to Charles the Fifth, she was disappeared after the Glorious Revolution and but for an oversight by the binder operator she would have been silenced forever.

another - curled up asleep by the wall, but Ron thought he was dreaming already, climbing into his bed with the gratitude of an old whore tired of punters and short on luck. There Ron slept, sinking beneath a waking dream where the moon was only so much sterile love set above the earth to haunt hormonal flow and the surge of a lunar drunk sea, a black moon made of grave sides, a dream where nothing is possible with ever presently shifting contraries; a moon of hunted blood, duende: pena, amargo y soledad - duende.

Kisan Patel slept on maugre and despite intoxicated intrusions and dreamed of becoming a Tory councillor. Kisan had been breast-fed ambition and reverence for Queen Victoria. At school he had been blighted with a refreshingly unwielding diligence, leaving school with a clutch of grade 'A's and the honour of a brief captaincy of the second eleven. Kisan was a credit to his parents, his race and his school. Kisan had run away from home. He was going to make it big, any way he could. Kisan slept on whilst working on positions from the Karma Sutra in Mayoral dress hampered by a chain of office with a hard-on.

In the centre of the plain carpet the brown mouse woke from his trance.

He'd been flying, an eagle's wing hunting the wind above the Black Hills, Powder River Country and the vast open plains of the Sioux and Cheyenne, black with buffalo. A sacred time dream time, when he soared at one with the Great Spirit. The Great Spirit like the wind, felt but unseen, the Great Spirit like the air, empty but everywhere. The Great Spirit? The sun moon, stars the earth. The mouse had laughed when he first heard stories of how the white people tried to trap the Great Spirit in houses of wood and stone. How the Great Spirit was captured in a book. Only later did he worry that it might be true, when he saw the might of the white thieves tearing out the guts of the earth killing all things like a dark-hearted child and sending out diseases to kill the Great Spirit's first children. But he was wrong. The

Great Spirit was above and beyond in the land of brother bison, brother elk, where a horse is always dancing, where Sitting Bull is waiting for his returning children, where the white maggot spawned from a demon's turd never shall know, never shall go. Little Mouse felt his heart beating slower, felt his coat turn grey like the grass of winter, brown mouse knew it would not be long. He was passing on.

Uncle Salty's First
Downright Rude Intrusion

...There is a classic problem in literature, how to get from A to B. Fundamentally there are two biggies, necessity and chance. Necessity has traditionally generated the most numerous ploys of literature; the big '-isms' for example: naturalism, realism, various forms of psychological determinism. The ancients now seem more poetic by, more often than not, personalising fate in terms of the will of the Gods: from abandoned babe with swollen ankles to eye-gouging realisation. Yet, even the Gods are but a mask for disguising fate. Naked fatalism is necessarily the strongest form of determinism. In Njal's saga, there is never any problem in determining what happens next, it is determined already and that is its fascination. No matter what moves are made, how the seer Njal tries to stave off the inevitable, there shall be the movement A to B: Njal knows and has always known that he is burnt flesh. Alas, now it is not so simple. The movement from A to B cannot be so openly crafted. We seek diversion in internal movement and progression, from the noise of 'moo-cow' to the rambling of a menstruating woman or the movements and counter-movements of the precise, precious world of a Mrs Dalloway. Yet, for all the internal richness of mental machinations nothing is as patently determined as the confined life of Dalloway or Stephen's hungry wandering for a father and Bloom's need for a son. The means of moving from A to B have changed, but the movement is still necessary. A painfully traditional manoeuvre taken by many writers in overcoming if A, then B, is by resorting to the Will or more correctly acts of will. At the very end of 'Sons and Lovers', the young 'Lawrence' walks <u>quickly</u>. He chooses, he will move from A to B. However, all that is happening here is that notions of freedom have become necessary. Perhaps some kind of contra-causal randomness can liberate the movement of A to B. Yet, it would have to be that, a certain indeterminate leeway is not enough, we merely map causality in terms of probability and chance. There is but one answer, pure caprice: a man wakes up and yawns into a daffodil's bloom. Dada, certain surrealists and one or two examples gleaned from the Theatre of the Absurd clearly demonstrate the art of the possible when it comes to truly liberating the movement of A to B. But this is not my problem, determinism/indeterminism, my sole concern is with A. I don't want movement, change, progression, but merely to be. A novel where nothing happens. A novel opened, dissected, with all its predicates laid bare for all to see. Gone are adventure, moral progression, enrichment, a study of manners or the plight of man, pursuit of human freedom and countless other formulations of A to B. There is only permanence. Sterility...Is this enough? Consider every day the dawn rises, Sisyphus rises, yawns, scratches his nuts and proceeds to roll the boulder up the hill. All day long he fucks about rolling up the stone, as night draws in so does the boulder near the summit. In the last light of day the boulder slips from Sisyphus's hands and rolls to the valley below. Sisyphus descends the hill, curls up by the boulder to sleep. On the morrow he shall wake to roll the boulder back up the hill. And this happens day in and day out, it has always happened and it shall forever be. But my preoccupation is this, namely if qualitatively one day is the same as the next, if there is nothing true about day X from any other day or not true of one day from any other day, if and only if everything is true of one day as of any other day, do we then have no movement? Is this one day or no day or do such concepts make sense? Nothing happens, nothing changes, everything is. I want a novel like that, that asserts, 'that A' not once, twice or whatever number, but completely...Perhaps this is all my arse. Give me a pint of plain with a pickled egg in it and let me polish mi pit boots for the morning.

Sadly, Here Endeth Salty's First Intrusion

'Who the fuck are you?' Ron asked by means of an exaggerated yawn ripe with beer breath. Morning rested unwilling to become day against the speckled bird-shit-pitted window. Kisan was awake but apprehensive. He didn't want to become another victim of Paki-bashing and besides he had his pride, he was an Indian and a British subject and no Paki. His great grandfather, a rather well to do Senior Indian Civil Servant, had cried when the British had left India and here he was, his great grandson, living in the mother country, trying to earn his fortune and about to be accosted by person or persons unknown, perhaps he ought to write to the Queen.

'I said, who the fuck are you?' said Ron without the aid of a yawn, just a bewildered scowl or two.

With operose care Kisan considered the question, but was no wiser and startled the morning slumbering against the windowsill by several long drawn out bouts of cachinnation, which Kisan hoped would be loud enough to smother the embarrassment of who he was. Ron was up by now, allowing himself a rudimentary dig round his testicles as he wondered where he had mislaid his hat late last night. Kisan had stood up also and, making a bow that would have put a resting cabotin to shame, announced himself, enter stage right, 'I am Mr Kisan Krishna Patel.'

'You still here?!' an exclamation mark coupling with a half-hearted interrogative somewhere in the flow of surprise spat out into the early morn air, courtesy of Ron. Ron was still searching for his sombrero which by chance turned up, surfacing like the face of a drowned man from beneath the abandoned folds of blankets and sheets that had the consistency of unloved cardboard. 'Mi hat,' affirmed Ron.

Then he saw it, small, grey, grey-brown mouse dead by his hat. Ron knelt down and stroked the wee vainglorious beestie. He wouldn't cry, though he and the mouse had lived for a good while together and never a cross word atween them. It was a shame though that it wasn't quite plump enough to be considered esculent, but there you go, you can't have everything your own way. Ron put it in his dungarees bib pocket and promised to give it a good burial when he had chance.

'It's dead.'

'Yes,' agreed Kisan, shewing a polite line of smiling dog-yellow teeth.

'Right, don't piss mi about old son, what can I be doing for thee?'

Kisan sensed that this was his big chance. He cleared his throat, raked his brown fingers through his black hair and threw himself on the mercy of the strange man with the subsistent sombrero and dead mouse, though he did take heart that a person so loving to animals was to whom he was plying his entreaty, 'I am the only off-spring from a happy, though morganatic marriage and I have come to the Mother Country to make my fortune.'

Ron had to admire the wee brown man, he was bold as balls on a dog. 'Go on old son, I'm listening.'

What a friendly place, thought Kisan, two men after only having just made each other's acquaintance, though they have slept together, but none the less already a stranger was calling him son - oh brave new world.

'On reaching Blighty I traversed the country in a very accommodating omnibus till I reached a surprisingly declining town, Brattfud, where a cousin on my father's side had settled down after being forcibly removed from Uganda, which was all very well, save my cousin's house was rather over-endowed with occupants and work opportunities in the Brattfud were not exactly promising, thus despite my very best endeavours, I failed to secure work though I was not altogether despondent as my cousin suggested removing myself to this very fine and historical city where no doubt my mastering of the History of England would prove advantageous in pursuit of work in the blossoming tourist industry of which Caer Eabrac is so rightly proud but no sooner had I managed to find lodgings than I was made homeless. This as you may imagine grieved me grievously, but I am not one to stand in the way of progress: the house in which I rented a room is being renovated and refurbished to a very high standard indeed.

'Howbeit, it did rather leave me with a problem, namely where was I to seek shelter that night, but for once I was fortunate no sooner had I walked down the garden path, than one of the partners who is developing the South Bank Area advised me that very reasonable lodgings were to be had not fifty yards from my former recently restored front door, so it was thus that I arrived here late at night and unaware that I had inadvertently committed an act of trespass by spending the night sleeping in your room. I humbly beseech your forgiveness Mr...I am sorry I failed to catch your name,' said Kisan stretching out his hand.

'No you didn't, lad, cos like I never gave it you. Come with me and look sharp,' said Ron kicking open the door with a hastily sandalled foot.

Kisan did his best to look sharp. He sucked in his cheeks, which highlighted his fine cheekbones and finely chiselled chin, though lending his face a certain drawn look of inanition.

The stairs were tired with time and the dust huddled into darkened corners swapping mucky jokes: just hanging out with the boys. The air was only so much tired breath exhaled by a chain smoking God with emphysema and terminal halitosis. A weak pool of light wept from a skylight above and cast estranged shadows into the inalienable gloom of the stair head and hallway. Ron kicked open a door, stubbing his big toe and surprising two ageing hippy lovers attempting a bacchanal of hot knives and tarot card readings.

'Sorry,' Ron apologised to Kisan, 'wrong room.'

'It is all right my dear, Sir, a very comprehensible error that reflects upon the perpetrator to no ill effect,' Kisan assured with a gentle sweep of his right palm.

Next door was more like it, empty save for a skeleton hanging by the throat by a moth-eaten silk stocking and a dead crow trapped in the grate of the redundant fireplace, its wings still struggling to flap in the tug and flow of a lame draught drawn by the heat-hungry chimney. Kisan was pleased, he knew squalor when he saw it. He knew also that the only way for him now was up. Kisan didn't know much. Not that Ron had time for what the Indian did and did not know - he had work to do. Outside the sun was hot and plenty bright. The takings would be good on Gunnarsgate that day, of that Ron had no doubt. Back on his own floor Ron dumped, then washed hurriedly. On reaching downstairs Ron was surprised to see Calo standing by the gate. Rumour had it that Calo was to be travelling again; another vain bid to echo his father's, Arturo's, footsteps. But so much for rumour, for not only was Calo very much still on the scene, he was in earnest conversation with the now flamboyantly suited Indian. More surprises were in store when Ron heard Kisan address Calo, 'Yes, Mr Herne I shall see to it to your uttermost satisfaction.'

'Oh there you are, Ron. Ron, meet Mr Patel, my floor manager. He'll be taking care of things while I am away, including the banking. I want you two to liaise in my absence... Well, be seeing you.'

'Aye,' said Ron verging on the unimpressed, what did it matter to Ron if Calo was running around in a very second-hand Mercedes, who the fuck did he think he was – Rose Kelly?

Kisan waved a rather colourful handkerchief by way of goodbye. He turned to speak to Ron, as the car turned and disappeared at the top of the street, and commented, 'A most remarkable man is our Mr Herne, a veritable Babbitt and no mistake, and to think I only met him last night - a most advantageous chance encounter, oh most indubitably so... By the way, Mr Smith, my most esteemed colleague, are we not running a little late this morning? I take it that you are managing Gunnarsgate are you not, best be prompt now, run along for I would hate to remove a most honoured colleague to a more desultory position such as supervising mendicants on St Olaf's Street or poncing for malapert courtesans on the corner of Kirk Square. A very good day to you, Mr Smith.'

Kisan sauntered off in the direction of Kirk Square. Ron made himself comfortable in Gunnarsgate, listened to the wireless as he took the morning's money. A fire-eating female contortionist from Cleckheaton signed up for a full day. She was built of soft supple curves, but still Ron doubted that she had the stamina for a full day on the street, but hell it was no business of his, the kid had paid and Mr Patel would be round soon for his cut and taking the takings to bank. Ron sold floor space to a mute who made strange strangulated tones whilst whittling away his inner left arm with an antique razor blade. It was such a day that all the office workers pepped up on coke whistle to work and forget to donate spare change to begging cups. It was the day that Ron's dole arrived. He left his post on the corner of Gunnarsgate, went home to find his giro out of its depth amongst unsolicited mail and adverts for haircare products. Cashing his giro he bought a packet of ginger creams and sought out the company of Mrs Jenkins. Ron liked to keep his promises.

Uncle Salty's Second Intrusion

...Time and literature invite many different relationships. On one hand we read in real time, the last five minutes before dropping off to sleep, minutes sneaked on the bus, train, tube or before the children arrive home, and at the same time we are distanced from our temporal settings by our reading. There is a dislocation, a sense of distancing: the work is historical, the novel recounts a life from birth to grave, the work is one day of criss-crossing characters mapping Dublin city though it took you three weeks to read. Yet the more interesting relations are the temporal dimensions set up by the fiction. Time is given definition by events, but a work can exhibit many different series of events yielding a rich landscape of time or multi-layered time: time on many planes. In the novel Catch 22, divers chains of events portray time in different ways: missions flown, letters received, when and where was money from the war made. More worrying is the double time in Shakespeare's Othello. We follow a seemingly simple progression of events, yet below the surface we become aware of a greater length of time elapsing between given events, in order for the Moor's tragedy to take full effect, to have a meaning, to be possible. Time is not a dimension in a novel. Time is a hue, coloration, shade and light...

Here Endeth the Second Intrusion

Mrs Jenkins had loneliness etched into every wrinkle of her made up smile. She still wore black, a sleek number she had run up from an old pair of velvet plush curtains, but her mouth was semi-circles of seduction paint and her eyes were done in black outlines so startling that they drank in the light. Mrs Jenkins was pleased to see Ron, the children were at school, the room was empty of everything but memories and it was a hot afternoon such that her cunt ran like butter and her heart hoped for too much. She was unreasonably pleased with a twenty per cent extra free packet of ginger creams from Aldi. They were one of Ron's favourites too, but he didn't let it get to him. Mrs Jenkins bad Ron to take a seat as she removed an unfinished collection of hand made knickers and bras that were made from only the finest material - Mrs Jenkins was paid thirteen dollars per item and she was quick with her stitching; it took her mind off her ironing. Mrs Jenkins asked Ron why he had never married and Ron dunked his ginger cream into a fine bone china cup with a chip out of the rim as he always did and wondered why Mrs Jenkins was so pleased to make the same mistake twice. Mrs Jenkins assured Ron that all he needed was a good woman. Ron assured her, he needed a good woman like a new sombrero, that when it came to needing good women the only people he knew that were in the market were Terry and Jo, but even they at the moment only needed each other and anyways maybe it ain't a question of need, but greed. Ron didn't know what he was talking about, but he liked to splice a little rhyme to his speech now and again, but Mrs Jenkins wasn't put off that easily she played some old rare jazz when Mingus was just a lad and went by the name of Baron Mingus and seating herself collateral fashion she waited for a fresh cup of tea and another ginger biscuit with just that hint of spice.

The afternoon was balmy with sin and death looking for a bride. The augurs from the Met Office predicted a hot sticky night impossible to sleep in whilst sociologists gave a seventy-five per cent chance of riots in the inner cities. The odds were high enough to warrant the instigation of the Mobile Serotonin Unit. It is a proven fact that a significant percentage of aggressive monkeys have a genetic constitution such that they produce significantly less serotonin. Of course, the Mobile Unit wasn't employed to catch monkeys, they just rounded up young men, boys, women, and even lasses and pumped them full of serotonin when nights were hot and long and impatient with discontent. It produced significant reductions in street violence and social conflagration. Now who's afraid of science?

Adolphos Jones for one, last time they pumped him full of that shit, he couldn't get a decent hard-on for months, maybe there were other drugs in the serotonin, maybe it was part of some plan to stop the underclass breeding, well they may nail the others, but they weren't nailing him. He surfed along on a hot sirocco wind sultry as a kiss from the black whore of Babylon with nothing on his mind but the power of his limbs, they got his brother, they gotten his daddy too, but they weren't getting him. He had a piece strapped beneath his Italian shirt, designed in Scunthorpe, no shit top designer, see he wears the label on the inside, and a flick-knife supple and quick as a cobra's tongue, they took his sister, they gotten his mammy too, but no they wasn't getting him. He had a smile as sheer as the shine off the edge of the razor blade, he had wits honed by survival techniques learnt at the edge of the world, and as he moved he made no more noise than a shade, he was half dead all ready, they killed his wife, gotten his only child too, now there was two wise-heads standing on the corner selling shit-rotten crack-cocaine, they'd poisoned his cousins, gotten most of his best friends, but they wouldn't get him no they wouldn't take him, he was the night panther and he was on the prowl.

A single shot sang out into the night, bulbous brain laced with splintered skull ripped from his head and coated the alley wall like human jam. They got him, oh yes they gotten him after all.

Kisan was a mile away when it happened, but he was assured his cut. Calo would be pleased and the bank balance was looking healthy, still he had other things on his mind like supervising the skip sifting. It was done in fifteen-minute shifts. He stood in the dark whilst the homeless waited in line for their chance to rumble amongst the supermarket skip of their choice, sometimes fighting, jostling, knifing for a place in the queue. But there was little need, there was always too much food thrown out and even the rats got fat when all the humans had gone. Kisan wasn't happy. His idea of being a businessperson was not standing outside in the dark timing chandalas with a second hand stopwatch. A young thug with a scar for every year he had been on the road took the job. He would time the line and in return take one item, anything he wanted from each skip-diver after they had dove, though the money collected be handed over to Kisan naturally. Kisan knew he had picked the right man, he looked aggressive, but shot through with serotonin, he was as harmless as an octogenarian granny with her false teeth out. Kisan merged into the sweet black night hot as a lick from red tongued Kali. Kisan to other matters had to attend.

Chapter Five - I Believe

They were in the pick-up. Ron was driving and Kisan was collecting Calo. Kisan thought this a most tiresome waste of resources, but seeing as how he couldn't drive for shit there was nothing he could do. Ron could drive. Kisan could not. It was as simple and as short cut and as certain as that, to be sure to be sure.

'It's discrimination.'

'What is.'

'You having a licence and being deemed as fit for driving upon Her Majesty's highways and me as having no licence being so denied the aforementioned privilege.'

'Who gives a shit!'

'I do.'

'It wasn't a question.'

'Well do you give a coprolite and this is a question?'

'A what? And that is another question.'

'A stool? Excreta – really your English English idioms are so–'

'No, I don't.'

'Ha! In that case let me drive.'

'You could get arrested.'

'In which case, if such a possible outcome is not desirable, then it must be the case, contrary to what has been gainsaid that you do in fact give a shit.'

'For fuck's sake then drive.' Ron pulled over onto the hardish shoulder of the M62 and let Kisan take over at the wheel, anything for a quiet life. For once in his life he wished he could have indulged in a tadge of racist resentment, but this was logically denied him, if he thought about it. He tried not to think, but it was no good. He did think, it was a blatant contradiction and his resentment had nothing to do with race, just invective against a widehead, clever shit who couldn't drive for potatoes and nearly wasted them both trying to undertake a caravan whilst returning to the motorway. This thinking business was still getting to Ron. Hence the attractions of moronic knee-jerk reactions, but no, he wouldn't wish self-contradiction on himself and anyway, in a strange way, he liked the wee Indian shite after all.

'Do you think,' said Kisan after a lorry nearly did the business on them, 'that if a policeman was to see me driving like this we could be arrested?'

'Yes.'

'Yet if I had a licence, everything would be as you say hunky-dory.'

'Yes and no.'

'Please do not be so illogical.'

'Yes, if you had a licence things would be hunky-dory, but no, I do not say hunky-dory.'

'You just said it twice.'

There were times when liking the wee shite and coming close to killing him were becoming all one and the same to Ron. He looked up at the wee Indian sat on his cushion driving the three-tonne pick-up like a maniac with a Hollywood contract and he couldn't help admiring the spunk of the man – bold as balls on a Mexican hairless hound.

'Tell me, how long would you think it would take for me to get this Her Majesty's Licence to Drive thing hunky-dory?'

'The way you are going about fourteen months if you were lucky – hunky-dory,' said Ron, feeling as he was saddled with this new expression, he may as well get his money's worth.

'And how long would it take on the black market to procure such an item?'

'Hold on,' said Ron, reaching for Kisan's mobile phone and dialling. 'Hello, is that Dodgy Phil?'

'Yes, is that Ron?'

'Yes.'

'What you want, mushe?'

'Driving licence.'

'Normal, Public Transport, Heavy or All?'

'Hang on, Dodgy, I'll just ask,' Ron asked. Kisan said he'd take 'All' if the price was right.

'Is the price right?'

'Oh aye.'

'See you at the next Happy Fat Bastard with the White Hat.' Ron turned to Kisan and assured him that his licence would be ready in about twelve minutes and less if he stepped on it. Kisan, thinking that this beat fourteen months by a long imperial chalk, stepped on it.

Kisan drove the pick-up kicking like a horse into the parking area of the next Happy Fat Bastard. There, waiting to meet them in a second hand Jaguar with the clock turned back a few times for luck and lucrative selling-on deals, was the boyo himself, the gaje of gajiz, Dodgy Phil straight up from the Smoke, doing a bit here and there and luckily in the area for a bit more of wheeling and dealing, know what I mean, governor.

'For "All" we are talking a thousand notes,' said Dodgy.

Kisan did not bat an eyelid. He batted a straight wicket in deed and thought and pulled out a wad thick enough to choke a bullshitter. Business was brisk. Dodgy, after passing a hundred sheaves to Ron for luck, left in a cloud of exhausted fumes.

Kisan was pleased. He pocketed the licence, marched straight up to a big sixteen wheeler and broke in. Ron was impressed; he had no idea that the wee Indian was a Kalichor.

'Pass me up my cushion, kind Sir.'

Ron passed up the cushion. Kisan hot-wired the big truck and steered it out of the parking lot like an expert. He drove smoothly, carefully out of the Happy Fat and rejoined the flow of motorway traffic. Ron was impressed, which made it twice in one day, perhaps he was becoming more impressionable as he grew older. Nah, he was just running sort of a wider range of human emotions and natural responses, not that he was arsed. What the hell, he got back behind his pick-up and drove back home. Kisan could pick up Calo on his own.

Bugger Calo, Ron had problems of his own. He was worried

about Gran for starters. He hadn't had time to go for her pension that week. He stepped on the old gas pedal and was done for speeding – a hundred notes. Ron could have spat, but he was out of saliva just then, as luck would have it.

Interjection From the Side-Lines, Matey

Yes I did know Mr Ron Smith and speaking personally and not professionally as you understand, after all I do not want to jeopardise my Civil Service pension, as it is the wife wished me not to speak about Mr Smith at all, given the state of certain pertinent and indeed pressing enquiries currently undertaken by certain investigative institutions, howbeit, since you have asked and have taken the trouble to track me down, I feel honour-bound to hazard some sort of a reply, so without further ado, may I say, here and now and for the record, that personally speaking I quite liked the old mushe.

Mr Keith Horton, Alpine Grower

Ron was vexed as hell. A gasket blew just as he turned off the motorway. He limped to a scrappie mate's yard and fixed the fucker, but and all, it meant that he would be too late to see to Gran, get her pension and such-like. There was nothing for it, but to pop down The Albert for a pint. He scraped around his pockets and the back of the van to find just enough shrapnel to sell to his scrappie mate to pay off for the new gasket and a half on top, so all in all it hadn't turned out to be too much of a bad day. It beat sitting on the street. It was getting to him, bossing about low down scunts, drop-outs, beggars, thieves and mot-selling punks. What made it most irksome of all was some had taken it into their noodles to start calling him boss. He was no buccra bossman sitting in the shade, cracking the whip; he was just another one of Calo's flunkies. By hell, he needed a pork scratching.

The Albert was doing a roaring trade, which made it even less sense for it to be turned later into a themed tapa and winos bar, but there you go. A card game for big stakes was on in the front room, so Ron sought refuge in the back room and declined the offer of a good blowjob from a budding up transsexual. It was nothing personal, Ron just had a headache, feeling tired and didn't want to be pressured into doing someone that he didn't really want to do. I mean, he didn't want to fake it – how insulting can you get?

'Get fucked!' said Ron, and the transsexual hawked her ass over to a more likely looking customer in the far corner, twiddling his Victorian styled wax tash with his left hand and his todger with his right – what it is to be ambidextrous.

Meanwhile back in the front room the action was hotting up.

The factotum of the town, Provost Selim the Grim Biggleswick, was a cool cat and decidedly did not drink in The Albert. It was for this reason that he was playing beneath his tie-dyed blond wig a game of call-girl stud with the rest of the lads from accounts-fixing in a far corner of the front bar, just against the shove a bus token board.

'I bet one brunette, big jugs.'

'Raise you a blond, with a plucked minge.'

'I'll cover your blond and raise with a mulatto who likes to be spanked.'

'I'll cover that with a two Thai lesbians show and a bondage schoolie.'

'I've shit out.'

'Can't cover, no way.'

'Time to see the Missus instead.'

'Make a change.'

'Ho. Ho. Ho.'

It doesn't matter who is speaking, all sexist bastards anyway, and besides mentioning names could be positively libellous at this stage of the game. Suffice it to say, the winner picks up the cards, arms himself with a bumper Nodder pack from the toilet and goes out to pick up his winnings and exotic strains of VD. Such is life.

Ron bought another packet of pork scratchings.

'May I buy you a beverage, my friend?'

'Kisan, be my guest,' said Ron, surprised to see the wee fellow taking time out from earning his next million. Kisan walked like the diminutive popinjay that he was, is and ever shall be right up to the bar, just like he'd been practising, 'Eh up, flower, a pint of your best frothing supping ale.'

'On your bike, Paki bastard!'

Ron was up on his feet, vaulting over the bar and hitting fast jabbing lefts and crossing with hooking dangerous rights. The poor fuck didn't stand a chance. He was down like a sack of Granny Smith apples Newtonian First Class and things were looking decidedly a job for the homicide boys from satellite TV when Kisan intervened. One thing Kisan couldn't stand and that was mindless violence, violence for profit, a job, a bit of brass in pocket, or just protecting one's interest, that was all right, that was business. But, lumping the crap out of someone without the profit motive, why that was so uncivilised.

'Please desist, kind Sir, none of my bones are broken and I am sure the barman would gladly recompense our good selves for his rudeness by letting us allow him to buy the imbidations on the house so to speak,' said Kisan, helping himself to a small vacuum-packed packet of cashew nuts. The barman was in no mood to argue. Ron stopped rearranging his features and poured himself a pint of mild.

'A pink gin for me, old cove,' said Kisan familiarly.

'Ah good, khusty-khosko, I see you've spoken to Ron about the takeover,' said Calo, walking in and ordering a treble Jamie with ice – ice!? What a moron, anyone would think he was an American. Ice in a good whiskey? What next, soda, an umbrella and a table-dancer with a pierced belly button?

And so it came to pass that for a time Ron became the barman at The Alberto Camus – existential angst theme tapa bar and all round good pisser. What was left of the former barman was scraped off the floor and thrown out with the ashtrays' dross. Calo smuggled in a couple of homeless hopefuls to work long hours and below union rate and the wheels of commerce turned to grease everyone's hands and everyone was happier and none the wiser, save the barman and curiously Ron. Anyway, push comes to shove and it's back to the action.

Calo had another whiskey: ice, soda, little monkey on a cocktail stick and a floor dancer with a maraschino cherry stuck in her navel. Then he left. The two homeless gave free deoch all night to Ron and Kisan, seeing as they were management of sorts and they had witnessed the way Ron had sorted the last barman.

'Calo tells me you used to be in the habit of contemplation, earnest and erstwhile pensive deliberations?' ventured Kisan.

'Aye,' said Ron.

'Do much reading, peruse weighty tomes of philosophy?'

'Now and again, well sort of, had a bash and what have you.'

'What precisely to you mean, old chap?'

'I am precisely decisively somewhat illiterate, hunky-dory,' said Ron adjusting his sombrero over his eyes.

'Ah, I see, my old pukka muka. And if I may be so bold, what did you tend not to read in those far off halcyon days of mental gymnastics?'

'Berdyaev.'

'Any others?'

'Unamuno.'

'And?'

'Train timetables.'

'And may I trouble you with one further question, now that we are and have become drinking companions in the chance Dickensian manner?'

'No.'

'Tell me, is Arturo still travelling?'

Ron rose unsteadily to his feet, started to wave a blurry finger at Kisan and promptly fell over. Luckily Tracy had come in for a last orders of Tequila, Babyslam and a pickled egg and managed to pick him up and drag him off home to bed.

Kisan flexed his supple fingers, wrists, inspected his nails. He had one further pink gin for the motorway and then departed. It was closing time after all.

Another One of Salty's Asides on the Art of Shirt Box Writing

That's it you see, to write like a wireless, a radio slipping channels, the dial moving at random picking up stray stations, a veritable Babel of tongues, musics and motion of particles through the ether – is a wave a particle? Discuss, answers on a unified field theory please and hand in before things get too heavy to reach the speed of light. And that's the point see, so much static, so many strands of discussion building a finely randomly woven texture of nonsense, quite literally none sense. Some puissant puisne banging his gavel down, defining the limit of what can be said or unsaid or just mulled over in silence without words. And the answer, just to let the dial slip and let in the noise. Simple as that: the tune, the threnody, the mere shimmer and semblance of sentences, statements and propositions defying any mapping, truth-functional or otherwise, leaking none the wiser out into the echo of deep space, leaving only the once said. Simple as that. Or not. Sound. Sound. Sense and Sound…Shush…

It was hard work sleeping back at Tracy's, all that beer had Ron up every five minutes pissing in the sink. But, that was the least of it. Tracy was still heartbroken after losing the bairn to Social Service Upward Mobility Adoption Agency Enactment Stature 234, subsection 9. Bit of a bastard that one.

Ron tried to comfort the lass, but he was useless. The drink on him can't have helped and his co-ordination had gone with the walnuts: putting his arm around her, he succeeded in poking her in the eye. No, the real disappointment came when Tracy said, 'Ron, I want another one. I want a bairn. Do it to me.' Ron was having none of that. He'd brought bairns into the world and look where it got him… He didn't precisely know where, but he'd be damned if he'd take another risk in that direction. Notwithstanding all that, it was hardly fair on the brat, neither of them having a pot to piss in and the chances were that Social Services would move in again – no way, amiga.

After hearing no, after trying straddling Ron, sucking, slapping and teasing his decidedly deflated prick yon lass really started yelling. It was then that Jo or maybe Terry came hammering at the door wanting to comfort her.

'Why don't you let 'em in – woman to woman sort of thing,' said Ron, pissing in the sink again and missing.

'Exactly! All they want to do is to stroke and comfort me and then the next minute it's tongues up my arse and finger fucking... I want my bairn back, Ron. I'm a crap mother, it's better off without mi, but I need that child. It's the only thing that keeps me going.'

Ron doffed his dick on a tea-towel and crept back to bed. There was naught he could do. It was a good job the lass was dead.

Ron woke up about midday with a storming head on him and an empty bed. The mouse was back ghost-dancing for all he was worth. Shit, Ron still hadn't called in on Gran. He grabbed his battered sombrero afore putting his best sandal forward. Little Mouse was dancing. Today was a good day to die – again.

Since the twinning ceremony, all round piss-up and a bit of goodwill and crooked commerce thrown in, with some piss poor northern shite-hole of an Algerian-bashing, non-place in France, the commuter village, Diddleton, all but swallowed by linear development, had been re-christened the Faubourg Did-le-toinne, which quite frankly meant fuck all to Ron who never went there anyway.

Ron set off Granwards with every intention of calling in on the old love. Just as he rounded the corner into her close he was waylaid and brought up sharp by the screech of tyres. Calo pressed a button and his window lowered, 'Get in, Ron, there's a job on.'

'What about, Gran, I've got to call, it's bin-'

'Business, Ron, big stuff and I need you.'

Torn by family loyalties Ron dithered, but at the end of the day a job's a job and he could always call back after. He jumped in and Calo headed off to yon side of Did-le-toinne. So, it came to pass that Ron visited commuter-ville. But no one were right bothered.

A Quiet Word in Your Ear in Case You're Confused from the Microsoft Binder Operator

I was once down the club in Benckley to see Uncle Salty and quizzed him about some of his stories with dead folk in them and not doing dead things and these people weren't ghosts or barguests or boggarts or the like. These were real people knocked over by a tram in the first part of the tale and there to welcome their husband home later on when the collier would be coming in from the pit. Salty shook his head and got a bit aggressive and I can remember his words clearly upon that situation, 'How much of a bairn are you lad? Are tha still a babee and shat yer pants? Tell me do you think these people are real – figments, lad, fucking figments existing only in my narration. I can do what I fucking well like with 'em. They don't exist, they subsist through me. I mek 'em dance, layke, fuck, screw or cry and they can die too. It's all up to me, lad. They are not real, don't be so fucking sackless like some gormless bairn sucking on't tit.' After that we had a game of fives and threes which I won, so it wasn't all wasted. Dear Auld Salty, he had such a way with words, but couldn't get a score-draw to save his soul. I miss that man, his drinking, hard cussing and his pit boots polished like glass. His like will not be seen again. He was real. He is dead. He's gonna stay that way, but he made a mark on me – God Bless, Uncle Salty.

On the mean linear development Main Street of Did-le-toinne an unlicensed drug-dealer lies sprawled in her own blood, by the right hand, fallen from her clasp, lies a .357 Magnum 158 grain 1235 muzzle velocity mother-fucker with muzzle energy rated at 535. It's a widow maker, it's an orphan creator and it paves the way for death to make a fast get in and get away. But, it didn't do this mother no good. She'd sold her last packet of skag, skank heroin top, and she's lying in her own blood and she won't be getting up.

This kid, nothing but a bairn, comes up, stares, crouches down, looks to see where the back of her head should be. It's not there. He pokes her gingerly with his red shoes, but the lady is not for stirring. Good. His little hands make the Magnum. Expertly he checks the bullets and gives an excited whoop.

'John-o, Tim-o, Judy, come here.'

His friends come. They'd been hiding low while the killing gotten done. The little lad in the red shoes spins the gun. They stand around in a circle. It's not a fair point. The gun lies between Judy and Tim-o. This time it's John-o's turn to spin. It's a fair point. Little Red Shoes has won or rather lost. Little Red Shoes has got to point it to his head and pull the trigger.

'Jason! Jason, get your arse in here right now, tea's on the table,' goes this mother's voice.

'Oh, Mam, I'm playing.'

'Get yourself in through this door this minute or I'll tan your arse for you.'

'Sorry,' Little Red Shoes Jayce apologises and puts the gun back by the unlicensed drug dealer's hand. The rest of the kids tut and grumble, but they know it's not Jayce's fault. Little Red Shoes gans home for tea and the rest of the gang just drift.

Calo drives past and takes the left turn up to Brick Farm. Ron takes a grimy finger and scratches underneath his battered sombrero. The first time that he is in Did-le-toinne and it is something of a mystery, but. But, really, Ron's not arsed either way, truth be told, his mind's adrift again.

It was this, Ron is fumbling through this house clearance when he catches sight of this box of books, not that he can read, but he takes a look anyway. He mumbles over the letters and manages to make sense, this thick weighty tome in his hands, *The Complete Works of William Shatner* and that's the moment, that's when the epiphany starts kicking in. He gets to remember the dook and that strange dream and he has a wee laugh about it, nothing too jovial, but a bit of a chortle nonetheless just to be going on with. Then this worry starts to nag at him, for there is this dream kicking around his head, there's himself and Calo in Did-le-toinne and they driving down main street where by happenstance Ron looks out of the window to see this dead mother sprawled on the pavement and they drive on.

They take a lane out of the village, not far mind, but out from the dorms to Brick Farm, a recent sold sign buttressed by the wind and the whole place looking a tadge desolate and all set up for some downbeat period drama. Calo pulls up to, almost right to, the door, because there's not much of a front garden. So be it, amen and all the rest of it, Ron finds that Calo has bought the farm, not that this is any of Ron's business, but it is something to be going on with.

And that's where he's wrong, for Calo takes Ron out for a walk around, shows him the fields sloping up to yonder wolds. Calo takes his thick brown fingers and crumbles the soil in his hands to show Ron what's what.

'See that.' Calo breaks the soil in his hands.

Ron looks but is no wiser.

'See the grit of chalk in the soil – poor farming land, a bit of rough grazing is all, but that's the past. This is perfect soil: viticulture, is what I'm taking – good draining chalky soil. The hills behind protect and provide rainfall, the global warming thing provides the right temperature – this is the start of a whole new subsidy scam.'

Ron sees a rabbit making to dash through yonder hedgerow and wishes he had brought a shotgun. Ron's partial to a bit of rabbit. While he's thinking about that sort of thing he gets to thinking about Gran and that last taste of aichi – be worth a poke about, make the journey worthwhile.

But, Calo has other matters on his mind. He wipes his hands on Ron's dungarees after hearing the approach of a heavy lorry and walks back to the farmyard. Ron's looking for a handy stick when he's beckoned over. Ron guides the lorry back, which pulls up to a nicety.

Kisan jumps out of the cab and gives a merry salutation or

two to Calo and a mere nod of his head to Ron. Kisan has really come on. He's made his first two million by now and a bit more on top.

'Don't just stand there making the place look untidy – open her up,' says Calo to Ron in his best music hall tradition voice and Ron is not laughing.

Kisan talks business with Calo. Ron opens up the back of the truck. Inside, gleaming, several gaily painted caravans stand. Ron takes a deek and bad dookerin comes over him. It's a moment of a complete lack of epiphany, that at least he knows. He helps Kisan remove the caravans and waits knowing that there is more to come and none of it good, it's too much like what happened last weekend and that was bad enough.

Ron called one Sunday at the caravan. Calo was away on business, but Manush and Tchai were in as was Arturo's wife, Rawnee. Rawnee insisted on showing Ron all the improvements recently undertaken by Calo. Firstly, the floor had been lifted and proper foundations laid. Secondly, out went the sides and in their stead walls were erected, forming many myriad rooms. Lastly, the roof had to go, in its place was built a second storey topped with a roof of Welsh slate made.

Ron said it looked just like a house. Rawnee asked Ron if Arturo was still travelling. It was that bad.

Another thing too that got to Ron, Manush barely spoke a word, just sat alongside his computer gazing blankly at the screen-saver, having fun. The boy was a born fool, but a nice one, always a smile for Ron and some sweet babble, but this day he just stared at the screen, this computer of Calo's, a maze of bent figures and cross-indexed tax evasion. The fool-boy remained spellbound by randomly generated images and Ron passed on by, disappointment and regret tugging at his heart. Then too, Rawnee's hair, cut shoulder length and dyed gold – and Ron remembering back to the first day he stood by her side, two of them out collecting wood by chance, and hot southern wind blowing her long coal-black, crow-black hair about her, seeing her then, bundle of sticks in her arms and a hot, sharp churi cutting deep within his heart. Ron stole inside her bedroom, looked with disgust at the likening creams scattered over a dresser. He didn't say anything, but Rawnee sensed his scorn. Rawnee insisted that it was just business, but Ron wasn't so sure. Only Tchai remained the same, only more growed, and put him in mind of arranging something of a marriage for the lass. Maybe when Arturo returned things could be sorted, perhaps not.

Rawnee and Ron took the old lurcher for a walk past the scrap to get some fresh air. There was something on Rawnee's mind: she leaning against this pile of tyres and there's a tear to her left eye and Ron looking away and feeling guilty.

'Only hope for us all is if Arturo comes back, Calo's getting out of hand and beyond himself.' Rawnee took the corner of her red skirt to wipe her eye and Ron couldn't help looking at her sturdy brown legs and this twinge of regret kicks in. 'So what I want to know is when we can expect the return of Arturo?... Don't stand there looking gormless, tell me. I have to know.'

Know, knowledge, gnosis – it was familiar territory, but Ron had given up on it. He scraped the heel of his shoe on this bent and twisted bumper and gave it his best shrug. Rawnee threw her arms around him, held him, clung on to him, pulled his face towards her and kissed his hard thin lips.

It was a good job Ron had had a bath that day. There he was saving time on the launderette running the warmish ferruginous water into the auld Victorian tub and jumping in, red shirt, dungarees and duds still on. He soaped up, threw in a couple of squirts of Our Mam's washing-up liquid and had a right good scrub. Christine came up from the room below the stairs and my, she was looking peaky. She just walked straight in and threw up in the toilet bowl next to the bath. She tried to apologise, but another chunder got in the way. Poor lass was in a bad way, she on the clodgy, shitting, pissing and vomiting and Ron had forgot his towel as he stood there drip-drying trying to bring some comfort to the wee runaway.

Finally, in between a puke and a fart, Christine managed to get in a full explanation about how she hasn't been feeling too well, can't keep anything down, sick every morning and strange cravings for pieces of apricot jelly smeared with Bovril – no, she's not been feeling very well at all. Really, said Ron, patting her head avuncularly, and offering her his bath water should she want to clean herself up. The girl grateful, but bashful, her never having known a man. Not to worry, said Ron as he picked her thin, but filling, frame off the clodgy and dropped her in the bath; she still wearing her spew-stained nightie. Ron nipped down to the room below the stairs and pulled out a thin hand-towel and some clothes from a cardboard box. Ron helped the lass. He didn't want to, he didn't have to, but it was something done. Christine gave him a wee wet kiss as he flannelled her down and cleaned her up as best he could. Girl was ill and suffering, they looked into each other's eyes and knew that any day now the poorhouse beckoned. Girl stroked Ron's coarse hand and lay back in the tub. Ron flushed the clodgy and the guts of the auld house rumbled. It was time to close the door on this other tragedy.

By the time Ron had walked to Rawnee's and the bairns he had dripped dry which was a good thing as not everyone is into that wet kiss thing... Rawnee pinned Ron up by the bent and twisted Hillman Imp and gave him one hell of a tongue sandwich. Her hands slipped beneath the bib of his dungarees and started milking his cock. But it was no good, Arturo was travelling and that was that. Ron broke free and together, man, woman and old lurcher nashed back to the caravan for Sunday dinner.

There was a stranger in the house, but slightly less defamiliar to Ron, who quite liked the wee greedy Indian despite all that had happened at Brick Farm. Kisan had called, dropped some merchandise off for Calo and invited himself for dinner.

Just to show that it was a social call Kisan took his beloved Luger P 08 and laid it underneath the statue of Our Lady of Egypt before he tucked into his Yorkshire puddings and onion gravy. The wee Indian was less his old jubilant self and more his newly acquired speculative, self-doubting, angst-ridden in flight from and to a sense of being in the world self, which was a bit of a gobful all told and no wonder the onion gravy started to repeat a little on him. There was no doubt about it, as the carrots, sprouts, roast beef, horseradish sauce, roast and mash were dished up his mind was crumbling rather too much histolytically for dinner-time small talk.

'I greatly fear, warm-hearted hosts, that I have grieved you deeply by my otherwise hasty actions in carrying out what I had deemed to have been my duty. My zealous conduct has alienated you, Ron, my first true friend in this cold-shouldering country, and I have, I think, brought death a closer step nearer to me – look, for example, if you will, how far I have fallen and so enjoy your English beef. Is this not my soul disintegrating, falling away into the realm, dark with death and unclean? Unclean to me, to you and doomed now to fall even lower as I endeavour to comply with my dreaded contract and…'

The rest of the family tucked in and Kisan, in between mouthfuls of traditional Sunday dinner, continued with his melodramatic monologue bewailing his fall from grace. Ron, though, would at times prick his ears up, just in case the wee man was taking the piss, for he had not forgotten the incident of Brick Farm after the caravans were unloaded, Calo passing an angle-grinder to Kisan, Kisan changing the blade to a cutter and proceeding to cut through the thin skin of metal of the lorry's insides, the sides folding back like foil and out pushing their way through to freedom, men, women and children. One old Raya, too keen, trying to force his way through when only half cut, receiving a slice across his chest for his trouble, anger and pain flooding the old warrior's eyes, Kisan backing off, the Raya stumbling forward, Kisan whipping out the Luger and making a third eye through the wounded man's head, a wail sounding loud as a thundering gale, men, women and children carrying the fallen man to one of the caravans, bound quickly in white sheeting, wood reived by hook or by crook and the caravan aflame to the sound of the singing of Jelan Jelan, Ron helping, Ron singing too, but all awhile there's Calo, patting the wee Indian on the shoulder – the Vinland, land of Vines baptised in blood, Calo thinking on this as good dookerin, Ron feeling the curse of burnt black blood, sharp as iron, and the little wee Indian never the same after that, spitting out his heart over the Sunday dinner with worse contracts and commissions on his mind.

'Pass us the pepper,' said Ron. Kisan passed the pepper, Tchai passes the Indian a rag of cloth, tells him in no uncertain terms to blow his nose. A traditional Sunday dinner - one of the staples of Northern culture.

Ron gives Kisan a hand to unload afterwards. Load of junk really, but there may be a few bob in it or not. Ron sees this box of books, house clearance, on top there's this weighty tome, worth a peruse if the man could read, but he has a bash nonetheless, mouths away to himself till he gets the title at least: *The Complete Works of William Shatner*. Pile of shite, Ron throws the book back, turns to find by yonder fridge-freezer with the ozone leaking out of it Kisan talking to Tchai, a certain presentiment ominous but fleeting disturbs the surface contours of his mind. Ron shivers, Arturo is nearing, but a match is made after all.

Little Mouse knew about time: time was, time is, time be and he knew all this was wrong. Little Mouse knew no time but dreamtime, time that sees all always and at all times. Man, woman, child, animal, spirit is not a line, is not a sequence, but a point, a squashed dot on the picture of the maker, running the outer ring of that dot is man, woman, child, animal or spirit.

When Little Mouse dances, he shakes and vibrates and circles, covering, creating, making and breaking time over and over again, bringing the circle not to its end or beginning, but to its total instantiation.

Beyond this thing Little Mouse knows nothing. He sees evil

spirit in spider's nest, he sees some Jewish girl kick and struggle as a black fly in the thread of spider's nest, and all he can do is dance.

The dance goes on.

On yonder bed Ron lies, scratting in his sleep, stumbling over words given to him from deep dreams and Little Mouse feels his fast heart begin to break.

It is not over. It has not begun. Little Mouse is his own dance and the ghost of his dance and the soaring song of his own spirit pinned to the static fabric of time. Little Mouse.

Ron is away with the fairies: two camp cherubs buggering the arse off one another with tiny todgers and wings flapping like merry hell – humming birds on acid, speed, coke and a lot of enthusiasm to boot. Ron don't mind; it's good to see folk enjoying themselves, even if they be imaginary. What worries Ron is that into this dream is coming the nightmare of what happened the other day on the street, where for once he is back working taking the takings and allotting pitches, that's what's doing the lad's peanut in as he lies there sleeping off the old Sunday joint.

Ron don't smoke much mind, but after a good feed at Arturo's place, there's nowt he likes better than to take a slow stroll home by the river, watching the bloated corpses of dead dogs get pulled downstream by the current as he rolls himself a little number with a king-size buzz. Lately, Kisan has been putting him in touch with some right headgear, sweet smelling grass, with a tour de force top of cannabis oil soaked into the shreds. It's some smoke. Can't blame a body for sleeping like the dead after a lungful or two of that splendiferous spliff.

So that thing in the street, well maybe it something and maybe it nothing, but either way it would take another book to be doing the job right, but here's some of it to be going on with, not that it adds up to much or little, possibly nothing at all, but there's two ways to be looking at this now, though neither help, so anyway, a little of the truth can't harm, well not as much as the whole truth, nothing but the truth, so help me God to help myself and all the rest of us poor bastards down here without a pot to piss in and really that could be half the story why this old Italian Punch and Judy man takes a wander down Gunnarsgate to entertain the little ones.

So okay, this gaje fails to get a permit, but that's not what's bothering your Ron any. It's the kids. It's the bairns. It's the youth of today sat there in a ring around old Marco who is going through the performance like a good un as all them youth out there is rolling up, fornicating and fighting and putting on a better show than wee punch knocking the holy hell out of his Missus. Old Marco crying, old Marco seen it all and worse, this Italian half-Jewish vagrant, and he saw the inside of a death camp, though but four years old, but none the less he seen all these things and it breaking his heart bad-bad to see so much potential evil realised as pure brain-fucking numb nothingness, like the eight year old selling his sister for a football sticker, bottle of coke and a couple of tabs of E. Old Marco has enough, borrowing Mr Punch's rope and hitching over the end of this lamppost and only then do the kids get to put their hands together and show appreciation for the show.

'What you let this cart stand there for filling up the space of prime begging territory? Bullshit chandala man, you want Calo to kick your arse, old cove?' admonished Kisan, turning up to do an inspection and bugging Ron a little as he was enjoying the show.

'The day Calo kicks my arse I rip off his foot and club him to death with it!' said Ron, coming on strong and evil, getting near to losing his cool one last time.

The whole street sucks on silence. Kisan backs off, the kids titter nervously for a wee wee while afore disappearing. Not anyone banked on this, the rumour is out there. A challenge has been made. Ron walks over to the orphaned show, looks inside and out. It's just something to do while the sound of his blood thudding through his head slows down to a quiet, steady ripple.

But, that ain't the thing that's really bugging Ron. It's more the show than the showdown that got to him. The huddle of kids getting high and bad no longer meant a thing, but the quaint antiquated ritual of poor Punch stuck in his guts. The echo of Punch's own march to scaffold reverberating in the swinging body of Marco dangling from the lamppost on the corner of the street – aye, that too got to him, some splinter of ice in the heart. The beat and swing of Punch on the gibbet, the choking, writhing body of Marco, his red tongue turning blue-black and his eyes like comical toads bracing themselves to leap from his skull – there was something to this mystery. It wasn't the way to do it.

Time waits for no corpse on Gunnarsgate. The ghouls from the bodily parts re-servicing centre arrived just in time to rescue the eyes and Chomp Doggy Dog Snacks Ltd managed the rest – some son of a bitch wasn't going hungry that night.

But, that wasn't the thing that mattered, no, for no sooner were the eyes scooped out, did not this antique dealer move in and try to strike up a deal with Ron over the remains of the show. Ron was having none of it. Ron was all on for trundling the cart off, wrapping its mannequins in white rags and torching it, that was the thing to do. It was what his mother would have wanted and that reminded Ron of the aichi still to be found and tasted. Whilst Ron was thinking about the best place to find a bit of aichi Kisan moved in and clinched the deal. The cart was loaded into the back of a three tonne pick-up, but as the truck clumsily sped off Punch was shook from the truck. Kisan was busy counting notes. Ron scooped up the wee fellow and hid him inside the bib of his dungarees.

Ron was relieved of his duties on Gunnarsgate. It made no difference to him, wandering back to his room to see how Christine was getting along. Last time he saw the girl it was looking time all right: could be any day, could be any hour. Sometime soon Ron would be walking the girl to the workhouse and perhaps that would be an end of it. Ron couldn't tell, he couldn't be sure and he was certain of that at least.

Punch and Ron get on not so bad, but Little Mouse is having none of it. He knows bad medicine when he sees it. Little Mouse huddled in his hole in the skirting board, hoping to hell that one way or the other it would all be over, for Ron at least. The ghost-black buffalo were seen roaming the red rug last night, the hooknose and chin of the mannequin had the face of the dead moon, Ron was sleeping, but he couldn't catch good dreams no more. Little Mouse's tiny heart beat fear, he tucked his head on his knee and wept.

In his dreams Ron found himself caged up, swinging from a hook set in the roof of a caravan while at the front Mr Punch drove the horse, making miles, pulling further away from the east, travelling ever onwards, moving through the lines of gibbeted men and women, past the cooling ovens of burnt flesh, ignoring the lines of chained women, men and children working mines, working steel mills, working worse than slaves. Punch sang, Jelan, Jelan, and Ron didn't know all the words, but knew the tune. The horse stumbled, the horse buckled at the knee, but onwards, ever onwards drove Mr Punch, only stopping one time to shoe the horse in human teeth. Ron sang from his perch, Ron cried aloud, Ron bit his tongue and died drowning on his own blood, but the caravan moved on.

Ron woke spitting obscenities and trembling from head to foot. A mist of sweat made his mid-wheaten skin glow. He rubbed his fingers over his face, smelt his skin and sweat and knew that it wouldn't be long. Standing up there was this sharp dry crack; Little Mouse lay dead, squashed beneath his foot. Ron shrugged, bit his lip, laying the mouse on a dusty empty bookshelf.

A Remembrance of the Binder Operator

There was a time when Great Uncle Salty and I were discussing dreams. There's a reason for this seeing as Great Grandma had a talent for dreams, picking horses, reading tea leaves and the like, but that wasn't really the substance of Salty's argument. Great Uncle Salty had it in for Freud and there's no two ways about it – con man. Fraud, is what Salty called him, a fable, a myth, a contrived nonsense and a pack of lies that continues to pollute and pervert society. Doctors, medicine, psychiatry have no truck with Fraud. Psychology mentions his name only to dismiss him as a practical joker and the man that cooked the books, his own books. Philosophy also takes a fair poke at him if required to drop a match on this man of straw and his tissue of lies, mixing metaphors over mixed drinks, no doubt. To Salty there were only two jokers left that took Fraud seriously: con men after deluding 'patients' with diatribes and to hell with diagnosis and the intellectual pygmies of academia – certain literary theorists. Salty cleared his throat, raked back a gob of phlegm, spit and pit dust and spat in the fire. It was comment enough and I never dared asked him why dreams played such a part in his own work. Perhaps, it was the influence of my Great Grandma that held the key, perhaps, this is all my arse.

Ron struggled downstairs to the room under the stairs, knowing that something was wrong, something torn in the fabric of his time. The small squat was clean and tidy and not empty. In the place of the later ailing Christine and her rotund belly, a young girl lay, eyes like startled deer and protectively clutching a small kitchen knife of the variety that does be sold in Jacksons for under a pound. From the future he should have known that this was his first meeting with Christine – but that wasn't it. From the past he should have known that this was his first meeting with Christine – and perhaps this wasn't it either. It was the present that counted. The rip in time didn't mean shit, seeing this young girl clutch this knife and stare so. The present was asking more than what did he know. Specially, as it is well known that Ron knows nothing.

'Runaway?'

The lass merely nodded in reply to Ron's question. Sadly, the old charvo shook his head and thought about ganning out for a pint, after all thoughts cost nothing. Ron boy told the girl not to worry and left after giving her a bigger, better and sharper knife of a kind that does be sold in such old fashioned but excellent grocers and hardware store specialists as your man Stubbs in York, which is well worth a visit after perusing the gothic delights of the Minster, the horrific Clifford's Tower where they massacred Jews and the all too specific delights of that tram car whiz round Viking York at the Jorvik Coppergate Centre, famed for its queues, meticulous reconstructions and fuck all else. Not so much as a penny to scratch his crabs with, Ron set off for a walk by the river, where he sought distraction in skimming half-bricks over the bows of that prat still rowing atween both banks for half a crown and a mention in Yankee tourist reports of the city. One smug fuck, and Ron threw a breeze-block just for variety. He hadn't had as much fun since standing on one of the ring-road by-pass bridges to piss over the side and this open-top sports car received a bit of a spray to send it on its way. Ah, life wasn't all sorrow, woe and mindless tv; there was always pointless violence and hatred of your fellow man too.

Talking of which, your man Kisan is getting more than a tadge worried about Ron, but this is not the place to go into it. Try the next chapter.

The Next Chapter

So there's this house clearance to be done after the inmate takes a dislike to the inside of his skull with a matchlock. Rumour had it that the old boy was some kind of arms enthusiast, shootist and do it yourself gunsmith. So much for rumour. Your man was in fact and in fiction the missing, unknown and unnamed sleeping, eternally sleeping now, leader of the Angry Brigade. Och well, enough of the mystery lesson, leaf back a couple of issues of *The Manchester Guardian* sometime in 1972 if you really want to know about the Angry Brigade, but that won't help you much as this boyo eluded them all, just sick of heart that everyone had forgotten about the struggle, tired of heart waiting for the special forces, police, MI5, MI6 and MFI to catch up with him. It just got so boring staring at the front door with a Beretta 92 9 mm automatic waiting to shoot it out with the inevitable, dying gloriously for the struggle. No one came. For Lord's sake, every year this man would send Christmas cards to ageing imprisoned Baader-Meinhof, to mad-dog Reilly c/o Stonecutters Way Belfast, and to Marco Di Bebaldo puppeteer and Red Brigade commander. Every Christmas but no one came – the back door primed with a booby trap of homemade explosives, primed with a vial of acid set to break when the handle turned. And no one came. Is anybody there, said the milkman. Is anybody there, said the man that came to read the meter. Is anybody there, said this Mormon missionary all the way from Wetwang up in the Wolds of Yorkshire. But yon mad was buggered if he was waiting to hear a question from the powers that be from the proximity of his front doorbell. Truth is no one took the red menace seriously any more. The only red that was a worry was world debt and would the First World, Second World, Third World and Disney World cough up the readies in time to avoid total economic collapse as we know it. It was a long shot, but the auld matchlock was up to it, blowing out the man without a name, cause or reason not to bite the bullet. And that was that.

Kisan, good man and entrepreneur, pulled up to take an artful dekko at the suicide scene. He'd been tipped and given the nudge-nudge, wink-wink, and the what's-what, by a regulation bent copper and had only half a day to take the goodies before the authorities moved in to re-house the corpse and inform the nearest of kin that their death duties were due in – no more freeloaders in this society, everyone had to pull their weight, even the deceased.

Kisan had brought Ron along for the ride. It was the least he could do now that he had a personal contract out on him. Kisan felt guilty and more besides especially as Ron would be a veritable marriage relation not too far away tucked in the future. He'd been discussing her uncle's fate with Tchai and he promised to try to look after Ron, even though he knew it was hopeless. As for Ron himself he wasn't arsed either way. He had never been scared of being born and saw no logical reason to be scared of being dead. The only thing that got to Ron was that last bit of aichi for Beebee, that was a thing he was in the position to bring about and effect in the world, but so far he had failed to bring about a satisfactory conclusion to the business in the other hand.

As for the business in hand, it involved rushing around like a blue-arsed fly throwing anything of value in the back of the three tonne pickup. Kisan was not disappointed. The house was stacked with guns galore: some that couldn't fire for toffee but were worth a fair auld whack at auction and others that were maybe a bit behind the times but could still do the business, such as this classic Luger. It was some piece, felt good in the grip, toggled for action and maintained with love. It was some tool, handy for a pistol-whipping if called upon for close-up work. Kisan was happy as Larry the Lamb in a field of clover. He'd always appreciated German craftsmanship in comparison with the cruddy, crude exports of the British Empire that were shipped out to India already obsolete and over-priced. That Luger - Kisan had this childish impulse to pull the trigger, to let off a couple of bullets just to feel the kick of precision engineering. Kisan had this mad urge to take a kiss from red-tongued Kali, run amok and kill, but instead he caught sight of Ron struggling to read by one of the bookcases.

Kisan, kindness itself, read out a few of the titles to old Ron. It was the least he could do and all he would do, no way would he stand in between Calo and his kill.

'*Nacirema – the Bid to Reclaim the Nation*, by a Bunch of Southern Twats, *Explosives Like Grandpa Used to Make*, *The Hungry Anarchist's Cookbook*, *James Bond's Manual for Boys That Haven't Growed Up*, *Chinese Regional Cooking* by Lao Tse Q'ien – do you require me to read any more?'

'Nay, just stop waving that gun around.' Ron started packing the books, wondering whether it would be worth making another effort to master reading. Ron had always been partial to Chinese food, specially northern cooking. He once had Shantung shredded pork and chicken in Old Capitol sauce and various other side dishes and he had never forgotten it. Ron had always appreciated Chinese culture and wished he could have breached communal divides even if it was only to say how much he appreciated a good stuffing: food, Wu Shu, and a little Chut Sing Tong Long and Q'an Kuen. It wasn't to be. Ron would be dead before the next Chinese New Year where he meets this young woman and her brother, thereafter becoming lifelong friends – such is life.

'Ron!'

'Kisan?'

'Ron, look here, there's a chuffing Redhawk, built like a cannon, chambered for .44 Magnum with a 7.5 barrel of bad ass bastard, go get 'em Floyd, man-stopping son of bitch, all out heavy wear, just the gun for you, Sir, by the built in bar billiards table!'

'So.'

'So, bloody damn well take it and no mistake matey and arm up, you born fool or what!' Kisan had lost patience with Ron finally. He had done his best. He would now have to tell Tchai that it was all over, it was ended, any day tomorrow.

Ron finished off packing books. He knew where he could get a few quid for such books on the market, cash in hand and no questions asked. He needed a pint, even though The Albert was some kind of tapa bar, he was dry as wood rot and tired of tasting spit.

The twain packed up, made off and didn't come back. The job was a good un and the police, hot on the heels of various estate agents, moved in on the scene.

Little Mouse woke on top of the redundant bookshelf. Oh bugger. Little Mouse was not best pleased to find that he had returned once more to the musine life of a wee rodent. Truth was there were no longer enough Sioux in the world to be returned as such. Little Mouse, though wishing to join his brethren, would have settled for another nation, Navaho, for example, but truth be told there were just not enough Native Americans left anymore. Little Mouse wiped the tears from his eyes and skated across the shelving to take a nibble at the hook-nosed puppet.

'Nibble me again you bastard and I'll pull your chuffing whiskers off,' said the puppet, which was some subtle trick of deception and spatial-temporal ventriloquism as right that very minute the puppet was stuck in the bib of Ron's dungarees in a paralytic universe not a spit and a fart away.

Ron was so dry that he couldn't help but envy the river water passing away to some other horizon as he traipsed the same bit of turf without the price of a drink, nor pickled egg, nor so much as an old pork scratching tucked in the folds of a pocket somewhere. That river was poison and would be the indubitable death of him, but he could have stooped down and drunk nonetheless and to hell with what is to come. He was dry. Times were tough, since they shut The Albert down, where there was always a chance of some mushe being in to put half a pint of something and more behind the bar for old Ron, for the memory of that man he used to be.

Gey posh and right gradely were some of the residences that

cloaked the riversides. Ron helped himself to an opening of some rich burgher's gate. Before him and a little to the right was a koi pond, further down the path, the paved flags took a graceful stagger to the left so as to avoid the croquet lawn, thereafter the path connected to this marble flagged patio, with various earthenware vessels containing sweet-smelling plants or pots of herbs. It was quite some gaff.

'Go on, you daft bugger, get thyssen in, lad,' said the puppet from the bib.

Ron didn't need no second bidding. He tried the handle of the French window and was favoured with the door swinging open. Never let it be said that Ron lacked manners. He wiped his sandals before he entered the room. Man, it was some carpet. Little Mouse could have feasted on the rich wool to his heart's delight; that Little Mouse could have fancied himself once more roving and reiving the high summer prairie grass of his youth, Little Mouse could have had a whale of a time, but he was busy scampering down the bookshelf at the time, several miles away and anyway, no one invited him out for a walk. Them's the breaks it seems.

Ron stood in front of this rather elegant Scottish dresser knocked up by Joseph Barns, a master craftsman of Northallerton and much sought after in auctions. Tidy piece, thought Ron as his hands ran along the oak, continuing till he found a Stewart crystal decanter of *Radharc na Beinne* single malt. An elegant Stuart crystal tumbler was found also on hand, enabling Ron to partake of a preprandial drink without resorting to swigging from the decanter and shewing himself up as a somewhat uncouth boor.

'Take a seat, you tosspot,' advised the puppet.

Ron walked through the dining room, equipped as it was with an antique English yew table with Davenport legs and Cornish beading fringing the sides to where a family of four and their King Charles spaniel watched something soporific on cable TV.

'There's an old Bogart film on Two,' Ron advised.

'Really?' said the master of the house.

'Aye, you soft sod, t'auld *Big Sleep* – a classic, man!'

The mistress of the house seemed vaguely concerned to hear words of such an obscene nature issue forth from the bib of this stranger's dungarees, but she was though a big fan of Howard Hawkes and so, what the hell, they changed over to Two and everyone was happy.

The film ended much to the satisfaction of onlookers and the mistress announced that luncheon would be served in twenty minutes. She ran through to the kitchen where a Chinese chef and his sister confirmed that indeed twenty minutes would be all the time necessary for some sumptuous feast to be served upon the Old English yew table of the dining room fame.

'May I pour you another whisky?'

'Yes you may.' Ron drained the dribble in his glass.

'May I suggest you try the fourteen year old *Sean-Bhlas na h-Uisge Bhui*, the only single malt from the lonely isle of Innis Todaidh.'

'Your suggestion warmly welcomed, kind Sir, such a drink shall answer me handsomely,' opined Ron, proffering his drained glass forward somewhat eagerly; nay, possibly with a hint of fervour to his manner and much noticed by the master of the house who appreciated the company of a fellow imbiber of choice spirits and in no short measure.

The First Psychiatric Report – Excerpt Only

The biggest obstacle to treating Mr Ron Smith was his delusion, persistently obsessive, that he was a Spaniard. Ron was about as Spanish as Al Jolson was Black, only less humorous, should you find Caucasians blacked up with boot polish in anywise something to stir merriment and mirth.
Dr A J P Khan, Bootham Car Park Hospital.

'Take it steady, auld lad,' advised the puppet as Ron, seated at the English yew table, was quaffing this glass of white served alongside the fish course.

'A mere table wine, really, but one from our own vineyard in Tuscany.' The Burgher re-topped Ron's glass.

'Careful lad, you can't trust Tuscans, arty-farty bastards to a man,' the puppet advised.

Ron drank, ate, and drank some more. It really was sumptuous fare and to hell with the doleful murmuring of the puppet. The meal was served by this Chinese sister who would have been a lifelong friend after the meeting of Chinese New Year, except Ron is dead by then...see below:

'Haven't I seen you somewhere before,' this Chinese girl said, standing in line waiting for the lion dance to begin.

Ron never forgot a face, but for a moment it seemed doubtful that he would remember, 'the maid – you served me dinner once at this posh house!'

'That's it,' said the Chinese girl, smiling. 'Enjoying the New Year?'

'Oh aye, I've always been fascinated by lion dancing and the like, everything really, ever since I saw *Enter the Dragon*,' confessed Ron, blushing slightly.

The girl laughed, 'My brother is dancing at the head...is the head. I shall introduce you afterwards.'

'Oh thank you,' said Ron, all smiles. 'I've a feeling that this could be the start of a beautiful relationship or whatever it is –

from *Casablanca* you know.'

'Sorry, Ron, it is not possible, you are dead and all this didn't happen, can't happen and won't.' A cracker exploded nearby and Ron who never was there was gone.

'Enough, lad,' advised the puppet, but Ron was having none of it, gutted at missing a tasty part of a possible future. With zeal and alacrity he accepted a glass of Almagnac – one for the road, and, draining it with one swig, tottered off home; the puppet chastising him almost every step.

Almost every step, for as they cut up a snicket a drunk collier lay slumped across Ron's path. He tried to help the old tope up, but the lad was having none of it. He was slewed up and three sheets to the wind, despite his pit boots being polished as glass. The puppet strongly advised him not to leave the miner in such a predicament, becoming quite vociferous, so Ron left the drunken collier the puppet for company, stuffing it into his jacket pocket, squashed up against pools forms and tab ends with just one smoke left in 'em. Ron had had a pleasant stroll by the river and a rather capital lunch out for a change. It was time to sleep things off, just like a siesta in the old days back home in Spain.

There was a thing and perhaps thing is not the right word, but anyway, so it is, like this or like <u>was</u> perhaps, keeping the tense for once in order and all of the rest of it, but now, wait while I tell you – one thing that Ron has never been afeared of is a sense of his own existence. This is in complete contradistinction to your man Descartes who posed the question of his own non-existence seemingly without self-contradiction and absurdity…well at least for bit. Ron was having none of it, down with those sort of problems entirely. All Ron had to do was to take his rather thick thumbnail and scrape the cobbled skin of his scrotum and pass the nail under his nose to savour his existence. Come on, course he exists, does his shit not stink when he's on the clodgy and squeezing stools from his arse? That smell from his balls, strangely earthly fruity and pungent; a real animal smell and there be no way of talking yourself out of that come what may with all the fine research conducted in the laboratories of deodorant companies and their ilk. The man smelt. He had a touch of the piles and halitosis, seeing how he never so much as flossed his teeth the once in his life, and he had big sweaty balls that could pump spunk for England should the need arise or more probably not. When he shaved was it not no longer than the day after when there's this clough of hair like black flints bursting through the sallow skin of his face; well neck actually, seeing how a fair bush seems to flourish around the neck region, and that time when he was living in Spain did not the beard he grew all mass and mangle together with the nest of hair up spouting from the chest and make no mistake it did, and let that be an end to it. Hair in the ears, hair in the nose and a couple of stray strands sprouting from the stalk of his cock which looks a tadge unsightly but what the hell, nothing worth getting the Immac out for or any other such product – the beast was still very much in that buck, your man Ron Smith, and lying there in a stupor farting and belching, suffering with the indigestion it was some cheek to suggest his very fictionality.

But for all that and this and even a bit of yon t'other chapter, Little Mouse knew the truth of it as he helped himself to a sip of the thick wax oozing from Ron's ears. Little Mouse knew it all, even his own ontological status and worse than this, Little Mouse knowing none of it made a damn, any second after the last he would be up there and dancing for the dead while your man Ron, that pisrogue of a fellow, would be asleep sprawled over the mattress that was his bed, not knowing shit as far as it comes to existence, sub-existence and the life to commence; all Ron would be knowing was that he was dry as a spinster's cunt and that was a very sexist, possibly ageist way of going about making metaphors, for despite the unread properties of his person he was quite a literate sort of gaje altogether was Ron. He once wrote a poem while in prison and not many folk can say as much nor as little and isn't that a pitiful set of contrasts that ever do be mentioned en passant and while we're at it. Wasn't much of a poem all told, but here's a snatch of it to be going on with:

> Every day looking from this window
> Out over the estuary of the Humber
> I see this pilot boat tack and shift
> Then move out of view, leaving me
> Wondering why not me too?

Of course the poor fuck spelt it all wrong, but there was this nice teacher from York who helped him with the spellings and how to hold the pen in the claw of his fingers in order to make patterns on the paper that prison visitors could just about muster into parameters of sense and possible sensibility. Ron was not impressed with his piece, but that is not the point of the exercise, the point is, if points must be made, is that there is this person from York, a generous soul, who can also vouch that Ron did exist, that there really was this Ron with all his imperfections, and perhaps, tracing a line through time, others may come forward also to point out the stages of life's way where Ron could have been found, such that those in need of verification could walk away satisfied. Points, points in time, draw the line and there's your man, or rather the shadow, the epiphenomenon of Ron walking out of the print to be known, seen and mulled over as if sub-existence was not a lack of a thing, but merely a different category of that thing's ness as being in the world, like the difference between numbers such as two or three or even five million and those numbers that do be proving troubling from time to time like the square root of negative pi – bit of a bastard that one eh? And by the way, just so you know, the wee pilot boat is still making that trip, tacking hither and thither along the Humber estuary from Hull itself out to Spurn Point at times. Continuity - if it should last forever would it be the same sort of thing as permanence - who could tell and who should care? Perhaps, none of this is even worth talking about, but to Ron, to

Ron asleep upon his mattress with his smelly balls, touch of thrush and the great hairy arse on him, all of this once meant something, for a time it was all he had left when he lost it all: friends, family and even his own name.

Little Mouse wept for shame. Tragedy thickened:-

Kali, Goddess of Death and good time gal, was a tadge bored. The Indian sub-continent managed mortality quite nicely thank you very much, ma'am, without any effort on her behalf, more's the pity. Now, listen up, certain strategy experts in the West and possibly elsewhere have even earmarked India and Pakistan as the most likely twain to go for an all out nuclear war. Stuff 'em, was Kali's answer, she was on her hols, cartwheeling down Gunnarsgate on all her hands and feet, rosary of skulls keeping time and hitting off-beats. She was hoping for a bit of action and wasn't long disappointed, Eric Newton, aged bachelor and owner of the corner shop and off-license, was in his bedroom wanking in something like comfort, propped up on pillows, pumping away with his rubber-gloved hand and a quarter pound of liver while flicking through *Homes and Gardens*. The lass helped him out, appearing out of the ether, her fiery red tongue licking the air, straddling his purple stalk and jerking the cum out of him in one quick spasm, arching over to tit-fuck his head between her black-black breasts. Newton gasped, Newton shot spunk and shit, thereafter giving up the ghost. Kali tore out his heart, ripping it to strips and chewing thoughtfully as she read the article on the possibilities of utilising alcoves and stair-holes and other erstwhile cupboards of wasted space.

Kisan was ticking off some substance vendor or other and it was getting wicked. This dumb fuck was cutting skag 60/40 when the ruling was clearly 70/30. Kisan was taking the arsehole to town and Lickle Lad was blubbing and crapping his shorts 'cos his mam's scales were wrong and they shot her last week, 'cos too Kisan had his dog-tooth churi out and was meaning business and lastly 'cos he had some kind of anal sphincter complaint after being buggered stupid for the past three years by the local priest –

it was that sort of neighbourhood. Kisan was having the none of it, slicing up the air and impressing on the youngster the seriousness of his misdemeanour, 'Go on, stand in the corner, turn round, no we don't want to look at you…' when all of a sudden Kisan hears then feels the hot, sweet as death, breath of Kali. Kisan shivers, the boy whines like a squealing pig as his throat is torn wide open. Kisan runs screaming, madness, black, death-black madness and the hot salt of spilt blood.

Ron is asleep dreaming of the Beebee, that last night she dropped six-five finally replying to his double six. Kali stroked his hair, recognising one of her own and that soon he'd be hers forever and possibly even a tadge longer. Profane kiss, the funky lips of her cunt she placing over Ron's open lips. She sticky with the grocer's spunk and the blood of the boy and Ron snores making her fanny fart. Red-tongued Kali laughing, black Kali, necklace of skulls, arches back and sucks cock, bites, nibbles, sucks hard drawing blood-clotted sperm.

'Ron! Ron come quick, give us a hand.' It was Tracy back from the dead again, knocking at Ron's door wanting something in the way of a bit of advice.

Other side of time, other side of town, there's this gangland gun war blazing and she wanting in on the deal – Kali gonna fuck those bullets dry. Ron wakes, the usual shit taste in his mouth after sleeping, cracking his old faithful boxer shorts a few times over his knees and putting them on, he waddles to the door, rubbing the grime back into his eyes.

'So?'

'I was just throwing myself through the window, feeling a bit down in the dumps like, when I land on top of this foreign git, his mates and their camels.'

'So?' said Ron again, just to be consistent.

'So get your fat arse to the door and sort it: you're the flat manager here, you're the concierge, you're the fat bollox that's shagging me, so get your butt to the door so I can commit suicide without having to contend with camels and coons blocking mi exit!'

Ron disapproved, there was no cause to be using such language, the bastard argot of empire acquisition, but more surprising than the latent racism of his current dead bit of totty was the fact that he now occupied some sort of official post.

Surprising or not, yon lass was in the right. Calo had bought the house and all its malcontents at a bring and buy sale t'other week. Owners brought leases or title deeds and buyers brought suitcases of unmarked notes. Kisan was the bagman and this was only one of the ways he made his first five million – canny lad, like. Rather than pay someone else for running the shop, Calo made Ron run the show but without bothering to tell or pay him. T'is for the lack of supervising these details that the likes of Rome fell or so some historians would have it; the sort that bore you to death in bars when you're trying to get nicely plastered or into the pants of something vaguely tasty somewhat opposite. Either way, Ron's going to the front door in his undercrackers and finding parking places for three camels as Tracy, or was it Shelly, goes flying through the air and ruins her bouffant hairdo and her chances of surviving to claim her pension all in one pavement human pizza and there's an end to it, though doubtless there might be a chance for some other minor appearance or so as the tales near their conclusions and Ron gets whacked.

'Anyway, what you fuckers want and be sharp about it, I was having this belting dream afore you jokers arrived,' goes Ron, scratting his balls like a cockerel working away at a lump of the old horse shite. It was a tadge rude of Ron, let that be said, but mun bear in mind that he'd just seen the demise of an almost loved one again; can be the likes of that for putting a pus on one and make no mistake, arrah.

Dr A J P Khan, Bootham Car Park Hospital, Interviewed by Uncle Salty

12th June 1992 (Excerpt)

...

Salty: What in fiction really annoys you?
Dr Khan: What?
Salty: You mean pardon?
Dr Khan: I know what I mean and so do you.
Salty: So…?
Dr Khan: So what!
Salty: You said to me, 'Mr Bestwhick, have you any questions?' and my question is, what in a work of fiction annoys you?
Dr Khan: In general, genres – that type of thing?
Salty: Professionally.

(Dr Khan strokes his luxuriant black beard for a second or two before replying.)

Dr Khan: Okay then, what really pisses me off is when writers confuse schizophrenia with multi-personality disorder; they have a schizophrenic character nice as Uncle Tom's apple pie one minute and a raving axe murderer the next – that is not schizophrenia, that is, if it is anything at all, a very extreme case of multi-personality disorder; what is more I have read several excellent papers that suggest that no such disorder really exists outside the labelling by psychiatrists of certain patients' behaviour. That, Mr Bestwhick, is what gets my goat.
Salty: Thank you, Dr Khan…

So there's these three beardoes hanging around outside with their camels on double yellows, though a couple of shekels have fed the meter, dead Tracy and Ron in his duds trying to make sense of the whole caboose. It has been said before, but it's well worth the reiteration: that this, all this, and specially this needs and would take a Jeffrey Fletcher to tell it right. Three saffron-skinned wiseheads with turbans, they stand waiting at the door bearing presents.

'We have come bearing gifts,' says one, sporting a royal blue turban and a simply splendid oiled and scented beard.

'I saw the very heavens point the way, heralding the nativity so long hoped for,' says one other, rich red turban and only slightly sparser beard.

'Coca-Cola – give me a takeout milkshake and fries,' said the last in black, who, not having a tongue of his own, had to make do with international lingua-franca, the Patwah of Latter Day Capitalism. Actually, this is bollox. That Black Turban had a tongue of his own. It was just no longer viable and apart from a couple of ageing egg-heads at the School of Oriental and African Studies no one else had a hope of comprehending a word the Black said. None of this was much of a help to Ron.

'That's as maybe, but how may I help,' said Ron in a vain endeavour to inculcate a strain of rationality to the conversation.

'Have you a virgin?' asked Blue Turban.

'You want a punch up the bracket?' asked Ron.

'I saw a sign, a flashing light in the skies, there can be no mistake, God does not play with lights,' said Red Turban.

'Personally, I thought that light was too fast for a star, more like a Boeing 747. What sayest thou?' asked Blue Turban.

'Big Mac topped with an egg over easy and give me a side salad on the side and hold the mayo, p-lease,' said the Alien Other.

Ron looked up and down the street just to make sure there were no hidden cameras and this was not some kind of wind-up stunt so beloved by station programmers with limited budgets.

But no, this was the genuine article and as authentic an incongruity as had ever crossed Ron's path by blind happenstance.

'Stop dithering, man,' said Blue Turban, pushing past Ron. Once through the door Red Turban took over, arms outstretched in supplication, following a scent, a sign, and the directions for the gas meter under the stairs. And, that was where the miracle happened.

'You a virgin?' asked Blue Turban, hopefully, a present tucked under his oxter.

Christine shrank back from the bizarrely garbed figure and drew out her bigger, better knife, her present from Ron, when she first arrived. Ron himself expected things to kick off and was priming his sandals for a nifty bit of sticking the boot in.

'You pregnant!' It wasn't a question, delivered like a bullet from Red Turban.

'Strawberry milkshake!'

All of a sudden, Christine burst into tears, racking sobs shaking her thin frame. 'I'm three months late, but I can't be…I've never done anything wrong, never had a boyfriend or nothing.'

'A sign, a veritable sign,' exclaimed Red Turban.

'Give it a rest, tha's getting on mi tits,' said Blue Turban shewing a remarkable grasp of the vernacular in such a short time.

Ron was nonplussed but felt as concierge that he had better do something given the strange set of circumstances that seemed insistent on imposing themselves on his morning's slumber. He made a pot of tea. Coming in with a tray of chipped mugs and one washed out jam pot Ron found them still arguing the toss and Christine still bewildered and far from a happy womble.

'Did anything happen, anything strange befall you, sweet sobbing maiden?' said Red Turban, turning on the charm.

'…There seemed to be a light all around me, then all of a sudden, there was this strange ringing in my ear,' confessed Christine.

'Right or left?…Ear, lass, ear!' said Blue Turban.

'Right.'

'By Jove, St Augustin was in the right of it again,' smiled Red Turban.

'Medium fries and a takeout large coke.'

'But I can't be pregnant,' insisted Christine, her chin wobbling.

'There's only one way to find out,' said Red Turban rolling up his sleeves.

'Oi, are you a doctor?' said Ron stirring in the sugars.

'No, he isn't, but old Balthi here is a dab hand with camels,' said Blue Turban.

'That's all right then,' said Ron, dishing out the teas, appreciative always of folk with a way with animals and Christine's legs were unceremoniously spread and Red Turban had a right good dig about.

'Damnations, a thousand woes,' wailed Red Turban.

'She not pregnant, Balthi?' asked Blue.

'Oh she is, indeed, but much too early, two and a half months is all.'

'I fucking well told you it was travelling too fast, that it was only a sodding plane, but oh no, Mr Balthi big-head knows best.'

'One Big Mac breakfast coming up.'

Christine politely asked Balthi to remove his hand and hid once more beneath the covers, struggling to hide her tears. Bugger, Ron had gotten the wrong mug and boy did he hate sweet tea. There was nothing else for it. The three boyos left, finding jobs in the area to await the glorious day. One chanced a job at a local panto, the other, a natural, worked for McDonald's whilst the third reconciled himself to working on the buses.

'You can stay here, if you want, there is an attic flat free,' Ron called after the retreating threesome.

'You taking the piss, man! I wouldn't house animals in this shitehole,' Blue Turban shouted back.

Ron didn't think much of this new malarkey of concierge. He went back to bed and treated himself to a bit of a hand job, the dregs of his dream still thickening his lingam somewhat noticeably. Well, Christine noticed it, dabbing away at her tears, not so much as having a bit of fagen, humping away and swapping bodily fluids and she still in the pudding club – there's safe sex for you. It's a mean old other-world.

Well is the opinion of veterinarians, horse-whisperers and others gifted in the treatment of our dumb brethren that Ron does be having in the main, which is in direct contradistinction to the gombeem pishrogues of fake quacks that does have the name of doctors. T'is common sense when all's told that those that be dealing with animal sickness are a superior type of healer to the white-frock and stethoscope brigade: point one – a human patient can tell a doctor what is in the way of ailing her/him, but even the most gifted and loquacious of parrots, the African Grey, would be hard put to give a blow by blow description of what sickens them. The only human practitioner that was ever doing your man Ron any good was the Witch of Llandewi Brefi when his back was out that time he was shovelling the black stuff for a bit of cash in hand in mid Wales. T'auld witch put it right, right enough and Ron figured she was a dab hand at animals too judging by the happy chicken clucking by her feet and the pet lamb that seemed to have the run of the place.

Ron was ill. The gaje was in a bad way, but there seemed nowhere to turn and nowhere to go. Even if he had an insurance scheme or three the lad would not have taken himself to any doctor. But, what ailed him most was not the sudden shooting pains in his gut or bladder, but something deep-seated in his dreaming. The heart of the sickness seemed to stem from there. His grandma Sbanck came to visit him one night in his dreams, playing this violin of human gut, bowed with the hair of a hundred Jewesses, playing this elegy, but not too well and really she was more of a one for playing the spoons and sometimes the comb and paper if they were pushed for something with a bit more in the way of an expansive melody line. Either way, Ron never found out what his grandma was after. Shame really as she could have given him the numbers for the lottery, some sound advice on the 2.30 at Doncaster and the fact that he only had three weeks to put his house in order and she did not mean the concierge franchise. Still and all, it was nice to see the Puro-Rawnee and she likewise, for eternity was getting on Grandma Sbank's nerves and after all Ron always had been her favourite. God bless, betti charvorro chal, said Grandma Sbank, see you soon. The tune was over, thank God, as Ron was not much of a one for the violin, the guitar being more his weapon to say nothing of the thin nasal whine of the pipes, that was the music that put fire in his blood, making him want to dance and whirr like a dervish, not that Ron played, but you can't always have everything in this life nor the life to come for that matter. Suffice to say Ron was in a bad way. If only his dreaming would let him be. Ah, to be, isn't that the question, or not?

A Few Words from Chief Inspector Bailehatchet

I must set the record straight, Ron Smith was never our chief suspect in the hunt for Arturo, in fact he was no suspect at all. Even when afterwards we made a thorough search of his premises we found no incriminating evidence, nothing untoward save an old Swedish soft porn magazine, black and white I believe, and there was some evidence to suggest that even this item did not belong to Ron, but had been put under the floorboards by the former resident, Seimidh Eoghan Dubh, a spoilt Jesuit from the parish of Gleann Colm Cille. Be that as it may, Ron Smith was innocent till proven shot.

Interjection

Salty received a reader's report, paid good money up front too; the pishrogue had the nerve to suggest that Salty was some kind of super-illiterate and his long meandering sentences were proving tiresome in the extreme. Salty's reply is hereby noted for posterity: 'Get fucked – short enough!' Personally, it is debatable if this is a sentence or not as too is its use of the exclamation mark as opposed to the question mark. Still my presentiments are with Salty. This should have been an end note, but as stated earlier the Binder programme got the better of the compiler and not everything as presented here is in its right place. Not even fucking close! Is that another short sentence? Debatable or not, perhaps, maybe.

Chapter Somewhere Near the Middle

Fast scurry of fast feet bouncing, thumping up the nest of stairs, drumming on the landing, approaching. No knock, no nothing, the door bursts open and Tchai confronts Ron.

'How can you live like this?'

Ron has no answer to life, his how of life nor his why of life: life is an open book, Ron is illiterate – the sort of readership that God is after. Ron looks at Tchai and despite himself a happy tear milks his eyes. (One tear, two eyes – that some lacrimation) Tchai, dark Tchai with the deep brown skin and huge sloe eyes, hair blue shimmer of black, trim and hard, wiry and strong – the best of the three children: Manush the idiot, Calo the cruel, Tchai slender princess, brave hearted and true. (Good enough for a panto – eh?) Tchai, who cares, what's in a name.

Tchai stroked Ron's hand, concerned, annoyed and pissed off. She knew it would be useless. There was no way back, but she needed help. Kisan was at the tapa bar, drinking himself a little nearer to death with only his Luger for company. Tchai withdrew her hand, drew it back and slapped the side of Ron's face. His sombrero fell off. Tchai pulled her hand back again and slapped one more time.

'You are supposed to ask, to interrogate first, then you strike me,' Ron advised.

'I'm sorry. I'm not used to this sort of thing. Anyway, I thought it would save time,' Tchai replied.

'Sorry, you right, my mistake.'

Tchai slapped Ron's face till her arm tired. Ron turned the other cheek. Tchai slapped Ron's other cheek with her other hand till that arm tired.

'Thirsty work,' commented Ron.

'Aye,' said Tchai.

'Fancy a pint in The Albert?' Ron asked.

'Only.'

'Only what – one pint?'

'Only my treat and I buy.'

'No,' said Ron, strangely, nay rarely, shamed.

'You want me to slap your face again?'

Ron couldn't bear to see more mindless cruelty, his beautiful Tchai hurting her hand on his face – what sort of bastard was he? Ron couldn't answer his own question, thank the lord it was only rhetorical.

Tchai treated Ron to a bucketful of sangria at Bertie's Tapa Bar. Ron liked his buckets. Soon, Ron's mood lifted, so much so that he was almost clinically depressed.

'What was it you wanted anyway?' asked Ron, just to be polite.

'I want you to have a word with Kisan. He's acting strangely, he's under pressure, and to be truthful I am scared he is going to do something stupid.'

'What, you don't mean-'

'That's right, give his money away and join the Socialist Workers Party,' said Tchai, worry puckering her brown beautiful forehead.

'Shit, you better let me have a word with him before it gets too late. Where is he?'

'Right next to you, buying the buckets,' said Tchai, pointing Ron in the general direction of his next free drink.

'That's handy,' admitted Ron, turning to have his word with Kisan, but Kisan getting there first with a rueful lamentation of his very own, composed without the need of a team of writers and fourteen re-writes, more's the pity.

AutoSummarize

The editor when shewn the first draft said that Kisan's lament needed much trimming. It was wordy, verbose in the extreme and so archaicly literate as to be non-literate, which is a tidy distinction to please any a follower of St Thomas Aquinas. The compiler, not trusting his own wily skills in the hard cutting department, took the easy way out and found another cute programme on his Microsoft Word package, up there on the drop down tools menu – AutoSummarize – with the 's' phoneme being realised by a now considered Americanism 'z' – interesting. Anyway, pressing this button a whole host of options become available. The most useful for the case at hand was the one where the summary, a reduction to a mere 25% of the original document, was saved and transported electronically to a new document. This was briefly read, before the old lamentation was cut and replaced by the autosummarized linguistic artefact. Everyone including the editor was satisfied with this state of affairs, except the compiler, for betimes this nag tends to worry him about the authorship of this work of fiction, given the use of the programmes Binder and AutoSummarize the text is now something of a bastard – half man/half software programme. This is but one stage away from computer authors or even perhaps to no authors at all, merely a pseudo-relationship compromised by kitsch and verisimilitude. Bit of an issue this one, but what's at heart is that Salty's work has been betrayed – this work is not a product of his intentions; intentionality has been rendered to impotent shadow and mere epiphenomen. Och well, for those who wish to peruse a copy of the document before the AutoSummarize got stuck in, kindly send proof of purchase and three Taylors Yorkshire Teatokens and answer the question, why does beetroot turns your piss pink? in less than ten words.

'So sorry,' said Kisan.

'Mine's another sangria,' said Ron.

'Drink is not what I brought you down for, talk to him,' said

Tchai, taking a hike to the clodgy as the need was on her. For a second or two she thought that the plumbers might be calling early, but thankfully t'was naught but pish and wind. Ripping a titbit of *Welt am Sonntag* from a nail on the door Tchai cleaned up and internally, introspectively, all mental gymnastics with the auld internal monotone speculated on the possible outcome of Ron's advice. This did not take long. Flush went the toilet - by Christ I wish I couldn't write like that.

Back inside, picking through the fried squid and olives stuffed with almonds whilst generously quaffing from another bucket of sangria, Ron was waxing lyrical, 'So?'

Kisan was falling to pieces. He'd lost his digit finger already and his left ear was looking shaky. Tchai had to act and to act fast. Failing that she hired a cab. Ron thought he'd come along for the ride. He'd had enough of playing house with a bunch of fuckwits, besides he felt sorry for Kisan, Ron knew the way senseless and sensible killing worked on a body.

'Cab for a couple of pissheads,' said the taxi-driver, which was kinda prompt and not a jot like real life. Who cares, you want real life go to a supermarket, it's there stacked up with the rest of the merchandise and don't forget your reward card.

Kisan and Tchai were already sprawled in the back seat chewing on tongue sandwich with plenty of lashings of the old saliva slipped in for good measure, when Ron spots the firm spray-canned on the side of the bullet-proof limousine: NSKK. Shit, no two ways of looking at this, Ron flipped, he really kicked off, man he did that, dragging the driver out and kicking his head to shit all the time bawling, blood-red tears in his ears, 'Tell me, tell me, who's the Fuhrer!' Ron was insistent, the man was not for telling till he had the tongue ripped out of him, by that time it was too late, thank God the driver could sign, his bust fingers working ten to the dozen, spelling, 'Calo, Calo,' though the comma probably wasn't included. Unluckily for the driver Ron was about as good at signing as he was at reading. He thought the poor fuck was signalling the birdy or some combination of the V-sign, either way Ron battered the life out of him.

Kisan and Tchai were too much down each other's throats to notice. Ron sat in the front and threw up – squid always got to him like that after the second bucket of sangria.

'Hey, who's driving?' Ron asked after patiently waiting for someone to show for a quarter of an hour or so; or so he thought in fact, for time flies when you're enjoying yourself and time waits for no man and if you can't do the time don't do the crime. Thankfully this reverie of cliché gets to be interrupted by Kali who is so impressed by Ron and his diligent antics in knocking the stuffing out of some sibling of the BDM, that she gets in and chauffeurs herself and themselves over to the caravan downstream of town just past the vicus. She's a dab hand at that trade seeing as she be putting death on the roads in no short measure and Ron has another digestive disagreement with his last vestige of squid: seafood – see it twice, ho, ho.

Ron forgets to tip, but Kali acts like it no problem, man, and see you later. Tchai carries Kisan inside; that man should pull himself together, but it may take superglue and a radical adaptation of the flying buttonhole stitch to make a right job of it. Ron has a jimmy agin some burnt stripped copper and thinks it's a good job he made of the match between Kisan and Tchai; one day he might even get round to telling them about it. Still, it's a grand night to be out, he thinks, as he passes inside to take care of a night-cap or so.

'Talk to him, Deiya,' says Tchai to Rawnee.

Rawnee just smiles. She knows, Ron knows, poor Kisan knows too that any day it all over, only Tchai, beautiful Tchai with the dark eyes won't see it. Rawnee pours Ron this drink of sljivovica. It's all bad news, but either way they get the dominoes out for a couple of games of 'first to five' followed by an equal measure of 'sling 'em'. What a quaint custom, thinks Kisan, as a couple of sarnies and pickles are served during and between play. He's still shaky, blurting some last minute news, unable to contain himself any longer.

'The worst of it is that Arturo is back. I personally had a message from him the other night. It was a most underhand affair – Castle Cabs blown up, torched, never operate again – some message, no?'

Rawnee looked at Ron. Ron looked at his hand, he was strongly suited in threes; that hand had distinct possibilities.

'You sure it was, Arturo?' snorted Tchai. 'You saw him, in the flesh? He told you to drop the happy matches?'

Kisan shook his head, 'Just a messenger calling in the dead of day with a mission to which I had to comply with all expediency.'

'You believed it? You acted on a mere message?'

'I have heard terrible tales of this Arturo. It does not pay to be circumspect – ask the manager of Castle Cabs.'

Tchai's temper was rising. She turned to vent her anger on Ron, 'Arturo is back and you just sit there? Have you got nothing to say?'

'Threes about,' said Ron, dropping his domino with a certain degree of smugness. Rawnee was knocking and knocked up a few more butties. Kisan had the only other three and Tchai couldn't care a gnat's chuff either way; she was more of a 'fives and threes' specialist.

To cut to the chase, Ron won. It was time to hit the sack; he had to visit the poor house on the morrow, as if his own house was not poor enough. Ron slept by the fire. Rawnee drew an old tartan blanket around him. Tchai lightly kissed his brow in despair. Kisan shook his hand and lost the nail to his little finger. Ron had a good night's sleep, that boy could sleep on a clothesline.

The Pudding Club

The pudding club, flat 23a, met every Tuesday, for lager, tabs and porno videos featuring men buggering the daylights out of one another. It passed the time. The laddettes ranged in age from fifteen to ninety-three. The club was open to anyone who was a woman and could take her ale.

Margery said, 'I have heard as like as not that they are on to Arturo.'

'Happen as maybe – Bailehatchet on the case no doubt,' said Doris.

'What does that Ron Smith say about it all?' asked Aunty Betty.

'Who gives a bugger,' said Doris. 'Last I heard he was about to be dropped in the shite an' all.'

'Really?' said Sharon; it wasn't a question despite being marked as such.

'Aye,' someone affirmed.

'Anyone got a light,' said Mrs Chandala Harijan.

There was a scramble for lighters and matches, till Margery put her foot down.

'Hush a bit and settle down, it's *Harry Gets His Hole Re-Greased* next!'

The laddettes cheer as a man. Bottles and cans are opened with obvious jubilation. Tabs are smoked down to the nubbins. Harry gets his hole re-greased.

And Ron could be in trouble. It might be the big one for our Ron. It could be curtains. It could be the final furlong. Then again, perhaps not, any port in a storm and it's half a dozen of one and six of the other and it's a game of two halves while we are at it as well, so perhaps Ron could be okay after all. But I wouldn't like to bet on it.

Chapter – Last Dance

Teotwawki had walked many miles, travelled over many lands, crossed the mighty black water in a Finnish freighter, travelling buckshee in his buck skins. The Great Spirit called him to make that walk. The Great Spirit was calling home his children. No star, no AA man or tourist information map drew him to that house – his heart, seeing with his heart finally, was how he found the house.

'Little Man with Mexican Hat, I have come to collect my sundered kinsman,' Teotwawki said to Ron.

'Come in, old lad,' said Ron. First time Ron had been so greeted and feeling quite charmed by it.

Teotwawki, son to Billy Two Bears, walked through the hall and straight up the servants' stairs, following his nose to the dank den of Ron. Ron trailed behind, intrigued, if this was some kind of assassination attempt it was damned original, worthy of the Master Arturo himself. Inside Ron's room, Teotwawki of true Sioux blood danced and chanted, by his feet Little Mouse danced. Ron bowed his head as a mark of respect and remained thus till the dancing stopped. Teotwawki scanned the room, saw panting Little Mouse and bent low to pick up his brother. Little Mouse knew he was coming home. Ron bowed, sad though also glad to see his companion go. Teotwawki smiled, gave Ron a hug goodbye and began his travels again.

Teotwawki, son of Billy Two Bears, walks the earth, seeking his brethren seeking return, called by the Great Spirit.

Three gajes in something like fancy dress walk out of this hovel of a hostel, a workhouse, where inside some brat asks for more cornflakes and is sadly disappointed and ridiculed by some fat fuck tucking into a full English breakfast. Worse was to follow when this young lad is sent to work for a fisherman off the Suffolk coast. Anyway, no time for diversions, Red Turban, Blue Turban and Employee of the Month walk out of this charitable institution and bump into Ron – the auld Dickensian coincidence thang kicking in again.

'What's the news?' asks Ron.

'That has got to be the ugliest baby I've ever seen,' said Blue Turban.

'If it were not for the most auspicious signs heralding the birth I would not believe that this is the One – bloody chandala bullshit man,' said Red Turban.

'Big Mac, gherkins and a double fries on the side.'

'I don't know, maybe if the babe gets a good agent, something can be done, but I wouldn't bet on it,' said Blue.

'To come so far, to suffer such hardships for such an ugly wee shite – tush!' said Red, mounting his camel – the things some camels will do for a good carrot.

'Hey, give some me doughnuts, butthead!'

The threesome buggered off down the road where a boat, *The Black Dog*, was all set to take them back to yon side of the Black Sea, which wasn't exactly where they wanted to go, but you can't have everything with a cheap package tour these days. Ron entered the poor house.

'Friend, relative, father, boyfriend, pederast, slave owner or paedophile?' asked this tasty young thing behind her reinforced mesh counter.

'Just a visitor, I want to see Christine: young unmarried virgin with a bairn, new born,' said Ron, tipping his sombrero.

'Sorry, I thought it was business. The bairn has been adopted by a merchant banker, his PA wife and their Czech nanny, can't reveal more details, except the mother has buggered off after being stitched up, taking only a clean pair of standard issue navy knickers and a small vegetable knife,' said this nice young thing.

'Erm, bit of a wasted journey then,' said Ron.

'Yes,' said yon canny lass.

'I suppose a date is out of the question?' asked Ron.

'Yes,' replied the batty, auld, stuck up, wouldn't touch it with a barge pole, slapper behind the screen.

Ron walked away. So much for the new man.

There was this disturbance down Gunnarsgate, the traffic had stopped and it wasn't even time for the rush-hour – traditions were breaking down fast. The reason, a high wire had been suspended from a gable end of this house on the corner of Gunnarsgate to this roof on the corner of Kirkgate. Walking the wire while a bear collected the money was Esmeralda Salamanca, a crowd-stopper to be sure and consummate professional. Kisan was for the moment impressed with this spectacle, but moments seldom last. A chance remark is what tore it; says Kisan to his henchman down on the street, 'So, Hengest, what's the cut on this?'

'Er, nothing, bwana, they set up in Kirkgate,' said Hengest, scratching his oxter.

'Bullshit fool, they not in Kirkgate now, we want a cut on this!' said Kisan, more than a little vexed.

'Er, sorry, bwana, but she's back on Kirkgate side now,' said Hengest, turning his attention to levelling out his testicles, his new boxer shorts playing up a bit.

Kisan said nothing. He reached inside his Russian greatcoat, pulled out his Luger and with consummate care shot Esmeralda down – boy the crowd liked that. This was entertainment; just like the movies, blood and guts everywhere. The bear collected a right hatful.

'Get the bear,' said Kisan.

'Can't. It's a protected species unless you hold a baiting license or a street-entertainer's permit,' said Hengest, breaking the back of a crab on his thumbnail.

The bear had gone, too late. Kisan swung the barrel of the Luger down and shot his man in the foot. Hengest limped off bawling, vowing vengeance amongst a clutter of expletives and cluster of curses.

'Now, now, now, my young lad, what's all this then?'

'You talking to me, you low-grade, nothing but a bribed

bobby on a beat, hitting the pay-off, getting all the favours from the girls, dealers and other pros – you talking to me?' said Kisan, hovering between incredulity, anger and a bit part in a nouveau film noir re-write.

'No, no, no, my young lad, I'm PC McGarry, I'm the friendly village policeman: tell you time, give you directions, rescue cats from trees – that sort of thing.'

'McGarry, fuck me not goddamn bullshit puppet of a congenital idiot. Go home now, please, take your flat feet and fine phatic pleasantries some non-existent place that never was and walk that walk. Go home please, this not the fictionality for you – change your name, become a postman, put on weight and stick a television in your gut, or what you like with fires – speak Cymraeg? Gaidhlig?'

'No, no, no. Now, now, now, young fellow my lad, just hand over that there illegal firearm and accompany me to the station. I'm sure a hot cup of tea and a word with the desk sergeant and all this can be sorted out,' said PC McGarry.

Kisan shook his head, Kali stopped his hand from shaking, there was nothing for it, a click of the Luger and PC McGarry was nothing but splinters, paint and broken strings. The crowd was really enjoying this act. They dug deep, then deeper and showered Kisan with coins. Not a bad old day after all. Kali licked Kisan's lips, squeezed his balls before seeking diversion elsewhere. There was this rising young stud with death as his only bride; that gaje knew all the tricks to keep her in corpses – 'Calo, Calo, wherefore art thou, Calo?'

Kisan cleaned up. Traffic started moving again. Then this cab pulled up – NSKK. This blond youth steps out, salutes then informs Kisan that he is his new henchman, Horsa.

'By what authority?' asks Kisan, his Luger ready just in case.

'Calo sent me,' said Horsa.

It was at such a point that the dialogue became somewhat wooden, almost falling in to the trap of such quaint Hollywoodisms as, 'Take me to your leader.'. It is for this reason that the dialogue whereby it is established that Calo is running NSKK cabs and is the real big cheese in town, etc, etc, has not been included due to its lack of any discernible aesthetic value whatsoever. However, a note bewailing the lack of value and the crudity of the dialogue and the wee snippet concerning Calo's rise to power has been included to facilitate a modicum of understanding.

Scriptorium

Uncle Salty makes it known that the real readers for him, the real heroes of the page were those that hadn't a fucking clue. Take the Middle Ages there, the boyos in monasteries, a good proportion of them illiterate as be damned, but none the less zealously copying out word perfect (this was before any talk of software) the Bible and other bollox. To cover a book, the same book, end to end or perhaps just mere fragments and not know a tinker's curse what the marks on the page signified. Uncle Salty lets it be known that this is precisely, and none other, the very type of novel that he is trying to present to an illiterate public; namely, to read cover to cover and not know a damn. Gnosis or its lack: no longer a mediaeval pursuit.

There is a bear. It has lost the love of its life, Esmeralda Salamanca. It has these pockets stuffed with money. Money no longer matters. The bear stutters with rage. He sees limping towards him in his grief this shape of a man. The bear rises, rages, and lurches towards the human. The bear in the skin becomes bear, elemental and necessary bear, dream bear, bearness, as he charges the limper. The limper squeals in fright, runs as best he can, falling out into the middle of a road. A taxi stops, a hand drags him in. The limping man is saved, saved for a very special little act of revenge. The bear meanwhile turns out its pockets, growls at a neon moon, moves off to find a fable to die in – *send a girl with golden hair and I'll tear her heart out*. It's that blood simple, finally.

Several cabs are getting the squeeze. The independents didn't last a minute, but two other cabs are still holding out for custom. There are Wilkinsons traditional cabbies at the undercutting end of the market, but they are under pressure. Then we got the Hacked Off Co-operative, a sixty-strong group that's gotten organised: shares costs, pays dividends and prides itself on running a service, but… But any day they gonna get whacked. In the early hours the sound of limping was heard on the night that this message in red paint got sprayed, 'Burn, Warehouse, Burn'. This didn't mean a right lot as the taxi co-op was in no wise a warehouse. There were complaints to the council, but the problem was this, the NSKK was by far the biggest vested interest pulling the strings and greasing the palms and all that other monkey business that keeps the world of corrupt corporatism churning along. Most folk knew that trouble was cruising out there on the streets. And, the man behind the taxi wheel was a maniac or otherwise entrepreneur with his finger on the trigger and the goddamn tab running. But many of the general public couldn't spot the difference, but what the hell it wasn't that sort of competition anyway, no prizes in the offing for noticing this new streamline service moving in on Joe and Josephine Public.

Kisan noticed and he was troubled. He tried talking it through with Tchai, but she insisted that he had his facts all wrong. The stumbling block was Arturo. Tchai claimed he was still travelling. Kisan said he was in contact, though only through intermediaries.

Tchai was squeezing nits between her thumbnails, grooming Kisan's hair for the wedding. He'd been mixing with low-life again and wouldn't use a shampoo, said it was made by the same people that made nerve gas and sheep dip and that his nerves was bad enough and there was no way he was part of the common herd. Kisan was becoming a bit of an expert on the misreading of Nietzsche; all Calo's men had to misread Nietzsche, to generate a further series of texts, such as Nietzsche the Anti-Semite, Nietzsche as Hitler's educator or the Nietzschean guide to shagging whores and getting a dose of siph. No one minded, no one cared and in the end no one read. Nihilism reached a new level of readership with only the books absent to make things more believable. It was nothing to write home about, suffice to say.

'You say that Arturo is still travelling, but when some hood with a balaclava covering his face, unknown except by his hirple, when such as he comes-'

'A balaclava is not a hood,' Tchai interrupted.

'I know my potatoes as sure as eggs wait till the cows come home to roast, so don't piss me about,' said Kisan angrily. 'Anyway, this gorilla-'

'What some kind of revolutionary – a guerrilla?'

'No, underneath the balaclava he was wearing a gorilla mask. He was hot some so took a layer off. Doesn't matter – no es portante! – back to the monkey business.'

'Apes – a gorilla is an ape.'

'He's a fucking nightmare with a gun in his hand! Do you want to hear this or play on-liners off one another till the canned laughter is arriving?'

'One-liners – you're missing a silent, perhaps magic 'e''.

'Fuck this for a game of Sanskrit, listen up and let me tell you, please?'

Tchai relented. She was a sucker for a man on his knees with lodgers in his hair. It brought out the maternal instinct in her.

'So the hood in the balaclava wearing the gorilla mask, he says to me that Arturo says to him to say to me that I must plant a bomb at Wilkinsons' Cabs.'

'And you did?'

'Yes.'

'Why?'

'Because Arturo said.'

'Arturo is travelling.'

'You sure?'

'Yes.'

'Me, I'm not too sure, that gorilla wouldn't lie to me. Humans lie, animals haven't the capacity, it's all simple biology in the end, man is a poor excuse for a bunch of molecules hanging out together and that is that. No, that great ape wouldn't have made a monkey out of me, and besides, it was crippled – you've got to support the disadvantaged, life's hard enough for them as it is without folk making out they are some kind of congenital liars. Calo, listen please now, Calo he's figuring some way to fix those types for good. It's bad, Tchai, and it getting worse by the day, so your devil may care attitude is no balm for me, though I may try a shampoo if the infestation continues.'

Tchai bit her lip. She looked at the emptied computer seat gathering dust and wondered again about that home to which Calo had sent poor stupid Manush. Nothing had been heard of Manush since and bad rumours circulated about such camps, though most tried to ignore the facts, the figures and the rising number of the disappeared. But surely Calo or Charlo as he liked to be now called wouldn't have hurt his own brother? Yet Tchai's heart grieved, Rawnee was broken, hair-tearing grief-stricken and Ron didn't know a damn what was happening to his family…

'No, Tchai, let me be telling you, Arturo is back, Charlo is out there as well and no one can stop him, but someone is putting me in the middle, by Jove, dirty scoundrels. At the moment, I'm Number Two. I know too much, but that is a dangerous place to be too. So when I go, when the tug of war rips, there's going to be nothing left, but damned bullshit lies and my nits having to find a new home.'

Tchai ripped out a knot of hair, 'Listen, you dumb fuck, Arturo's travelling and they playing you for a fool.'

Kisan smiled. He had his answer at last. He shook his head foolishly and didn't believe a word.

Tchai had to talk to Ron.

Stop press. They don't really have that so much so more, now that it is all electronic – they stopped the stop press. A couple of keys pressed and that's all the last minute fix the last minute is needing. Well, more or less. By the way, the stop press has it that the Co-operative was found guilty of torching Wilkinsons. The Co-op is barred by the greasy palms of the local council, Wilkinsons is scraped up and put in a box and buried, enabling the Charlo's NSKK to be at the wheel. How the mighty have fallen.

Ron had a day off, not that he had a job, but he was always busy. There were drug-licence wars, there were pimp battles, there were take-overs, stake-outs, entertainers' contracts, contracts involving Calabrian hit men or women (it was an equal opportunities employer making the pay-offs) there were the casino wars, building contracts and bogus trade unions and none of it had anything to do with Ron. Ron had other things on his plate, like a severe case of halitosis, followed by a debilitating debacle of flatulence and aesthete's foot, the slightly poncier version of athletes foot, darling. Aye, Ron had had it tough while the Charlo's Civil War raged, but not so you would notice.

Anyway, Ron had a day off and given that he'd promised himself to visit Bebee he did so. Gran was in, which was lucky, as Ron had tried ringing and had not found her in, but that was nothing to go on as she wasn't very good on the phone, press button B and all that nonsense. Ron made a brew which Gran did not drink. It was the same old story, Ron blew the dust off the dominoes and waited for Gran to reply to his drop of double six, Big Ben as it is known to some, a familiar colloquialism enough, but Ron hadn't a clue why it was so called, maybe the municipal library would be having some tome or other to be explaining such mysteries, a dictionary of slang perhaps or even an encyclopaedia of games, that would be the very order of book to be at the unveiling of such passing perplexities. Either way, Gran still hadn't replied, perhaps she was knocking.

Anyway, Ron couldn't sit there playing silly buggers all day, watching the vermin run through Gran's hair and clothes, waiting for a domino such as a six-five or six-two to be played. Ron volunteered himself to go for Gran's pension and could he please be borrowing a tenner for the week to come? It was the usual question and Gran didn't gainsay it or otherwise show disapproval, which was all very well as far as Ron was concerned, not that he was in anyway mercenary, but a little helps and anyway, Gran herself hadn't touched the other week's money, still there in the biscuit tin in the pantry, not doing anything in particular. No, a tenner was no skin off Gran's nose, not that there was much left – the rats had been at it and a tidy job they were making of it too.

Anyway, Ron toddles off to the post office up on St Olaf's Square, for it has been a long time since Ron were in that neck of streets and plazas and thought the change would do him good, variety being the salt and pepper and cruet bowl of life's humdrumanity. Ron was a tadge delayed in making it to the square as some nonce with dyed blond hair nearly knocked him over whilst Ron ambled down a pedestrian zone. There was this march on in the square that was a long time passing down Sigurdgate – a town youth rally funded and sponsored by Charlo and the Society for Eugenic Development. Ron liked a nice tune, but these fuckers were about as pleasing to the ear as an Orange Day Parade jamboree without the aid of paracetamol. It was all the same to Ron, he wasn't doing much that day except avoiding being run over again; that prat had driven past again just missing him and even popping a few shots from a trusty semi-automatic with the serial numbers filed off in all the right places. Ron remembered his green cross code and consequently negotiated crossing the road without so much as a flesh wound. It did not stop Ron though, from shaking his fist, giving the birdy and mouthing rather loudly, 'Bloody hit man drivers!'

Anyway, march over and in the post office is where and when the real fun began. In front of Ron is an old woman who has lived too long. Her pension was not being renewed, thereafter she was advised not to make a nuisance of herself and hobble along as best she could to the nearest workhouse. Then it was Ron's turn for the humiliation.

Between the text, the intertext and the testosterone Ron Smith hadn't a monkey's aunt what was going down. He was flung to the ground, a pistol popped against his head, while the whole post office seemed to be full of tear gas and lachrymose armed police marksman. Ron was fucked.

Sidney Weable's Two-Penn'orth

One time not too long after the death of Salty while I was at trying to make sense of all this, I jumped on the train at York and travelled on a cheap away-day to Benckly. I saw the auld hus and the new people that were in it and making a neater job of it than auld Salty had been doing in his last years; the only thing he ever took pride in were his auld pit-boots – tha could see thy face in them. After the hus I took a gander, ending up at t'club whereby I wetted my whistle. A few of the auld lads recognised me from the funeral like and I fell to talking with a character by the name of Sid Weable or Sidney for short. See, there was this thing that had been perplexing me over much ever since I started to read through the shirt box, namely, why or how in heaven's name did t'auld Salty get started on the writing game. It was Sid Weable that acquainted me with something of an answer. When Salty were able he would gan along to the worker's college and study literature and literature appreciation. He had originally signed up for mathematics but that proved too hard for the lad. Of course this is not a full explanation, but it provided me with something of an answer, perhaps that's for the best when all said and done – t'auld Salty has a right to his secrets.

A Hirple in the Dark

Kisan is lying there in the dark and he doesn't sleep so good. Tchai has gone home to comfort Rawnee, grieving still for the taken Manush, but then who comforts Kisan? Kali red-tongued Goddess black as burnt blood takes the wee manikin in her arms and slaps his lips against her lactating nipples. Well it's not everyday you have death sitting in your lap, but Kisan is not impressed. There is work to be done. He hears the telltale limp of the man in the monkey suit. The creak on the stairs, the soft pad of fur and the panting of breath behind the mask – every night and every other night and tomorrow night too marked out. Tonight there shall be another killing gotten done, tonight someone else, some business, some politician or just someone dead. Arturo wanting this killing done. Arturo wanting it all and Calo doing nothing. Rumours said that Calo and Arturo were one and the same. Other rumours too dark to say, speak or whisper quietly over in the cold lone hours…that say – that say too much. Yet all the while Tchai swearing blind that Arturo still travelling. What did she know – nothing. Kisan knows, Kisan knows the hirple, hobble and pitch of the wounded foot crossing the threshold, knowing too that any day the order will come through to silence himself so. Kali strokes his hair lank with fear and sweat. Kali's fingernails slice the thin skin of his nipples quick as a bullet. Kisan screams. Monkey laughs. Mad house. But his killing gets gotten done.

Quiet Time Is No Time

Ron is surprised and disappointed. They could have had it all. They fucked up and let him live. So okay he's doing a couple of lifetimes for social security fraud in some maximum security prison. But, they let him live, stupid move. There is a chance that one day Arturo is returning and then...

Then there shall be no more then. For the moment Ron no worry and no get depressed though he mumbles a prayer or two for Beebee. He wasn't to know that she died six months ago. No one ever tells Ron anything. Ron just thought the old lady was taking time over her dominoes. But, they fixed him good. He was caught, social security fraud first degree, and he was banged over and he wasn't going to get out in a hurry. But picking oakum sure was piss-boring.

Ron could have stayed like that a long time. Ron didn't mind the dull routines of slopping out, slopping on the slop at breakfast, dinner, tea, or picking the oakum. So it was a meaningless existence, but Ron had given up on thinking anyway, so what the hell. He deserved it. The only thing Ron missed was the occasional beverage of the hard stuff and a comfortable wank in private. Ron was no hero. He had it coming, all of this meaningless pile of shit. Ron never asked, demanded or fought for more...

Well, not for a long time and that's another novel. Still, things would have remained much the same for Ron, but for two visits.

First visitor that paid a call to your man Ron was Calo. Calo greased the right palms and had Ron transferred to a soft cell where Ron could masturbate to his heart's content in peace, quiet and a plentiful supply of mansize soft tissues. Calo got him a cell with carpets, television, walk on through bathroom and some poor whore who would come in once a month to pull his pud, give head or just do a jigsaw or two when Ron got lonely. Calo fixed Ron up good and was there to welcome him to his new pad when mi-lado gets transferred through.

'Sit down, Ron.'

Ron sat down, looked at Calo and thought briefly about busting his neck, but gave up, turning the television down instead: six hundred and sixty-six channels of fuck all worth watching.

'What do you think?'

'I don't.'

'Ron, you're sore, you've got every right to be mad at me, but what could I do? You made the move or so I heard and I don't know if it's true or not, but it matters not, either way, you pay, 'cos I can't afford to lose face.'

Lose face, that was it. Calo hadn't only bleached his hair blond, but his skin was worse than fair, it was putrid white. Calo had changed. Calo was lost, but so far Ron couldn't care.

'What could I do?'

Ron shrugged. He couldn't be arsed. Calo, the cheap white prick, then does something useful. He pours Ron a drink. There's a case of wine and Calo brings out a few glasses and pours themselves a drink of Chateau Brick Farm. It's drinkable, but then again so are most poisons. Ron does nay care. He sups it down and helps himself to another.

'Listen, Ron, you safe here. You watch telly, you drink, have some other inmates over for cards and I'll send a girl now and again, case of wine every week too. But you stay. You ever make out and I shall have to have you killed. Your choice.'

Ron squeezed a spot in his ear. He turned up the volume. Calo was gone. A pretty young whore came in with a jigsaw of Beverly Minster. Ron and Sharlene did the outer edge and a bit more while getting incredibly squiffy. On the telly you could buy a his and hers electric toaster at super low new prices just by ringing this number 0800-0910235 and giving your credit details. It didn't add up to a hill of beans any of this, but so far Ron wasn't dead. He had a couple of useful pieces in his hand and his glass was half-full.

Hit

The factotum of the town, Provost Selim the Grim Biggleswick, had won again at call-card stud, beating off a transsexual nun on an exercise bike with a trampolining dominatrix with one leg assisted by her every orifice open leather fetish dwarf. It was a close call but the amputated leg just clinched it. Provost Selim the Grim Biggleswick collected the win large. He was on all fours, trolleys round his ankles and his short fat circumcised prick was whupping it up the arse of Thumbelina as Dirty Denise the long hopping dominatrix cracked the whip and hit the ceiling. Just as the Provost's balls are about to burst in walks a small slim man in a Peter Butterworth mask and blows him away with a classic German Luger.

A bit like a headless chicken what happening next, despite the back of his head being missing Selim the Grim continues to pump away for several seconds afore finally thumping to the floor with every sign of coitus having been achieved. It is a vexed question whether the late provost gleaned any satisfaction or not, which takes things back in a way to the Reign of Terror. Parisian physicians would have vexatious arguments as to whether after the fall of the guillotine the severed head was alive, albeit for only several seconds, or not. Side bets were made, reputations questioned or sullied and sometimes pistols were drawn, till some widehead came up with the solution of putting the matter to the test. Thereafter, after some aristo received their short back and sides physicians would rush to the basket and stick pins in the head trying to elicit some kind of response. Shock, surprise and downright anger were recorded, but also contended. A new impasse was reached, which was only breached when a famous physician ran foul of the powers that be. He being a sporting gent and consummate scientist agreed to give a sign, to wink if it should prove that he was to a degree conscious after a bit off the back had been taken. Drum roll, the drop of the blade, roar of the crowd and a posse of doctors gazing in wonder at the head of their colleague blinking in the cold morn's light. Sadly, this did not settle matters, for is a blink the same as a wink, perhaps a single blink may be construed as a wink, but two blinks? To be sure, to be sure, matters were never truly resolved.

Although the Halifax gibbet was to some extent a precursor of the guillotine it has not been recorded whether the vulgar quacks of the time in the last place on earth God created, Yorkshire, similarly speculated over these matters. As for the criminal fraternity the best they could do was to arrive at this merry ditty: 'From Hull, Hell and Halifax, may the good Lord deliver us'. This was shorthand for the prison of Hull, the fires of Hell and the gibbet of Halifax. Ron, though, was still enjoying his prison stay. He had completed several jigsaws, found a station that specialised in repeats from when the BBC was still worth watching and had even undertaken a little creative writing, nothing too grand, just a wee poem or so.

However, there be no gainsaying it, the factotum of the town, Provost Selim the Grim Biggleswick, was dead as a wet winter weekend in Cleethorpes. Thumbelina recovered her composure first, dominatrix was still bouncing, she whipped through the Provost's trews and Harrison Ford jacket like a dose of runaway vindaloo stomach. Dominatrix was slowing to a nicety. The hit man was daubing the name Arturo on one of the walls not covered by chains, handcuffs and various blow-up cut-outs of former Cruft's Champions – some pad!

A crack split the air. The hit man clutched his hand and howled with pain. Thumbelina laid him low in the balls. Dominatrix took a swing with a ball and chain. Hit man dropped like monopoly stock under investigation. The women screamed, 'Arturo is travelling, Arturo is travelling – dumb fuck!'

The hit man didn't hear so good. His mask slipped and the face of Kisan was revealed. The damage done, the hit man limped outside, out into a waiting Mercedes, ditching his Luger as he fell inside the car. The driver sped away and the hit man took off his Kisan mask – canny bastard. Kisan was set for the fall.

Second Visitor

Everyone likes a visitor. It took Tchai a lot to make that visit. Her mother was going down fast, mad with grief, fear and clean hot hate. Tchai was keeping her there, alive, still breathing, still opening and closing her eyes, washing and cleaning, eating and shitting and everything else it takes to take another twenty-four hours. Tchai was more than all Rawnee had left. Tchai was nearly all she herself had left, save this tiny piece of broken hope she held out for Ron. Ron had to come through.

It took months to squeeze the address of the prison out of Calo or Carlo as he preferred to be called and even that was changing, yesterday on the street she did hear Charlo, then Carlos and Carl, then Chas – Charlie, so Charles couldn't be too far behind. There was a sale on a piece of Pangaea and Tchai knew that Chaz wanted in. She made the move, tracked him down at the auction and drew a bead, telling him straight that he was going to get an extra belly-button, although she did this in a whisper so that nobody could know. Chaz spilled addresses and grudging respect and just like you sometimes get on the movies, even offered to cut her in on a little of this or maybe that, but Tchai made like she wasn't there. She had this piece of broken hope, held back and buried deep from when she nothing but a child in Arturo's arms. It had to hold. It had to come good.

She stood in line like the rest, got her bag and panty-line searched by some jerk with three butts and a couple of extra chins, but she was carrying nothing more illicit than hope.

Ron looked good, relaxed and his dungarees clean for once. No, Ron was doing okay in his own way, asking nothing, getting plenty of nothing and nothing else seemed to follow from that save empty tautologies with nowhere to go. She sat down. Ron smiled. Ron could do that and make a few friendly noises off his own bat. There was a chance and it wasn't good. Ron had put on weight, shit he looked good and then this doubt, had he been bought off, was none of this any damn good? Tchai looked across the tab-burnt Formica table and opened slow.

'You heard about the Mayor?'

'You mean the Provost?'

'Selim the Grim is last month's obituary column.'

'Really?'

'Yeah, really, yeah. What I'm really talking about is good-time Charlie the Mayor, local charvorro-chal made good – they used to call him Calo.'

'…So?'

'So, did you know?'

'Listen, Tchai, it's good to see you, but-'

'Tell me, did you know!'

Ron hung his head, picked a tooth, a tooth that the prison dentist ought to take a deek at sometime maybe next week if pain starts to kick. The dentist don't get a look in, 'cos Tchai slapped Ron hard across the mouth making one lip bleed.

'You learning too fast, Tchai, getting the slaps and questions in the right sort of drill – Calo been working on you too?'

A voice, a quiet voice, tense but hung low in the air, scared to be overheard or just scared to know – a question insistent and low, 'Did you know, Ron?'

'I could have guessed. I could have made that effort, but I didn't do any of that and no I didn't know and so, what's the next surprise you've got lined up for me to fall over? Want to know if I'm bought, if your brother is treating me well – is that all you came for, Tchai?'

Tchai's eyes got moist, but she couldn't cry. Tears were not going to solve anything yet. 'Listen, Ron, they framing Kisan for the kill, for the knock-off on the old Provost.'

'Makes sense.'

'He didn't do it.'

'He got paid enough by Calo so he may just as well have done it and maybe more. Understand, when contracts get accepted, sooner or later your own name gets a contract of its own: too dangerous, know too much, and besides, why should I care when

Kisan had a contract out on me. It's blood money either way – hit or be hit. He just didn't know when to disappear or how.'

'No, that takes an expert!'

'Or a coward, Tchai, don't forget that,' and it was Ron's turn to turn the volume down, keeping it low to the ground.

'So, you not going to help?'

'So, that's right, I am not going to help. Kisan, if he isn't caught yet, then maybe he can still make the break. He's got brains, money and no right to live anyway.'

Tchai wiped her eyes dry. She'd expected no more, but she wasn't done, not even started. She had to work on Ron and she had that brittle piece of bust hope sticking in her side, making her mood evil, making it strong.

'Mother cries every night. She prays sometimes too, but not every day. She isn't strong enough for that. She prays though and someone sometime should answer just a little of what she asks. Ron, you're strong and hard and dead inside, but Rawnee, she's soft and hurting and you just sit there so fucking smug I could take a churi to you and cut your dead heart out.'

Ron flinched, flinched and moved like he had been struck hard that time. It no longer felt good on the inside. It no longer felt empty. Something was happening there and it wasn't the argument. He'd been through those and beyond, so many times it was just routine. Tchai was there, she was making the pitch and something inside was coming undone.

'Can't go back, Tchai.'

'She not crying for you,' the girl said and Ron sat up, 'She crying for Calo, for me, for what they done to Manush.'

'Manush?'

'That's right, Manush, stupid, child-minded Manush who did nothing but smile, hold your hand and gaze his life away. They took Manush. He's gone. Some home for special people like him, but not home, not us and he ain't never coming back, I know. No one comes back from those camps – not ever.'

The black pitch in Ron's eyes burned. He knew. He knew too

that Manush, the laughing boy with the empty smile and honest love of a fool-child, that betti charvorro chal wasn't coming home.

A bell sounded, sounding strangely solemn and still in the hubbub of the visiting room. Ron grabbed Tchai's hand quickly, pressed her soft brown skin to his lips. Tchai left, walked away and didn't look back. Ron waited to be called, then moved patiently and paced back to his cell. There was nowhere to go, but back.

?

What would answer thou most timely at such times is an aporic stroll away from all goodly habitation, a copse or a wet meadow given to deep ploughing thus affording some shelter from wind or unwelcome onlookers seeking diversion at thine own distress. Once some chance haven found with the heel delve such a scrape as deemed necessary and down with the breeks, squatting low, posterior possibly pointing higher than the crown, and put thyssen at ease. From a scrip or otherwise purse take not a few handfuls of best goose down and afterwards consign to the scrape also. Lastly, cover with leaves, grass or a sod or two perchance; hide thy business well. 'Tis good advice and well meant of use whether travelling or no.

The Buffalo They Coming

The warder knocked and let in the whore. Ron knew that it wasn't quite the end of the month, but he couldn't be sure. He was though pleased to see her, despite it not being a good day to call. She was a slender brunette, though a tadge plump around the middle with the sun sending some curls deep gold and even others had a strain of red to them. If she wasn't exactly tall then she had the height at least on Ron and Ron wasn't small, not for his generation and the hard times they suffered; not exactly the best of times either, but not bad all told nonetheless or so some people say, whilst others would if they could, and do, affirm the contrary. Sharlene was her name, thought most called her Shaz or Sharon, shag-bag or fuck-pig or sweet thing or beautiful or other such kind things even when they hardly felt sentimental. She was that kind of girl. She was no kind of girl, though still young. Her youth seemed somewhere else, that happened to this other person, a long time ago, maugre it had been nothing over a twelvemonth since she got the job. She walked over to Ron, but more of a glide. She was unnerved, just a little apprehensive, perhaps adding something a little ungainly to her tread. She was at Ron's side. She stood above. Ron lay on the couch. He sat up.

'I want a good hard fuck.'

The girl didn't say anything. Ron saw the dimples in her hand as she rested on the table whilst she removed her shoes, one by one, dropping, thudding to the floor. They were puppy-fat hands. She started to shift the skirt above her waist, dug her painted thumbs inside her knickers and began to pull her panties down.

'Stop.'

Sharlene smiled. She placed her skirt neatly about her, rubbed her hands as if unclean and gazed down at Ron expectantly. Ron said nothing. Sharlene spoke, a hot gabble of speech.

'Knew you weren't like that, Ron. Knew you'd always treat me different not like the others, they just want it, anyway and every way: mouth, cunt, painful buggery. Knew you-'

'I'm just like them and worse. Don't be fucking stupid. You're a whore. I'm a punter. A dirty old bastard more than old enough these days to be your grandfather – crouch down, I'll fuck your lips.'

'Ron!'

'Don't cry. Don't fret now. I don't want sex.'

'S-sorry, Ron, I don't like it when folk talk like that. It's worse than doing things. It makes me feel worse, worse than anything. It's-'

'Why whore? Why a prison punk – worst of the lot?'

'It pays the best – money…' Sharlene faltered, seeing the look on Ron's face. She began again. She didn't like the story, but she began again, 'Mother was not mi real mother. She was the second mother to me. My real mum was going to cut one of my legs off, so that we could go begging and get more money. Mother, second mother, was coming home from work, sweet factory, stopped my real mother who threw me at Mam's feet in disgust…Mam took me home, raised me up like her own and on her own. I owe everything to her. When she got bad and the money started running out, she'd starve herself just not to see me go without and go to school and…And I was no good at school. And there we were the two of us: Mam with all her social credits used up and me too young to get any assistance. A social worker said they'd take our Mam to the workhouse, but I weren't having that…So, I whored…I whore. I get the best money. It breaks Mam's heart, but we're saving. By the time I'm twenty-six and investing well, we'll have enough for a little shop, sweet shop or something. I'll maybe find a widower, divorcee or lonely bachelor – I like kids. If I stay clean and keep saving, then in six years Mam and me we shall be free.'

Ron shook the anger from his eyes. The mind-numbing banality of it all. A story heard before a thousand times over in all the tongues of Babel. A fat child of a girl, cheap fetish wear and badly shaven calf, fucking prison skags and perverts. The thinking was gone. Thinking never mattered. There was something black and sinister inside him and it wanted out. Suddenly, the urge to smash the bland white face of the girl through the prison bars – suffering, pity and hate sending him twisted. Kill all and every and each living thing – to stop, simply to stop it all and nothing more, nothing less, not ever. Ron ripped a split nail from a finger. A tiny, meagre trickle of blood ran down his finger. Ron laughed.

'That's better, have a good laugh,' said Sharlene, scared. She had been studying Ron curiously. She'd seen 'em go before, last time she was nearly killed but for a warder chancing to hear her screams. She was no child.

The laughing faltered. Ron raised his head at last, 'Open a bottle and get two glasses, Sharlene.'

Sharlene did as she was told. She busied about, poured the wine and clinked glasses with old, crazy Ron.

'Look what I got you,' said Sharlene, pulling a small jigsaw from her bag.

'Shouldn't be buying me presents.'

'It were only £1.50 and it's all there – Scunthorpe Cemetery – unusual eh!'

Ron had delved and graved a few holes in Scunthorpe Cemetery in his time and that was a funny, curious coincidence at the very least. Ron laughed, drank from his glass and got merrily squiffy doing a jigsaw with Sharlene till it was time for her to go and see a couple of special clients on the locked upper ward. Ron drank on.

Manush.

Ron drank alone.

Manush.

Ron drank on.

Manush.

Ron drank till the drink ran out.

Manush.

Ron wouldn't get maudlin. He had no use for tears nor sorrow nor regret nor rewriting his illiterate life with ifs and maybes and maybe nots. All that was finished, washed up in the past over and done, past pluperfect and all that jazz, what was finished was finished then and now and tomorrow too, should anyone be counting.

Ripping and shredding sheets and blankets was easy even if pished and Ron wasn't half-ways drunk. He never felt so sober. There was not a lurch nor tremor to his actions. He roped it up, made a good knot and swung from the window kicking his desk away. Two hundred and fifty pieces of Scunthorpe cemetery lay scattered on the ground.

The drop was never going to be enough to snap Ron's neck. Old as he was he had some bull-neck on him yet. Strong too, he struggled and kicked for two hours. Someone should have heard him, but any warders spare were busy trying to take a homemade knife away from some sex animal up in top wing as he sliced away on a prison punk. Ron kicked and choked and his eyes bulged, but no one was looking.

There was blood in Ron's eyes. He shut his lids but he could still see blood. His tongue felt like a hot dead weight in his mouth. He felt cold though, creeping cold moving through his body. He opened his eyes one last time, something made him look, a scamper, something was running around his cell.

Little Mouse made it through the tiniest of cracks. There was his old roommate, the great gormless crackpot, swinging from some candy-striped sheets and making a right arse of it.

Ron found strength enough to mouth, though clamed with blood, 'Today is a good day to die.'

Little Mouse couldn't be impressed with this. He streaked up the leg of the kicked desk and began to dance. Little Mouse danced and danced till his paws blistered.

A voice in Ron's head, dance, Ron, dance. Ron is dancing, following Little Mouse. Dance, Ron, dance. They danced man and mouse in great unstable gyres falling through time, all time and no time. The centre dissolving and re-forming, constructing and deconstructing itself and its selves and all questions of selfhood.

A dance. A chant. A dance.

Hey Hey Ha Hey
Hey Hey Hey Hey
Hie Hie Ha Hey
Hey Hey Hey Hey

Ha Ha Ha Ha
Hie Hie Hie Ha-Hey
Hey Hey Hey Hey
Ha Ha Ha Ha

Hey Hey Ha Hey
Hey Hey Hey Hey
Hie Hie Ha Hey
Hey Hey Hey Hey

Ron followed Little Mouse. Ron walked that walk, through the tall buffalo grass, from across the dark plains of the restless black water, across to where the Black Hills stand like guardians greeting the Great Spirit, sheltering man telling tales by the pungent fires of dried dung made. Ron was dancing. Ron was free of Ron. There was no going back. Little Mouse had shewn him the way.

The Death of Kisan

Outside some idiot was walking straight down the middle of the road proclaiming that a saviour had been born unto them. Kisan had nothing better to do than to hide behind his curtain, so he sat back, listened and had a damn good belly-laugh for the first time since militant Hindu extremists blew themselves up with a homemade atomic bomb as they tried to blow up a mosque in Wath On Dearne. Verily, I say unto thee that a child is born, brought into this world not for the sake of the Father, but for sinners here on earth in this peak and trough boom and bust to dust fallen into stagflation post-industrial whore of doan mess wid mi natty dread, spa, Babylon: businessmen, captains of industry, high financiers, owners of monopolies of computer software and internet access, barristers, solicitors, bank managers and insider traders – nudge nudge wink wink – howbeit verily fucked too as I say unto you. This man was better than a freak show and how Kisan did clap till a juggernaut rounded the corner, knocked the maniac flat across the back, squeezing the head off his shoulders, it coming to rest by some naked kerb-dancer out begging for tips and pricks or otherwise erstwhile Johns.

    Kisan stopped laughing and it was no accident. He heard a telltale tread coming up the stairs. A slip-jig beat of cripple creaking on the landing and nearing, a pushing open of a door, a scream from a wæ Asian's lips, the kick of a Czech M52 automatic, a snigger then a curse. The assassin forgot to unmask himself before wasting the wog. He made the bullet-ribboned corpse a present of his monkey mask and his Kisan mask and a little stick of Blackpool rock that he meant to give to his bairn the last time he saw him – bad for his teeth. The assassin was nothing if not a conscientious and high-principled father, nothing he'd not do for his family. He hirpled away, down the twisting servants' stairs, out the back kitchen, across the auld stable-yard and out through the gardener's gate opening upon

Jack Pilesgross's snickleway, thereafter he made his way down to the river to finally follow his last order: putting a bullet in his own brain, the kick sending him over into the river so as to drift downstream and out to the oceans where crabs would take the eyes first and eels too would get their fill once thoroughly rotten. Charles the Fifth, Calo, wanted no loose leads, nothing to tie him to the hit. The assassin's last bullet had bought his family some future and for Calo, a hundred percent animosity. The hit was professional, too professional and some folk are overly conscientious for their own good.

Kisan was dead.

As for the street outside:-

The juggernaut driver was spot-fined for driving without due care and attention. The driver consoled himself in the arms of the naked kerb-dancer. Across the other side of town, a valetudinarian gardener called Bob Fossgit planted out a couple of clumps of daffodil bulbs beneath his cherry orchard. It was one of those days right enough.

Kirkyard

In the reiving black of night, in the shadow of an owl's eldritch screech, as a hag moon of gaunt bones made marked time, a shadow, nay shade, passed the blea kirk's gate to search with a dark lantern for the name of a lost grave.

> HERE LIES
> THE GRAVE
> OF THE
> UNNAMED
> CONSCIENTIOUS
> OBJECTOR

Lang ago Ron had delved graves here and got recompense for it. It was dour work, but welcome work should he be travelling that way. The kirk was dear to him as being the place where Puro Deya Sbanck dropped his own Gran, coming untimely into the world beneath the shelter of an auld yew tree growing deep in the resting beds of the dead. Folk of Kirkdale shunned the place of a night, but superstition was bread and butter to Ron and he relished the whine of wind in the trees and flurrying flight of bats twisting about his head. The dark, superstition and the dead were well found friends to this wraith of a man. At last, he found the grave. Using nothing but his hands he lumped at the earth, ripping it apart like a rabid fox unearthing its mother. The grave was shallow delved that way by Ron for such a night as this, when even the dead lie but lightly at their rest. Ron struck wood, a cold dead tone silenced by the blackness of the sky swollen above. Ron pulled and tugged and ripped at the lid till it exploded open with a crack of dry bones and dry rot dust. Unsheathing the lantern Ron espied his long buried name typed neatly inside an old Spanish passport, but Ron hadn't come to reclaim his identity; he just needed to borrow for a while the ghost of that lost self of many years gone by. He ripped open an oilcloth, making sure his old tools were still in working order. He left by melting into the cold mist of midnight. This cold dark shade was travelling home at last.

Next day two local archaeologists noted that a grave had been disturbed, but went about their business just the same. There was their own digging to be done, history was being lost while the present could take care of itself. School kids, mere bairns were blamed for a time by some, one lad even admitted it and was suspended from nursery school, but the auld folk knew different. The auld, the wise and the mad shunned Kirk Dale's kirk's kirkyard – the alliterative tradition was not dead yet.

Nuevo Drom

The rot of dyed gold in Rawnee's hair was pulled out in clumps. Tchai looked on, silenced by her own quiet grief. Earlier that day Tchai had driven into town in her old white van with its borrowed passenger door of pastel blue, parked up in the stable yard and ascended the servants' stairs to find her husband dead, mauled by bullets and painted for death in his own blood. Tchai had torn her own hair then. Later she wrapped her Kisan in a white sheet, laid him to rest on the floor, promising to return with kindling, petrol and wood enough to disperse his soul.

Neither mother nor daughter cry nor do they speak, content to let grief break their nails, tear their hair and humble the slow persistent thudding of their hearts. They do not care to raise their heads as the front door is opened. The whole room dims, a shramming mist gusts at their feet and the bare bulb above flickers then dies like a wind-blown guttering candle. The fog thickens, glimmering strangely, faintly luminescent with chill blue light. Nothing is colder than their hearts.

This fog reeks about them, strangely bringing some old stale warmth, hint of faded dungaree, crushed sombrero and scarcity of good soap. Mist, silence, myth weighted with presence, shadowed and sketched in the form of a man. Silence grows old and breaks…

'Rawnee…Tchai. There is a car at the end of the lane, two of Charles's men sit and wait, searching for me – Charles is taking no chances,' this voice said.

'Charles, aye Charles for Calo is dead…with the rest; came too late. That last visit and Tchai said you would come and perhaps you have, but it is all too late,' said Rawnee.

'Late, aye, and neither have I long now – so listen: I'll take the car at the end of the lane, the men inside will wait no longer for me; Tchai, drive to Brick Farm, buy a caravan and horse, torch the car and return here, Rawnee get ready; I'm going for Kisan-'

'Kisan,' laughed Tchai.

'What do you want now with us?' said Rawnee.

'To put Manush on his way. I need to find him, Rawnee, even if over late.'

Rawnee ripped one more chunk of gold from her scalp, walked over to the hearth where the shreds of a fire lamely glowed and threw the ball of hair to the ashes. A slight hiss, crackle and it was over. 'Take the Wolds road over Wetwang way, just through the village turn left, a farm track and by its side a newly laid track, where the track ends…you'll find the camps.'

Fog lessened, mist swirled then seemed to dissipate as the door blew shut with the wind. For a while, some frozen now, neither woman stirred, the raw smell of someone long lost to them hesitated a moment longer in the room afore disappearing one last time. They would never see him again, husband, father and deranged stranger. The fire was raked into life. A new bulb was found and in the bright electric light, two women readied themselves. Tchai drove off into the night. Rawnee sang as she hid coins, notes, jewellery in bundles of clothes. There wasn't much.

Mein Host

Step right up, one-ticket entrance fee guarantees access to all the atrocity exhibition has to offer, step right up. Sorry, folks, we never knew nothing no more. Over there, right just there, sample that soap, so creamy and white, twenty-two tonnes almost made every night, step right up. Steady, folks, don't rush, take care, take your time, sit down on the leather settees, the skin's not swine; feel too while you're there the quality of the bounce, upholstery, made of real hair. Sorry, folks, we never knew nothing no more. Outside looking through the window, see the garden grow, that bone and teeth ground up neat is the best treat to make the beets grow – something else we never did know. Step right up, folks, step right up, sorry but all the gold bars have gone on to Switzerland, you just can't understand how much work that took, strictly off the books – sorry, folks, this ain't no joke, we never knew nothing no more. Step right up. Experiments, experiments, you want the data and you can have it, just sign here to say, we never knew nothing no more.

The tour guide had finished for the day. Families, photographers, sightseers sporting a host of cameras and video equipment pillaged this atrocity for holiday snaps. A wind blew up from the east, coming in wet bringing low cloud. The tour guide withdrew to the hearth to where his wife had made a hearty meal of *Kohl und Pinkel*.

The visitors returned to their coaches and cars. There was a work camp up in Farndale, a typhus twin centre in yonder Rosedale and more, in fact a very full itinerary and they stepped right up.

From a swirl of mist a figure came searching the mounds of cold ash. He raked his fingers through the cinders, took a handful and by a burn, fresh and clear, he floated the cold, cold ashes over the water, murmuring Jelan, Jelan and his idiot child's name. He'd come for him at last; soon they could both rest. For the moment the wind twisted ropes of mist, tethering the figure to the present. Long time since he'd felt a tether, bit and the bridle and heard the slow thud of hooves dragging forward through the day. Time to move on. His son was gone.

Back at the *Kohl und Pinkel* mein host and hostess and hostess trolley were tucking in con mucho gusto, washing down the heavy fats with pilseners and *Alt Senator* schnapps as well as a little amiable conversation. The door exploded, a weight of mist condensing to fog, falling like a wave, The kitchen grew chill, hostess and host refrained from another forkful. With a sneer the host wiped his greasy mouth on the back of his blackcoat entertainer's uniform.

'So you've come at last. You finally decided to do something now that it is too late for you, for me and history too, but you come.' The host drank a swift cold schnapps, poured another and waited.

There was silence for a while. The meal grew cold, though the host continued to pick at his dish. His wife, vaguely embarrassed, worried about her reputation for hospitality, finally spoke, 'Please, sir, sit down, we knew nothing – all those things…well they happened far away from our Heimat…Look on the map, if you don't believe us.'

She received no direct reply. The silence proved eloquent enough. The old woman started to sob. Her meal was ruined.

The host was not so cowed. He picked his teeth and drank, reciting some vague meandering tale of an excuse.

'Don't confuse last time with this time. It is not so simple. Why pick on Jews? Educated, cultured, accomplished, hard working people – economically disastrous hitting on them. And some people do not learn from history, like that fat coon fool in the land of Blacks kicking out the Indians – only damn people that did any work, kept the whole Third World shit-heap on their backs. No. This time wasn't last time. I tell you a story…

'I used to get up at half-past five, dressing in the cold black winters with neither aid of light nor heat. I would breakfast on a cold potato and walk five miles to a pit. There I would work ten-hour shifts in seams sometimes no thicker than your waist. I would walk home: chop wood, tend to my garden, feed my animals. I would work very hard before my rest of sleep.

'In the summer months it was not so bad. Those walks on a morning in particular were beautiful; a balm to the soul healing the dark hurt of the black seams below. Now sometimes on my walk I would pass an idiot boy, the son of two idiots. A whole family unable to shift and care for themselves, relying on the charity of others to maintain life. But what a life. The husband mad, violent or fucking his wife in the middle of the street without a care for shame or modesty. The wife barely any better, hardly the sense to clean her own arse or put her babe to her breast. Too stupid to scream when raped, as she was from time to time.

'Less than animal – a degraded mockery of man…

'But the boy. He had a life. While I toiled below, he'd sit by the village drain with a rod of ash and a piece of string hooked with a safety pin waiting for shit to bite. It was a joke, such a good joke. But down in the darkness I could not laugh. I worked hard to keep these half-humans, or other such useless mouths – dumb beasts sitting in the sun: breeding, breathing and having fun.

'Six foot five I stood, but by the age of twenty-three I walked bowed. I have no regrets. There has to be a solution to the problem of useless eaters…'

The host was not answered, not directly. The silence weighed heavily, seeming to swirl and thicken with the mist. The hostess laughed, an embarrassed short bark of a laugh. It was not mirth.

'We saw nothing…nothing.'

Her head was snapped back. A spare fork gouged out both eyes. Then, she was spared. The man drank another schnapps, shook his head, murmuring, 'Regret nothing.'

He fared no better. He lived, though his tongue was torn out, left to lie idle amongst the *Kohl und Pinkel*.

The mist grew less intense. The range began to thaw out the room, bringing real warmth to the seated twain. There was though still silence, rank with damp, old sweat and long held hate. An empty phrase from the blinded woman would sometimes puncture this, but not to any lasting effect.

'…Saw nothing…nothing at all…not here.'

The host did not reply to his wife's lame whisper. It was time to pour another schnapps.

Vulgar Boatman

He'd pack it in soon. The river hardly ever now spoke to him. He was getting old too; arthritis setting in and how his bones ached sometimes in the winter as he rowed from bank to bank. Rough weather seemed to spread out from the opposite bank, an onrush of white mist spilling out over the water, over to him. A distant shout, sounding strangely dull in the fog, hailed him. He pushed off the bank, bowed his back and blindly rowed to where he hoped a fare lay waiting. It had been a hard day; tourists were fewer since the Enabling Act of Charles the Fifth.

'You!'

The figure said nothing, but jumped aboard, barely rocking the boat, his wide, battered hat pulled down over the eyes. Ice sharp dread clutched the heart of the boatman. He gibbered more to himself than to his fare. He couldn't look at the figure, shrouded in river fog. He couldn't take the two gold coins for the passage. Finally, the boatman could take no more, blind with fear, a dry scream stuck like a spike in his throat, he ran terrified, lost in the tenebrous Stygian chill.

The boat was tied, waiting, ready; there was so little time left. This shade of man sank into the night.

The gate linking the stable yard and Jack Pilesgross's snickleway opened with a barely audible whine. Footsteps faint across the cobbles, climbing the servants' stairs without making a sound. The footsteps halted briefly before Kisan's door. A faint susurration and the door gently blew open.

Kali was under the sheet with dead Kisan. She was bored, disappointed and thinking of trying Florida's Disney World adventure next year for her holidays, apparently there was this ride that was guaranteed to shrink the piles off you.

'You too damn late, bloody bullshit fool,' said Kali, rising to fix her eye make-up, her mascara was just a tadge smeared. 'You not saying any damn thing to me after all I have done for you – well fuck me in the teeth…Go on, make a deal, be bloody noble about things for once, say, 'Kali, Great Goddess, take my life in exchange for Kisan's. I beg, I implore you, please, sweet, kind Kali."

A rake of bullets shredded the curtains, shattered glass and sprayed hunks and chunks of plaster. Kali gave her lips a lick of war paint.

'You still got some bloody balls. I venture in better clothes you would cut quite a handsome killer, something mean and so damn Spanish…Okay, have him back…Take him, go on. He was always bloody damn useless, even when he worshipped me back in India, eating corpses from funeral pyres, begging bowl of a skull, eating shit sometimes to try and cure himself from life's distractions. Bloody bullshit fool dead and he still not happy. Take him. I have to go, can't take any damn more of this climate, my feet are cracked and sore, and had this damn bullshit cold yeah ever since I arrived. Cheerio, good fellow.'

Kali gave the face a gentle slap and a small chaste kiss on the cheek. There was a taxi waiting downstairs and she was pushing it to make the plane in the fog, the vale of Eabrac was one giant ghost town thick with mist.

Kisan was rudely shaken alive. He didn't seem surprised or scared, that's death for you. Slowly he collected his things, various bank books, bullets and his old trusty Luger. It was all business as usual and a contract is a contract.

Softly, in silence, they descended the stairs, the back door and the back gate barely creaked. They sped down Jack Pilesgross's snickleway, running blindly in the fog. The boat was still there. Kisan sat in the bow brooding deeply. The far bank neared. They were without the city walls, far from prying eyes and the open road lay before them.

'What now?'

'Walk by the river to the caravan park. Rawnee and Tchai are waiting. Travel the back way to Whitby. There is a boat, the *Black*

Dog, booked to take three travellers to the Black Sea, accompany them and re-cross the old roads back-'

'Back, you mean right back – back home?'

'You can live like a Rajah. The money you made here makes you like a Mogul – you'll never do without again.'

'But…But I left. I don't want to go back. What about America – land of opportunity?'

'A land of thieves, chors, oath-breakers – White man make Hitler look like amateur. No, when you can't travel forward, travel back – it is the only thing left to us.'

Kisan no longer brooded. He stood up, leapt ashore, drew his gun and shot point blank at the heart. The body was flung back in the boat, but strangely the boat didn't move.

'Why did you do that?' A dwarf came forward out of the mist.

Kisan pointed his gun. His hand shaking like a willow tree.

'Just answer, then walk on.'

Kisan felt suddenly shrammed to the core. His teeth rattled in his head.

'C-commission – it was my last commission from Arturo.'

The dwarf laughed for a while and Kisan's cheeks burned with shame.

'Arturo was it? Arturo! You only met that Raya when it was too late. Go on, flee, nash! Get going. Nash!' said the dwarf and Kisan sped, slipping and skating along the towpath.

The dwarf stepped lightly down into the boat. He closed his friend's eyes, folded his arms and taking the oars pushed off from the bank. The river was thick with white luminous fog. A small boat drifted downstream, out to the great black water. It was over at last. There was no coming back.

And so a breaker in of osses, knife-sharpener and grave-digger was not buried.

Part Two

The Jester's Tale

Chapter Ones - they wouldn't have made the arse of it like I did. They could have learnt and been exposed to such wonders too. I am afraid after rescuing me from the crack of the arse they were very disappointed with their find.

The man found himself alive between the curlew's cry and the sigh of the sea. Above, seagulls keened as they weaved white and black against a blue sky. Coarse sand of powdered shell made marked his soft brown skin. 'Ah,' Man breathed in. The Man breathed out. It was not a bad place to be.

Slowly and unsure, the Man sat up only to fall back, collapsing on the sand in wide-eyed alarm. He rubbed his smooth bald head in evident disbelief. He tried again, this time feeling himself fall back to earth, he flung his arms back in panic. On shaking arms the Man sat up and gazed around him. His eyes were drawn to the ceaseless shift of wave on shore. Edging himself forward on his bottom and falling back from time to time, the Man arrived at the edge of the ocean. He squealed as cold skilting wavelets lapped against him. In panic he tried to move out of the way of oncoming waves. He slipped and fell, drinking in mouthfuls of chill seawater. The Man retched and started to cry salt tears. Dejected, the man edged back towards the sand. He did not stop till he made it high above the wave land, collapsing amongst dry white sand and coarse marram grass. His thin chest panted heavily. His ribs stretched his brown skin taut and his emaciated arms hugged his wasted body to sleep.

The afternoon sun was warm and flies buzzed around his open mouth and nose. The Man sat up easily. He was a quick learner. He leant back on one arm, shielding his eyes from the sun with his free hand. The bright orb hurt his eyes and soon he hung his head and screwed his eyes tightly, blinking out the strong sunlight. The Man was restless and crawled hither and thither. The Man was hungry, but he had no words for hunger.

The Man did not know that he was hungry, yet instinctively he placed object after object into his mouth: sand, shell, pebble. Luckily, down at the water's edge the Man came across edible seaweed, sadly the taste was bitter and he spat out his next mouthful. He fared slightly better pulling off winkles and limpets from an outcrop of rocks. These he sucked from their shell or crunched them, shell and all, between his powerful jaws. The Man had a full set of teeth, undamaged and unaffected by modern foods.

After eating his fill of seafood the Man crawled back to the sand dunes and there watched the day pass. The night was cold. His naked skin came out in goose pimples. And the man marvelled, running his smooth brown fingers over the tiny bumps of horripilation. He shivered as a new moon rose in the sky. Fitfully, the Man slept, slipping into a light hunter's sleep just as daylight tinged the sky pink.

After two days of trial and error the Man stood. True, he often fell, sometimes hurting himself, and then he would cry. On other occasions, a sudden fall would surprise the man and he would laugh aloud, loud guffaws of belly laughter. The first time the man laughed he startled himself and clapped his hands over his mouth. Later he learned to let himself go, thrusting his head back and opening his mouth wide to let the sounds rip from his body.

Though the Man could laugh, he was far from being in a secure position. At night he froze and when one day the rains came he learnt how to cry as, miserably tucked up in a heap, he spent the day trying to shelter from cold, wet rain. Yet, the rain probably saved him. His diet of seafood left the man permanently athirst. As it rained, the man opened his mouth, trying to chew and bite the raindrops. On the following day, above the sand dunes, he found a peat bog where at last the Man could take his fill of drink and slake his thirst.

The Man had food and drink, but slowly he was starving to death. He lost too much energy trying to keep warm at night. By the fourth day, all the winkles had gone from the rocks near the shore. He made a tour of the island trying to find other rocks bearing the strange crunchy fruit. Luckily, he found food for another day, but that was all.

Slowly, the man toured the island and thus it came to pass that he learnt that he was not so isolated. At low tide the island was linked to a much larger island by a sandy causeway. The Man ventured along the sand. On reaching the other side he looked back at the island and smiled.

The new island was much bigger than his island. On the new island there were sheep, cows, houses and two shops, though the man did not have words for those things yet. The Man only had words after he was taken in by the crofter and his wife.

Hay was taken in by very traditional means upon the island, stacked in round mounds next to the cattle sheds. Thus, it was that the Man was found early one morning by the crofter as he came to feed his cows.

The crofter was wary of the brown naked man. He thrust his pitchfork forward and asked in no uncertain terms what the man was doing buried inside his haystack. The Man just stared open-mouthed. The crofter shouted again more loudly. His wife, hearing the commotion, came out of the house. She saw her husband threaten the Man who had by this time begun to cry: pained, unintelligible animal noises came from his throat. The wife took off her shawl and wrapped it around the Man. The crofter bade her beware, that the Man was a wild foreigner, a brown heathen and not to be trusted, but the wife took him inside just the same and sat him by the fire.

To the Man the house was a source of constant novelty. For half an hour or more at a time he played by the tap, turning the water on then off, hot then cold, till led to the kitchen table by the wife. In front of the Man the wife placed a bowl of porridge. The Man stared at the food, not knowing what to do, though, feeling its warmth, he cradled his hands over the steaming bowl. The wife made vague eating motions and finally the man understood and fed himself as best he could without using the spoon. Afterwards the wife cleaned the man as if he were naught but a sackless bairn. After all, he was a brown heathen.

The crofters had no children of their own and so adopted the Man. Luckily for all concerned the Man was a quick learner. By the end of the first week the Man had mastered the spoon and fork as well as the basics of the potty. Not that they had a proper potty, but the auld milk pail, made by the tinker MacPhee, sufficed very nicely indeed for the business in hand. More importantly, the Man's nakedness was immediately brought to check. The crofters were rather set in their ways regarding nakedness. The occasional mishap with a potty was forgivable, but walking around shamefully parading nudity was a veritable sin. The old crofter's clothes that the Man was forced to wear made him look pitiably thin. His wiry frame barely filled out the breeches and Guernsey – would a clotheshorse have filled out the crofter's clothes the more. This said however, though the man was barely but skin and bone, he was remarkably strong. Soon the Man could wield a pitchfork more ably than the crofter was ever able in his brea rude youth. What is more, the Man had a special way with animals. At first the crofters put this down to the fact that he could not speak, that like an animal he too was dumb, but even after the Man had mastered speech he still showed an affinity with animals.

It was spring and the crofter lost not one lamb or ewe that year thanks to the Man. Some instinctual feeling or understanding assisted him and guided his actions. Gently, he would tease out a badly placed or breached lamb, easing it out of the womb, breaking it gently from its membrane and out into the cold world. The crofter knew the Man was gifted and lavished great praise upon him. This got the back up of several of the crofter's neighbours who did not trust the strange, wee, brown fellow at all. Some spoke of how the brown fellow had bewitched the old couple. This was the first pain that the Man brought the crofters. His second was his leaving.

The Man had finished his porridge. He tapped a meaningless tattoo on the base of the bowl before pushing back his chair from the table and standing up. 'Mother, Father,'[1] for so the Man had taken to calling the crofter and his wife. 'I have decided to leave you.'

Both parents were dismayed at hearing this news, for in a very short time they had both come to care for the stranger. And he was very handy around the croft, brown heathen or not; after all it was not as if they were harbouring a Catholic.

'When will you go?' asked the crofter, a hint of despair in his voice, for when all's said and done there was the hay to consider.

'After the hay is in, father,' said the Man. 'After the corncrake has raised its young, after the green grass has turned to hay and been gathered in, I shall leave you. I shall go and inspect the world, for I have heard that it is a wide place full of many wonders; the mainland is full of noise. I am sorry, but I need more than just the island. It has grown small to me…And too, there is a need in me to find… to my…' The Man's words petered out, unable to finish, to put into words some deeply held and hidden wish.

'Och well, the hay,' mused the crofter. 'At least that's something.'

Yet the hay was in and still the Man showed no sign of leaving the croft. The wife hoped that the Man had changed his mind, but the old crofter knew different. Often he had seen the Man walking abroad at night, visiting each part of the island, talking out loud to himself, 'Will I ever come upon this place again.' Nay, the crofter knew that the Man would not be long amongst them.

When finally the Man left the island the crofters made him a

---

[1] For the sake of those not having the Gaidhlig, reported speech has been rendered into more or less standard English, as far as the author is able to use the tongue of Thieves.

gift of new clothes, a small pig-skin suitcase and what money they could spare. Fitted out and newly attired, the Man set off for the ferry. Only the crofter accompanied the Man on that short journey as his wife found the separation too painful. She kent finally that she would never see the Man again.

At the quayside gulls screeched noisily in the air. A few cars and trucks disembarked or boarded the ferry and the people of the island milled about chatting in loose informal groups. The man was fascinated by all he saw. Already he felt himself upon the threshold of a great adventure. He took and shook the crofter's hand, promising to write as soon as he had mastered that art. The Man bade him not to worry himself with that for he could not read the Gaidhlig too well and as for the tongue of the butchers he had no great desire to read such an unlovely language. The crofter bought a single ferry ticket and waved the brown heathen a cheeridh goodbye.

The crofter was sad to see his foster-son go.

Other islanders looked on and breathed a sigh of relief that the strange, brown abomination unto the Lord was no more living amongst them.

On the ferry the Man made his first purchase, a cup of tea and drank it at a window seat of the small in-board cafe. It was a six-hour ferry to the mainland, stopping off at several small islands on the way. The Man was never bored, constantly he scanned the horizon and at the next stop he was almost tempted to jump ship and explore the new island, but that it reminded him gey much of home. The Man turned his gaze from the small island and fixed his eyes to the slate-grey horizon.

As a dim outline neared and became town and port the Man's spirits rose. Never had he imagined anything so magnificent: the curved streets of shops, hotels and houses. He knew from his father that it was not the city, but the small town still delighted the Man and filled him with awe and wonder.

The boat docked. He had three hours to wait for his train. He did not mind as he lost himself amidst the bustle of the small tourist and harbour town. He made a second purchase, buying pies and sandwiches, some of which he ate straight away while saving others for the journey ahead.

Back at the station, he waited impatiently for the train. The piss-poor one-horse harbour town was beginning to bore him inexorably. The Man had no idea what sort of thing the train was and even less could he guess as he gazed down at the parallel tracks. The ferry had not been too surprising for often he had seen the ferry come and go from the island. On board the motion had seemed strange but somehow familiar, as it reminded him of his first few attempts at walking, the lurching uncertainty of imbalance. The boat had hardly been a mystery. Impatiently the man waited for the train. He was not disappointed.

It took the Man several minutes and a little help from the guard to open the train door. The Man was shaking slightly in excitement. The train was running late and the guard muttered, 'bloody foreigners' beneath his breath as he helped the Man on to the train and into a seat. The Man chose a window seat and watched the landscape pass by as the train sped through the country as fell late autumnal night.

The Man smiled.

He was happy.

His next adventure - the City.

Uncle Walter

I wanted to write a novel about Man, but the jester insisted that I write his story. Despite his diminutive size, the jester is a most insistent and persuasive kind of person. I wrote the first chapter of my minimalist novel before I caved in to the demands of the jester. He sits by my typewriter and presides over all I write. Even as I write this he pulls on his long nose and smiles knowingly. Ever since I inherited the jester I have been plagued by his smile. I never wanted the jester, but my Uncle Walter, my Uncle Salty, died.

Walter, or rather Salty as he was called, lived alone in the end terrace house of my great grandmother long since dead. This grandmother had always taken a certain pride in the fact that she lived in an end terrace house. She used to scrub the front doorstep every day. That was in the days before she suffered a stroke. After the stroke the house declined with her and after she died, the house fell to ruin. For the last ten years of his life Salty lived alone with the jester.

Salty had two hobbies, drinking and studying the football pools. This sounds a little tame, but it was Uncle Salty's life. The drinking was fairly constrained. Salty would patronise the local Working Men's Club at the bottom of the road. He did not just drink there, but would meet the lads and play fives and threes, dominoes or cards. But the pools was a different matter. The end terrace house was given over to stacks and stacks of newspapers. They were never allowed to be thrown out. While the great grandma had been alive, bed-ridden after her stroke, the home help had offered to clear some of the newspapers away, but Salty was so enraged that he threatened to take the poker to her if she so much as touched a bundle. The great grandmother managed to appease Salty and the home help agreed not to touch so much as a single issue. The papers, each individual paper, was a key to Salty winning the pools. He had a system. No one knew or could even follow Salty's system, but it existed none the less and when he died the skip-load of papers was testimony to his lifelong bid to win a fortune.

When he died Salty left little of any use, some clothes, a few crocks, newspapers, but to me he bequeathed the jester. The jester stands six inches high and wears a faded suit of red and yellow. His facial features resemble those of Punch and his deep-set eyes are bright and alive. His long curved chin suggests craft and the deep wrinkles of his eyes are heavy with mirth and merriment, despite which the jester rarely laughs these days. He is busy. He is writing a story. He is writing revolution, change and ceaseless turmoil. This he dictates to me and this is a very strange business. The jester has written much aforehand and yet still he craves more. For me I am tired of his erratic, nonsensical narration. His voice grates like a razor blade drawn against a blackboard and I don't think my nerves can stand much more.

The first time I heard the jester speak it was in a dream. I had gone out for the evening, met a friend for a beer or two and eventually got back early in the morning, tired and drunk. I couldn't be bothered undressing, but lay across my bed fully clothed. As soon as my head hit the pillow I was asleep and snoring loudly. The jester crept along my bookshelf, jumped down to my desk, jumped the gap between my desk and pillow and sat on my forehead, his feet dangling down to the bridge of my nose. The jester sighed, slapped his hands hard on my head and exclaimed, 'Just like Salty.' I don't remember much more. The dream changed, I fell into heavier sleep, but I did not forget the jester's warning.

On the following day, woken early by the singing of Mrs Aleppo my landlady, I promised to start writing my science fiction fantasy again. Singing is the defining characteristic of my landlady. When I first entered the city, looking for rooms to rent, the rumour of her singing drew me to inquire as to whether she had any accommodation available. I was in a pub taking the head off a pint, my battered pig-skin case by my side, when I overheard a conversation from the next table. It seemed that a young lad in his twenties had decided to give up his room for he could no longer abide his landlady singing opera first thing in the morning, that he was well again and able to move on. Though it was rude of me, I asked the whereabouts of the speaker's former lodgings. I hoped that the room might be still available. I had no contacts in the city and any address was better than none, plus the prospect of an opera-singing landlady was not so displeasing to me. Having written down the address and having asked for directions, I quickly drained my pint and left the pub.

On one of the roads leaving the city is sited the house of Mrs Aleppo. The day was hot and my pint poured from my pores by the time I arrived on Mrs Aleppo's front doorstep. I felt grubby and apprehensive. There was no doorbell and I knocked hard against the oak door, though making little impression. The house was possibly early nineteenth century and formerly it must have been of some grandeur when first constructed by an Armenian trader and financier. In the bright June sun it looked rather shabby and worn, not scruffy but well lived in.

There was no reply to my knocking, so gingerly I tried the door and found it open. I turned the handle and stepped inside, calling out hello all the while. Immediately I heard singing deep from within the heart of the house. Pure sung vowels echoed and welled throughout the house. I stood in the dusty hallway unsure of where to turn. Suddenly a door opened and a woman in her mid fifties backed out of a room, wheeling an antiquated Hoover – a model long obsolete, something from way before the days of the glorious Enabling Act of Charles the Fifth. She was still singing. I said hello, but my voice failed to carry. Mrs Aleppo practically backed into my case before she noticed me. She turned sharply and in loud tones asked who I was and what was my business. I mumbled that I wanted a room and she bit my head off, demanding that I speak up, for one thing she could not stand was mumblers. I spoke up and again I had to speak more loudly till at last Mrs Aleppo understood that I sought lodgings.

I realised immediately that my future landlady was a little deaf. It is my considered opinion that Mrs Aleppo is often unaware that she is singing, but carried away and lost in some silent opera where she plays the prima donna and what is more, plays to a full and appreciative house.

I was in luck and she shewed me to a room on the second floor. It had a wash basin and kitchenette, but no toilet. On each floor there was a separate toilet and bathroom. There was also the full use of the large downstairs kitchen while free cereal and milk too were thoughtfully provided for all her guests.[1] The most prominent feature was a simply staggering huge bed, so large in fact that it seemed to dwarf the rest of the room, which itself was far from small. Indeed, the room was spacious and the afternoon sun streamed in from a large bay window, for fifty pounds a week I could do a lot worse. I paid a fortnight in advance and Mrs Aleppo handed over two large keys, my room key and one for the front door which was rarely locked on account that visitors could seldom be heard, but were rather expected to walk in and knock at the room they sought during the hours of visiting.

At first I wanted to waste no time in unpacking, but the dust swirling in the air put me in mind of cleaning first. On the ground floor was a utility cupboard built under the stars, where the Hoover, dusters, polish and bin-bags were kept. I fumbled vainly in the dark, searching for cleaning products, till I struck a match. Sadly, I noticed that even in this out of the way hidey-hole someone had vandalised a wall; a girl's name had been crudely carved into the plaster. Despite my sinking spirits I availed myself of duster and polish and set to work cleaning my room. After half an hour I gave up. I had merely succeeded in moving the motes of dust from one place to another, when it settled the

---

[1] Always we were called guests, though even now I am unclear as to why, perhaps, she thought that all of us were transitory, just passing through, maugre the fact that many of us stayed on and on and a few of us even died in her lodging house. We seemed more than guests and more than folk just passing through.

room was as bad as ever. Still not discouraged, I finished by hoovering my small patch of threadbare carpet. Unreasonably pleased with my efforts, I unpacked my bundle of clothes, small portable typewriter, books and finally the jester. I had moved in.

The jester was pleased with his new surroundings, deeming that a new start might be conducive to furthering his novel. Every new place he is the same, getting all excited about a frumth start, a new start, pregnant with possibilities. A new place is like a virgin piece of paper to the jester. The whiteness calls out to be filled. As often as I have changed rooms I have started the jester's story anew, with its endless loops of time and insane jumps of events. Alas, the story never shall be finished. His problem is that he can never be satisfied with the first draft. He is never prepared to let things stand for a while, but the first line, first paragraph and page must be perfect.

With any new place you start to discover niggles after a while, such as air rumbling in the heating system, draughts, or the queue for the bathroom in the morning or a hundred and one other petty irritations. As soon as these faults make themselves known the jester wants to move on. He screws up the first page and declares that it is time to leave. Yet, with each new place his enthusiasm surfaces as irrepressible as of yore, demanding to know at what stage the story is currently. The first time he asked this question I was dumbfounded, informing him that he had destroyed the work himself. The jester called me everything from a pig to a dog and worse, and I learnt to save the screwed up pages in a box, so as give some indication of his story's progress and in a bid not to incur his frightful wroth.

The jester was well pleased with my latest move. We thought that the landlady's singing might well aid his writing. He wanted me to describe Mrs Aleppo to the last detail, from her black and grey hair held tightly in a bun to her down-at-heel faded pink slippers tired of fluff. The jester was not content till he had a complete word picture. Whenever we heard Mrs Aleppo sing he would describe in detail the way she would stoop to dust, bend and straighten as she would vacuum or wash the stairs' paintwork. It was important to the jester to wreathe the singing in concrete detail so that it assumed a solidity of presence as if we were present at some stage performance. The jester hoped in this way to capture the dramatic now despite largely using the past tense.

Though Mr and Mrs Aleppo lived in, having the top suite of rooms, we never saw Mr Aleppo. As the weeks passed the jester became more curious and bade me imagine our hidden host in a variety of guises, none of which were exhaustive and none of which satisfied the jester's hunger. Mr Aleppo was a bedridden cripple, worse than a babe, who communicated by the blinking of his eyelashes. He had suffered a mental breakdown and could no longer bear to meet people. He was a scholar who only needed the world of books to sustain his existence. He was a tyrant who ruled the house through his minion and who would not suffer an audience with any other. Mr Aleppo was dead, perfectly preserved sitting by the fire in his favourite armchair, his pipe idle in his hands waiting for a light.

Though the jester never tired of imagining Mr Aleppo it was time we made a start on the novel. The jester was dissatisfied with the mechanics of biography. He couldn't have cared less that he had been won at a fairground lucky shot competition or that he had once pranced upon a diminutive stage to the raucous laughter of children nor that his former, boss, stage manager and buddy had been murdered – self-murdered, crushed by failure to please the demands of a feckless and ever-changing audience, outgrown of innocent delight in mayhem, mirth and a wittily placed, 'That's the way to do it!'. Nay, none of that, fellow listeners and erstwhile readers, none of this is relevant to him, for the jester's novel is the life of the imagination. The jester's life is the presenting of the unpresentable. At times he would write abstruse articles in certain journals that thought they were learned about how the mechanisms of presentation were in themselves incapable of presentation. I had not time for this. I wanted to get back to the Man and strictly keep things in the past tense. The jester thought I was a fool. I wrote pornography for a while when bills were needing paying. And the jester thought I was worse than a whore. Whores he could respect, dislike, pity, admire or even on occasions frequent, but my two thousand words or so of wank-assisting tosh only fuelled his far from latent loathing of me. I shewed him unpaid bills, bounced cheques and angry letters from the bank. He laughed, boldly stating that one day everything would be all right - had I not forgotten my mother's words to me, her only words of assurance. I thought him mad and I did not think about my mother or her vague ramblings concerning inheritance, trusts and the problems, the legal wranglings over *The Will*. I never knew what will she mentioned, but she drooled over both the definite article and the noun itself as if they were somehow magically charged. Repeating them now in my head I can hear my mother enunciate these words so clearly that I think to feel the spectre of her being about me still, some chill haunt of family madness. There are some thoughts that I cannot cope with even now after having been away and having witnessed such changes. I bade the jester to look once more upon my stack of unpaid bills.

The jester has no time for realism. Why should he, he hath neither need for victuals nor indeed a shelter above his head. In consequence, the jester has forgone all constraints. He recognises no authority but the internal monologue of the mind astray. The jester is a libertine incapable of restraint.

This time, when we started to write, the jester searched for archetypes. He sought some figure or character to rebuke the age. After several fruitless suggestions the jester hit upon Robin Hood. The task set, the outlaw was deemed too ineffectual a figure to challenge the hegemony of Charles Fifth's all encompassing rule, so reluctantly the jester agreed to reunite Robin with Little John. I had hoped to smuggle in more characters from the past, but unfortunately the jester proved obstinate. He did not wish to rewrite a fable from the twine of history, but merely to use the odd character here and there in order to further certain ideas: ciphers rather than characters have always been his constant concern.

The jester was satisfied, but not so Robin Hood and Little John. Sherwood Forest could no longer provide them with a living. The forest had become a theme park and tourist site unrecognisable as a den of thieves. At first they did not suffer too badly as, dressed in Lincoln Green, the two outlaws milked the tourist trade, jumping out amongst day-trippers, their staffs raised or arrow set ready to fly, receiving money, 'tips', in return.

Unfortunately, the Park Authorities were less taken with the idea. There had been complaints that young children had been scared and, what is more, they resented the initiative of others muscling in on their theme park. They tried to round Robin and Little John up, but the two old hands were not so easily caught. They merged into the forest and left the area hoping for richer pickings elsewhere.

The jester was not disappointed with his proteges' lack of success. He thought the whole scenario most amusing and looked with eager anticipation to the next adventure of the pair. For myself I was bored and saw little future in the resurrection of two archaic, anachronistic anarchists. To me their day had long been past, nothing further could be achieved by using them out of time and out of context. To be honest I was frustrated artistically and again made notes about the Man: bare unadorned man was my subject and I wrote surreptitiously. But it was to no avail. The jester always had a knack of discovering me at work; not even my doodles escaped his attention.

My latest work derided and destroyed by the jester, I sought refuge in a writer's group. Little John and Robin Hood were still in hiding at this stage, the jester had no further plans for them, so taking this opportunity I signed on the line. The writer's group was a mixed bunch, mainly poets desperately seeking any possible publication through the small magazines. There was an odd failed playwright, someone who hoped to get into advertising and the usual motley collection of piss poor pen-pushers, still stuck in the rut of writing as if born unto the last century. As for me, I infiltrated a small band of would-be novelists. There was Patrick Thistle who pretended to be Irish and was writing a book strongly influenced by Flann O' Brien, Joady who for a time refused to talk about her work, Kevin who was inspired by Dirty Realism, and I, a front-man for the jester.

The main group met once a month, but our splinter group met much more often, once, sometimes twice, a week. Frequently, we met in pubs discussing our work over drinks, comparing notes, hungry for suggestions and wary of criticism. The jester was not pleased. He demanded that I paid more attention to his work. Robin Hood and Little John were restless. It was time that I wrote again.

The jester was not my only critic. One night in the pub, The Wellington Inn, I think, seemingly a little drunk and out of sorts I mentioned my rescue and Patrick Thistle turned nasty. He told me that all that abduction shit had been done to death and was about as original as ending an absurd novel with, '…Suddenly I awoke. It had all been a dream.' Patrick said he had expected more from me than some sci-fi rehash and asked me bluntly what was the point of it all. I tried to explain that I wasn't talking about any literary project, but Joady patted my hand, indicating by a slight derisive shake of her head that it was pointless trying to talk sense to Patrick when he was on one of his hobby-horses. Later, we laughed about it, but behind my mirth was this concern that I was forever doomed to be misunderstood. I tried to write, I tried one last time to set the record straight, something beyond fiction and fact, something that someone would hopefully believe howsoever incongruous. I rebelled and the jester sulked.

That's it, I wouldn't play ball. I refused all entreaties. The Jester held his peace, bided his time, waiting for the opportunity. It came. His vengeance, that wrecked my life, that turned it inside out, dredging the worst of details of all my estranged pasts, is written, over-written, written between the words and silences of text, inter-text and subtext. Some of it has even been smuggled into what follows, so help me God.

Perhaps the above is a lie. All that follows is but a part of the Jester's revenge. And as for me, I curse the day that Uncle Water, auld drunk Salty, woke by the river to find a jester, grinning, skitting and recklessly laughing from the harness of his second best suit's handkerchief pocket.

Eden Crow

My girlfriend, large as life, was stood at the door, blocking the open exit, chewing very elastic gum, which still did not manage to contrive to hide her all too visible sneer. I knew then it was too late. The jester's revenge was already kicking in. I'd never had a girlfriend, though I once had a mate.

Sadly, you can no longer tell a story the way my father told stories, the whole damn lot of us in bed of a weekend's morning. He'd begin once upon a time and out would come some gem that made a lot of sense to him, but damn all to us though we loved to hear my father squeak along in that semi-castrated tone of his. I give you an example: there was this excellent story that began, 'Once upon a time there was this pigeon called Herbie…' I can't quite remember all the details, but I still have the story well enough, should need require that some day I verify something of the substance of this tale. Then and for quite some years after, well until the time I read Philosophy at Hull, I misunderstood this children's tale about this pigeon who tried to rally his fellows into living a more truly-pigeon like existence, away from the false associations of modern urban life, pecking corn from tourists' hands in Trafalgar Square for example and back to the life of winging freely about some distant cliff…Well, anyway, aged three or possibly earlier I never realised that this was some fine skit on Herbert Marcuse's *One Dimensional Man*.

But, this is purely by the way of example. This tale was not the tale that I was thinking about when first dwelling on the way my father started his stories with the ubiquitous, 'Once upon a time…' Strange though, as I try to complete this thought, once again I remember another tale, one that caused no short distress to my cousin Beverly, also a mere bairn and in bed at the time, cuddled up and ears open, waiting on my father's word as he told of the curious friendship between a black and white alley cat and this family of mice. The mice, initially scared, were lulled into a false sense of security by the lavish attentions of the tom who called upon them every day to swap news or deliver presents, perhaps a bunch of flowers or so, till the day they invited him in and he killed and ate the lot of them. My cousin Bev was heartbroken. She sobbed the pillowcase wet and my mother bad father to alter the story to change it somehow so that they all came back to life, that it was a joke and thereafter they all lived happily ever after. My father refused. He was, for a time at least, a man of principle.

No, it is the bed thing that I was thinking of. We have lost our sense of innocence. An uncle in bed with his children, nephews and nieces telling stories now sounds so decidedly dodgy and suspect, which it most certainly wasn't. The age where it seems so sadly commonplace that a father crawls over his wife to fuck his daughter, or where children's homes are a holiday camp for paedophile fraternities and the priest that is not a violent, drunken pederast is the exception that proves the rule. No, this age has lost its natural right to storytellers. It's not possible to tell the story straight.

The jester wants to break in, wants to say something, hurrying the tragedy along, but there is something more I want to say. I was sat atop my father's knees. We were playing humpty-dumpty, whereby my father would recite the rhyme and upon the fall the knees would collapse and I would tumble among the bed covers. Distinctly, I remember looking down upon my father's nakedness, seeing this mass of black curls and his short, fat, circumcised prick, a thing to me at that age that looked for all the world like some lone forgotten link of sausage. There is nothing I want to do with this memory, nothing depends upon it, no great movement of internal epiphany or any such thing, except to say this person, this man that I loved was my father and I felt how unlike, how strange, he was. Nowadays I could use such words as the other or alien or some psycho-babble from the post-Freudians, but it was the wonder then that there was this strange, outlandish lump that lived, breathed, talked to me and had nothing whatever to do with me. He was stranger than curtains, pooing on the potty, the yard outside and the girl I loved then, Sharon Drinkeld. This thing was not…simply was not.

It must not be imagined that I did not love my father. I did, but he was separate and different and seemed to be often away. He was unlike my mother who seemed and indeed always was there, whom I said that I loved up the central heating and back again. When my mother objected that this was not so very far, though it seemed to my slowly darkening eyes a long way indeed, right round the room in fact, I asked for something bigger then, to help my love along. She talked about distant stars, other planets, she talked me through a little of the universe. I said to my mother that I loved her up the universe and back again. She was impressed and kissed my cheek. I was a fool, a sackless bairn with little gorm over and above a babby at the diddies – this was before I had any tiny reckoning of the vastness of the universe at all. This was long afore I travelled a bit. And when at last I had some nous about what I had said as that child, I no longer loved my mother much at all.

What about the girlfriend, you fucking thick prick.

The jester is at me again…So, there I was with this sweet young thing chewing gum, looking for all the world like she despised me already and this young woman was my girlfriend. She seemed packed down hard and miserable with it and I still didn't know what kind of stunt she was intent on pulling.

'Aren't you going to invite me in then?' She walked in all by herself, took the beige chair, part of the three-piece settee, though the room was one piece short.

'Careful-'

It was too late. She fell through the arse of the chair; a couple of supporting bands had gone and I had been meaning to have words with Mrs Aleppo, not so easy when the woman was deaf and drowned out your own words with opera from Monteverdi to Puccini. There were a couple of snags to the room all told, but

I hadn't the neck, face or cojones to just say a few simple words. It wasn't even as if Mrs Aleppo was somehow uncivil, unreasonable or some kind of rack-renting landlord backed up by the boys with the baseball clubs. I had been through all that, not that that was the worst place I had lived, there was the roof provided for me by the step-dada, that didn't work out so well, and other places at other times too, where I had stayed for a while, regretting and hating every minute of it…but I'm losing the thread of it all again. Chairs, though, chairs right then didn't seem important and that's why I didn't bother having a blether about it with Mrs Aleppo that time the other day when I was bumping into her on the stairs. There was something quite else on my mind, though I can't for the life of me be placing it now, so. I helped the girl as best I could from the hole in the chair to the matching settee.

'Thanks, my name is Eden Crow, I am your officially appointed girlfriend. I am fully registered and have been certified by a qualified doctor that I am free from all known sexual diseases and/or of sound mind, though it must be said that I do suffer a little from thrush in the summer months, but that's not sexual and quite usual. Also I am not married or otherwise employed with any other, and shall continue to forsake all others while this contract lasts.'

The jester was pissing himself. Holding his toes, he tumbled round the room faster than a demented rat with a rocket up its hole. I wanted to crush him then, smash the spine and grind his splintered bones and blood into the thinning carpet pile. The girl was demented, delusional or suffering in some other way. For a time there I thought she was another deranged member of the household at straying through the wrong door. This thought really had the jester howling. I scowled at him severally, there was no cause right then for such mirth.

'Look, Ms Crow-'

'Eden Crow: not Ms, not Eden, not nothing, but Eden Crow.' She blew, then burst a bubble-gum bubble. For someone with mental problems she did not seem unduly distressed and I tried again to set things straight.

'Look, Eden Crow, I am sorry, but I don't know what you are doing here. I don't know you, casually, formally or in the Biblical sense. You are not my girlfriend. I don't have a girlfriend. Truth be told, I have never had a girlfriend, though I am not a virgin nor am I homosexual.'

'Do you consort with prostitutes?'

'No.'

'Have you in the past?'

'No, never.'

'Then what you do – rape somebody?'

'No, nothing like that for fuck's sake!'

I was angry. The girl wasn't mad. She was cool, business-like, knew what she was doing. It was some kind of sick wind-up and I was wrong-footed. She just sat there, waiting for some kind of answer. She had all the time in the world and she was being reasonable with it, patiently waiting for her boyfriend to explain something of his past sexual life. In a way, I couldn't blame her. Still surprised, confused and wary of whatever practical joke was running, I had to admit the sense of her questions. You just didn't sleep with anyone. The problem wasn't contraception or unwanted children. There was a waiting list now for bairns as infertility continued to rise. Indeed, so many underclass mothers had lost their babies under the auspices and regulations of the welfare office, social security and divers charities all concerned with the exclusive wellbeing of the child, that for the first time in a century the population of the underclass as a whole had fallen in real terms, despite this class's appallingly high birth-rate. These worthy institutions deemed it their duty to give such children a better class of life or just a better class. Nay, it wasn't pregnancy that was the problem, but sex – sex could kill, it was that simple. India, Philippines, Africa below the Sahara and the Americas had lost serious portions of their population through Aids or any one of its more exotic offshoots. It was there, this threat, the little death entailing the much bigger death, and this threat having been around for so long that no one really took it seriously till a crunch time would come: a new partner, becoming involved in the porn industry or prostitution. Then there were the conversations, lies, rewriting of one's personal history and the inevitable blood sample. In the porno world if you got the all clear you'd just hope to make enough in a couple of years in order to retire and get the hell out, even though knowing full well that chances were you'd pick a virus up in six months despite screening and go under within three years. Prostitution had better odds. You slapped on or slapped in a whole new regime of condoms, anti-virus sprays or lubricants and you just didn't have unprotected sex: sticking to the rules got you almost a hundred percent protection. Partners though, that was where the biggest lies and wanton acts of bad faith figured the greatest. People lied to their partners, lied to themselves, lied when the results came in and people, they just kept dying, lying and passing it on. Eden Crow was reasonable, she had a question that deserved an answer, but that still did not make her my girlfriend.

'Eden Crow, I think you'd better go, leave and shut the door.'

She didn't move. She chewed my dismissal over a few times and she looked like she didn't think too much of it. The jester stopped tumbling, scampered up the off-orange curtains and waited. He was still getting a rise out of this and that didn't help. It was making me more brusque and less sensitive, much more so than I am naturally. Eden Crow took out a small intensely coloured brochure. It was like a flyer. There were six girls featured including Eden Crow. She shewed me the leaflet and I read. I read about these girls' temperaments, intelligence quotients, hobbies and their vital statistics. I saw these girls too in casual wear, evening gown and swimming costumes. On the back page various nude, semi-nude or fetish-equipped poses were featured. There was Eden Crow in delicate lilac suspenders, fingering her labia with matching, colour-coded painted fingernails, though the nails themselves were probably false. I blushed uncontrollably. I had an erection too, felt cheap and horny as be damned. Masturbation, the thinking man's soap opera, sniggered the jester from on top of the curtain-rail. I passed the leaflet back. There was nothing I could say. Eden Crow got half way through a bubble and stopped. She'd had an idea. I could see that she was trying to help me to come to terms with all this.

'Statistics shew conclusively that men between the ages of eighteen to thirty-two are the most prone to suicide.'

'I'm thirty-three and I haven't had a suicide attempt in over six months and why the hell should anyone care, least of all you?'

'In a bid to solve this social problem the government, through its youth programme, has targeted these vulnerable groups, assisting them by facilitating authentic interpersonal interactions. It is to be hoped that these wider networks will function to break chronic circles of alienation and social isolation as well as promoting greater self-esteem.'

Eden Crow stopped. She had it all off pat, but no doubt the look of disgust that I couldn't hide hindered the rest of some other directive bullshit. The jester was no longer laughing either. He kept muttering, fuck her, fuck her brains out, dress up in lilac and screw her backwards. It wasn't nice.

'Look, if you don't want me or any of my cell I can get them to send more leaflets on.'

'I don't want anyone and if I did, I'd want to find my own girlfriend or facilitate my own interactive interpersonal authentic fuck-ups.'

Eden Crow gave a sigh. She tore a tissue from a cheap roll in her bag and deposited the small worn piece of gum directly in the centre. She folded the tissue around like a nappy, or a diaper, as we are encouraged to say now.

'You got a home for this?'

I took the wad and put it in the pedal-bin below the sink. We still weren't getting through. I wanted to walk over to the door, swing it open and... And I didn't too. I was low and lonely. All I had were the scraps of my novel and some shit the jester wanted me to write stashed and screwed up in a box. That didn't mean I was settling for whatever game was being played, but it meant I hadn't the moral courage to do the right thing. Something though didn't add up – the sums.

'Our government suddenly all concerned and philanthropic, after all this time and all that has transpired – it now wishes to save on people – save people? Bollox.'

'No. There's a charge. This is my first, so I only get standard rate – it's a scheme after all.'

'Charge? Charged to whom?'

'Whom – I like that, you don't hear it so much these days. You really are quite cute. You don't sound brainy or anything, but you can't be all stupid if you still use whom. And anyway, my services, administrative charges and introduction fees are automatically deducted from your bank account every month and at least one month after severance, unless marriage or dependants have been incurred in which case an official settlement has to be made according to the rules and regulations agreed between the various governmental departments and the relevant guilds.'

I laughed then. I should have known better for the jester had fallen silent, but I laughed. My Lloyds current account when last I looked was only six pounds in credit, my post office savings account had six hundred pounds, another month and I would have to go back to my old trade and to hell with pride. Some mistake had plainly been made, suddenly I was feeling so much better about the old deal.

'You want a coffee – proper one, with hot milk too, if you like?'

'That's kind of you. You know for my first boyfriend, you are not too bad – bit old and ugly, but what the hell, a job's a job.'

'Flattered,' I said and ground down some beans in my Czech coffee-grinder. Both the grinder and badly dented expresso maker were a present from my old man. After things fell apart at home, I never saw my father for quite some years. He'd been travelling mostly and trying to sort out his head after what my mother did to it, but anyway, one day he tracked me down to this tiny one room gaff in Todmorden. It was a rat-hole, no one called and people hid when the landlord called. Anyway, there was this deeply tanned man on the doorstep asking to be let in and did I know where – he mentioned my name... Well, that was it. He said my name and I sort of recognised the old cove. He took me for a pub lunch, said that he had remarried and settled in Spain, then shewed me pictures of his new wife and my half-brother little Arty, and we laughed, cried a little and when he went away he gave me this wooden Czech coffee-grinder and this two cup expresso maker from Ceuta. I miss the old man. I never knew him, not inside and up close, but I wish to hell that I had been a better son to him – too late now.

'How old are you?' I said. A strange nag at the back of my head made me ask this and this nag was more than just my fixation with the flow of time.

'Seventeen next.'

'I'm your first boyfriend? You raised by nuns?'

'No. I just prefer to make love and have successful relationships with women.'

'Oh. You want the hot milk or anything?'

'No just a single sugar.'

'Out of sugar.'

'Just as it comes then.'

The chair was fucked. There was nothing for it, but a little enforced intimacy, the two of us, squashed up on the little two-seater, sipping away at these coffees which were really quite good. That old expresso maker of my father's, it was still doing sterling work. Put your arm round her, you prick, said the jester, but I was thinking about my father, wondering if I should maybe try hitching over sometime to pay my respects, and my brother too, maybe it could be possible to track him down somehow, or write to him, write him -

The jester's crude interruption brought me back to the matter at hand. She was very pretty, a dark, heart-faced woman. There was a time when I would have given a lot to go out with/have an interpersonal authentic inter-relationship with such a girl.

'Tell me, does it not make it difficult being a lesbian and being my girlfriend?'

'Well, we'll see…I've got my name down on a lesbian list too, not that I'll be eligible whilst still seconded to you. And besides which, I've been through my training – I'm a professional.'

I left it at that, not wishing to question her professionalism. We drank our coffees. I washed up at the sink. The water is slightly rusty, but it looks worse than it is. I pottered about at the sink, making busy, hoping now it was all sorted that the girl would go. Sometime soon the administrative error would be spotted. I'd probably get my wrist slapped, but not as much as some unlucky civil servant and then I could get back to my cycle of depressions, being taunted and plagued by the jester, and also too, I really would try to write something more on the Man. He was still there at the back of my mind, demanding attention, needing to voice his own story, threatening to break out of frame to come and find me.

'So, you want me or one of my cell or another leaflet or what? You gotta have somebody, everybody got to have somebody, if they got serious money in the bank. Idle money is what caused the great crash – you want that again! Come on, I quite like you. You're saving me from some other cunt or the streets – that's what happens to us, if we don't make out: three strikes then we're whoring. So, what do you say?'

I put a bit of polish on the cup I was drying, put it away and looked at Eden Crow. She was taller than me, but most girls are. She seemed pleasant enough for an administrative error. I couldn't take any of this seriously and I didn't want her to take a stripe because of me.

'Sure, why not.'

'Good, I've got your number. I'll give you a ring when I've got us a date organised.'

'I haven't a phone,' I smirked, and put a bit of polish on the other cup before placing it by the other in the small cupboard above the sink.

'Your phone arrives Wednesday.'

Suddenly, there was a strange ululation coming from down the corridor somewhere. It was bad. It made me shiver and even the jester pricked up his ears.

'Jesus, I'm not staying to hear this shit. I'll be in touch.'

'Hey, how about a kiss goodbye?' I think I said it as a joke, telling irony, a little sarcasm and all that. Eden Crow scowled. She moved briskly towards the door.

'Listen, I ain't whoring yet. We take this steady. It's my job to build a proper, fully-functioning relationship – we build on this. Let us try to be professional.'

'Whatever you say, darling.' I blew a kiss and Eden Crow slammed home the door. The jester and I couldn't help it. We laughed aloud, danced and jigged. All this was bollox and the powers that be had screwed up big time. I was even allowed a phone. I had no one to ring, but a phone was at least a start. The only thing spoiling my sudden lifting of spirits was this drone, wailing and chanting that seemed to permeate the whole building. It drifted in from the bust window, it crept along the hall, the whole damn house seemed to resonate:

Hey Hey Ha Hey
Hey Hey Hey Hey
Hie Hie Ha Hey
Hey Hey Hey Hey

Ha Ha Ha Ha
Hie Hie Hie Ha-Hey
Hey Hey Hey Hey
Ha Ha Ha Ha

Hey Hey Ha Hey
Hey Hey Hey Hey

Hie Hie Ha Hey
Hey Hey Hey Hey

It was enough to drive a sane man bonkers. I'm not the most stable of characters it has to be said and indeed has been said. Things got bad when I lived in the sock, but the damage was done long ago, when mother and the step-dada took over from my father in the rearing of me. It's easy and a clichéd thing to blame parents or those that raised you, but I'm not going to do that. Thinking long over this, chewed it all over that time when I lived far away from all that is, realising that part of me had never been put together right, but it was my raising that made damn sure that I stayed fixed broke. I try not to dwell on it much now or even back at the time of this present part that's getting narrating, back when all of a sudden I had a girlfriend, something that at another time I would pray all night for, back when I had religion and lust and plenty to spare of unreasonable hope. I think it was all back there in that backed up time, but I'm not the man I used to be with sorting out the past, the travelling did that for me.

There is something though, something that needs talking about concerning that time I picked my mother up from the bottom of the stairs, a couple of ribs in and her mouth all bust open. That woman back then promised me that one day everything would be all right. She couldn't save herself from the beatings, but my mother wanted so bad to make sure that there would come a time when everything would be all right. In her wishes perhaps she was still my mother. She talked about her father, legacies or was it liabilities. She talked, but not sense. She was smashed, broken and rambling with worry. Yet, she promised. She was such a hopeless liar, but recently I have been thinking of her again and hope that perhaps everything is after all all right. I think that was the last I saw of my mother, but I can no longer be sure about the sequence of events – the travelling has definitely done that for me.

Transparent White

Woke to less drama on the day following, possibly the day after that one even – whatever. Chronology is not an issue here, not yet, that can come later if need be. I woke anyway to some kind of grey non-descript day which I think ought to have been summer, but I couldn't be sure then nor even now. Colour perception, the way I saw the spectrum, had been altered irreparably by my time away from all this. On coming back, I struggled to define where blues and greys, and greens too, separated out, becoming clear and distinct qualities in their own right. I was told by a specialist that my case was quite rare and may even be a linguistic, not a perceptive, problem. She could have been right this woman, for she had a fine collection of degrees and honorary awards decorating her surgery, furthermore she really seemed assured that her sentences actually conveyed some truth, relevancy and considered opinion. It was inspiring to meet somebody like Dr Loansrot. Her handshake too was very reassuring when we parted. She couldn't help me though and even today I make the same mistakes with blues, greens and greys, whilst also finding myself extra sensitive to other colours that I don't really have words for: beige, wheat, whey, tan, dun, wan, mealy, yolken, embered…The words are not there, but these colours are to be seen by me, perceived, re-seen and capable of being discerned, though others fail to see what it is I am trying to draw their attention to and neither can I tell them. Sometimes I do not always believe that it is my problem. In my absence the seasons have changed, pollution too has increased, resulting in much more dust clouding the sky, causing sunsets to at times positively scintillate as the sun dips below the horizon. Sunsets always used to be a fine thing in Tobha Mor or that wee strand near Ros Goill, but grand as they were, they cannot compete with today's long glowering sunsets and their radiant, lingering explosions of colours. It is the dawns that now are so lacking in substance, wan greys and simpering blues, delaying the light, hampering day, a sun limping across the sky, blinkered, wayward and worn with time. These dawns not worth spit.

As I say, the jester was up before me. There he was down on the carpet slowly practising his Qi-Gungs, absorbed and quiet. It's the only time his rather over-active mouth lets up. I used to joke that I found his Wu Shu more relaxing than he, but the jester wouldn't laugh at such a quip. He was content to breathe in and breathe out, his body becoming the breath of movement. I tried to get into it, hoping that it would help me to try to understand what had happened or regain a hold on my scrambled self, but after several redundant efforts I gave up, content merely to watch, propped on my elbow, head resting against the pillow as the jester put himself through his routines. It looks easy, but isn't. I know. I tried. I did at least do that once.

There was nothing for breakfast. Often I keep a little in, but it is not really a problem, as Mrs Aleppo has an open breakfast kitchen, providing a choice consisting of several cereals in addition to her own very excellent muesli. The only snag is that I prefer real milk, full fat or green top, back in the days when you could get it, while Mrs Aleppo and I assume Mr Aleppo are firmly into non-fat milk. It tastes like water, looks like pigs' swill, but you can't complain when the breakfast is free. Anyway, one of the other lodgers often happens to have a bottle of the real stuff going spare, including myself on occasions. It all balances out, but it niggles nonetheless. I mean it cannot be for health reasons, for she tucks into cakes, sweets, creams and has a milky coffee every morning. The little bit of fat saved on the milk is hardly going to make a difference one way or the other. But, it is not my place to mention this.

Tell the fucking story, you bollox – it's the jester again, at me, always at me and it doesn't help that I no longer know the story, which story too is another question and the jester himself is no guide, changing his tale to suit himself when it pleases. I don't know why he has to be so crude about it either. I am not a prude when it comes to language. If I stub my toe walking into something in the middle of the night, say I'm going to the toilet or something; anyway, I may stub my toe and curse, fucking bastard, or whatever. But the jester, it is as if it is all he has left. Nasty, cutting remarks, laced through with pejorative language and invective taboo terms. Tell them about the puff in the clodgy, you soft cunt – is just the sort of thing he'll shout, knowing full well what happened next when I got out of bed finally and toddled downstairs for my breakfast.

Some rooms do not have a full range of facilities, but there are a toilet and bathroom on every landing. There is a toilet outside my room, and without touching upon lavatorial humour, the English fascination with toilet jokes, I have found its nearness capable of arousing some interest. It is fair to say that often I overhear people at their ablutions, shitting, pissing or throwing up. One person in particular I could not help but overhear as often he was in there, groaning, sobbing sometimes in very agony. A handsome, almost beautiful young man/lad with soft hazel eyes - he really suffered in there. It was awful to hear him.

I pulled my door to and belted my old green dressing gown, when I heard the boy again.

'Christ!…Sweet Christ, no!'

I tried to walk past, but he cried again and the agony cut like a knife. I walked back and tapped gently at the door.

'I say, you okay in there?'

'Yes.'

'Sure?'

'No…no not at all.'

'Shall I call a doctor?'

'No. It's all right. I just have to…I must…Christ.'

'Is there anything I can do?'

There was a pause then. It lasted quite some time and I began to worry if the lad had passed out. I knocked again, gently.

'Oh Christ, it's so embarrassing–'

'Doesn't matter, can I help, that's all that counts.'

The bolt was drawn back, a crack opened and the tear-stained face of the boy appeared in the gap. It didn't smell so good, but obviously, that was to be expected.

'You couldn't come in and give me a hand?'

It sounded so pathetic and all the jester could do was laugh and clasp his sides. I wasn't going to, felt uncomfortable to be honest, but hearing that laughter I marched straight in and shut the door. My voice sounded business-like, like an old army matron or at least like somebody not scared about these bodily things.

'So, kiddah, what can I do?'

'My arse has gone to pieces again. The muscles have all collapsed and it's agony trying to stuff them back. I keep trying, but it's like trying to give yourself an injection, couldn't do that either, so I gave up on drugs – I just can't do it…' The young lad started to cry again.

'Don't worry, young fellow my lad, I'll do what I can.' I said this, sounding blasé and confident, but I had never so much as put a plaster on anybody before.

'Thanks…'

'So…'

'Erm, get that tube, squeeze some on a wad of paper. I'll bend down and touch my toes and you stuff it all back in. Be quick, but try not to be too rough.'

I did as told and the jester was pissing himself, choked with laughter, tears, huge, welling tears of mirth, streaming his face. The lad bent over, carefully I collected his damaged valve muscles –

Go on shove 'em back in with the old purple fellow, the jester chided, elbowing me painfully in the ribs.

'Christ!' the young lad screamed, but his muscles were back in place for the time being.

I washed my hands at the sink, hoping that the youth would not see me blushing.

'Thanks, thanks a million…hazards of the job, you know.'

I knew, patted the lad on the shoulder and left. The jester, like some professional Northerner, like some WMC stand-up comedian, wouldn't let it rest all the way downstairs and during breakfast: should've slapped some salt on it, let him know what his arse is really for, fucking nancy puffda...

It wasn't clever, amusing or in anyway entertaining, but the jester knows what I think about gay-bashers, racists, bigots in general and he works on this. He baits and baits till I start to lose it, get mad, sad, depressed or evil to know. He pushes me all the way.

Come off it. You were beginning to get a chubby on, fancied slipping that queer a crippler.

I ignored the rantings of the jester and ate my muesli, looking through the papers, trying to find something worth reading. Jester wouldn't let up. It was a relief to hear the approach of Mrs Aleppo, singing as usual and seemingly happy with the world.

'Morning.'

'Morning and how are you today, had a lie-in I see.'

He's been up the arse of some up-hill-gardener – been a busy morning.

Mrs Aleppo was having none of the jester's cheek. She spun round, grabbed the runt by the nose and threatened to cut it off if she heard another peep from him again that day. Mrs Aleppo was close to me. I could smell her body. She exuded this strange heady scent of honey or saffron or something sweet and fragrant. I loved to be near Mrs Aleppo. She ruffled my hair, gave my forehead a peck, 'Well done, now eat your breakfast, lover boy.'

Like a third-rate sitcom the spoon dropped from my fingers. I gazed up at the warm wheaten features of Mrs Aleppo, a thin playful smile graced her lips and her dark brown eyes seemed so knowing; they drank you in, but not so that you felt threatened. You wanted to be in Mrs Aleppo's eyes.

'You've heard?'

'Ah, I may be a little deaf, but I hear things. It is good that a man, still not so old, should have a girlfriend, a girlfriend at last – eh.'

'Suppose so, but-'

'But nothing, let me tell you, before we took over this place and turned it around…Well, not quite like that – the Big Crash and everything, you know.' Mrs Aleppo paused mid-flow, she wasn't making sense, but I was used to that. 'Anyway, this property developer went bust trying to develop this house, but before he tried to convert the place, it had been a rats' den of tiny rooms, squalor, and the only ones who lived here were those without hope or nowhere else to go. True, one or two were not too bad, but they were only passing through, cheap place while they saved to buy better, that sort of thing. There were young girls aborting, homemade job, people throwing themselves out of windows or down the stairs or just going quietly mad, never leaving their rooms, lost inside their own crazy heads – one fellow hung himself, not discovered till the ruddy smell proved unbearable. Since we took over and turned this place round, we have not lost a single guest yet. We don't want to lose anybody. This girl, Eden Crow, she knows her job, she will keep you safe – I know.'

'But, Mrs Aleppo, I-'

'No! Don't complain, not to me, at least. Eat your breakfast and be bloody damn glad.'

She went off singing. And so it was official. I had a girlfriend, Eden Crow was my girl and everybody seemed quite happy with the arrangement.

Fat, old, slapper! Fucking foreign tart, the jester called after Mrs Aleppo. I blushed crimson and hoped she hadn't heard. She was a beautiful, kind, generous woman, this was the happiest and best digs that I had ever come across, but the jester was intent on causing trouble. To my shame, I began to curse the memory of my Uncle Walter, hating and distrusting his legacy.

It's Good to Talk

Eden Crow, strangely enough, was not the first person to call me on my newly installed telephone. It was my bank manger, such a person as almost to be unknown to me prior to the coming of the direct line, though it may be said that I must have seen at some time in the past his signature on some at least of the many letters that I had received, instructing me amongst other things that I was overdrawn without asking for any such facility. I seem to remember too what was most galling about such letters was that on top of the problems of my 'illegal' borrowings, the bank would make a charge for drawing attention to the fact that my account was not in credit. This was a most unfortunate practice doing nothing to alleviate my various financial crises. Still it was nice of Mr Jonas Blenkinsap to contact me and I suppose it is my loss that I don't play golf. Mr Jonas Blenkinsap did assure me also that it was such a perfect morning to be out there on the green, a brisk eighteen holes before lunch. Alas, I had to disappoint my bank manager and to be honest I had found the morning somewhat irregular, though not in the slightest displeasing.

'I thought I would bring you up a cup of tea, hope I haven't woken you,' said the lad with the hazel eyes, placing a china-blue cup upon the bedside dresser.

'No, it's quite all right, only dozing. The jester was up pouncing about doing his Qi-Gung – can't really sleep when he's doing all that deep breathing and grunting stuff.'

'Looks good though, maybe I should do something like that to relax after work.' The lad seemed pensive, concentrating on the jester's slow graceful movements. 'Hard night, entertaining some Thailand Tigers over for a business meeting: smaller than the European penis, but hard as nails, you could bend an iron bar on a couple of the ones I had last night if your wrists were strong enough…Sorry, I get so crude.'

'Ah, I suppose prostitution does that.'

'Prostitution! Whoring – I am a whore. Prostituta – Latin, could have been a priest, but didn't believe in God. I hate that.'

'What have I said?' vaguely aware that I had somehow touched something of a raw nerve.

'The way people dress up the sordid or the taboo in Latin, Greek or technical terms. Prostitution almost makes what I do sound clean, clinical, professional with a capital P – whereas in fact I'm a street whore, working a pitch, from home too and dish my cards about all over town. A cunt smells as sweet even if called a vagina.'

I didn't know quite what to make of this outburst, clearly this discussion, albeit one way, was rousing deep emotions in my new-found friend. I didn't really know what to say, how to deal with such a situation. I have this suspicion that I have always been this way, though I can manage, hello, good day, or any other number of phatic phrases, even with total strangers. 'Sorry, I suppose it's hard these days to find the right terms, you know without sounding judgmental or prejudicial or-'

'It was like this, when I hadn't got the grades and the careers facilitator invited me into his office to discuss my options: 'Get your backside in here Fertin Squirtworthy and don't be all day about it, lad.' I went in, sat down, got told off, 'cos I hadn't been invited to sit down and old Ali Bhangqat says to me, 'the only thing tha can do on a computer is piss abart playing games, tha hasn't gorm f't Civil Service, nor are tha robust enough f't Army, whilst thy hand/eye co-ordination and other wise dexterity is abart as gud as my Aunt Fan, so them factres that are left wun't touch tha wi' mine – so what we gonna do wi' thee, lad?' Like everyone else in my position that morning, I shuffled my feet and tried to avoid his eyes, looking out the window or at the photograph of his ugly wife, but beautiful daughter, on the mantleshelf behind his fat bald head, alongside his certificate from Darlington University, but he was having none of it. 'I'll tell you what tha's gonna do, tha's gonna whore, lad, and put bread on't table. Be a man. Be self-employed. Stand on your own two feet. Pretty lad like thee, should mek a killing...Or would you be interested in drugs?' he said, his voice sinking low. I shook my head no. 'Thought not, never mind, lad, fill in these forms and get thyssen a gud patch.' He was a coarse blunt bastard Ali Bhangqat, but he told it like it was. First day sucking cock, having me arse opened up like a Terry's Chocolate Orange, I knew I wasn't anything to do with an old, classical language like Latin, language of poets, mother church and fund for the establishing of scientific terms. I was crude, unlovely Anglo-Saxon with all the derogatory punch of its impolite lack of breeding: whore, cock, cunt, piss and shite. You don't upset me, calling me a whore. It's what I do. Dress it up, put a polite Victorian lengthy tablecloth on it and call it prostitution, then I know that you are insulting me, that you can't deal with what I do.'

Fertin was crying. I felt awful. I drew a protective hand around him. His shoulders felt thin, bird-like and wasted. Holding him close I could feel the thud of his heart.

Can you not shut that cunt up, I'm trying to concentrate, the jester called from the carpet, Golden Rooster Stands On One Leg, or some such position.

I tucked Fertin in bed, went to my small sink, ran the water till it became a little warmer and soaked and soaped my flannel. I cleaned the mess of teared, smeared make-up and mascara. Fertin's tears subsided to a little blub, then ceased. I got back into bed, putting my arms around him. I suppose we dozed for a while.

'So you are gay after all.'

I sat up rubbed my eyes, took a good slurp of the cup of tea and told it straight, prevaricating no more and thus almost having my first row with my new girlfriend. 'Just because you find me in bed with an attractive young man, doesn't mean that I'm homosexual. I can't help the way your nasty mind works...' She wasn't listening and I wasn't that bothered, my tea was cold, good tea too, either Yorkshire or Tetleys, but I do not normally take my tea with milk and sugar, except in certain parts of Ireland

and amongst the old Dale folk who tend to have it very strong indeed and stewed to death to boot. Fertin had woken too and smiled warmly at Eden Crow. My girlfriend stopped scowling then and gazed with wonder at the young lad with the hazel eyes.

'I say you are never young Fertin Squirtworthy, Traycene Rumpart's cousin?' asked Eden Crow, though her question could equally have been marked by an exclamation mark. I perceived also that a faint blush lit her ruddy cheeks, making her appear rather callow yet not unbeguiling.

'I am that, Eden Crow, and I remember you, surprising you that time in the Wendy House, the two of you playing nuns and nurses,' said Fertin.

There was no mistaking Eden Crow's coyness now. Her face positively glowed through an equal mixture of embarrassment and dimly remembered pleasure. She shuffled her feet, ventured a few questions as to the wellbeing of Traycene Rumpart, Fertin's cousin, while I repaired to the bathroom, my bladder getting the worst of me. While urinating what seemed not a little copiously I could not but overhear some dull chanting accompanied by rather heavy thudding from above. It was as if someone were hirpling rather vigorously with a club-foot, not necessarily unpleasant to the senses, though the odd flake of plaster fell from the ceiling, but certainly something which activated my native inquisitiveness in no short measure. Wiping my penis end with a small swab of tissue paper and thereafter washing my hands as is my wont, I ventured forth, eager to track down this peculiar distraction. Ascending the landing above via the old servants' stairs I soon ascertained from whence the commotion came. Surreptitiously, I placed my ear against the solid oak door and quite unashamedly eavesdropped. The person inside was chanting, some mantra or doggerel while, I suppose, performing some antiquated ritual or other. Unwittingly, my hand strayed to the door handle and I was saved from making a most rude and unwelcome entrance only by the chance intervention of Mrs Aleppo.

'Wouldn't disturb that fellow just yet,' said Mrs Aleppo,

backing out of a room nearby, dragging her ancient vacuum cleaner. 'He does get most particular about his privacy, positively cannot stand it when people interfere, not that he gives a ruddy damn about the rest of the house. Still he is harmless enough, unless that is you prove to be an American, then it has been known for him to get not a little boisterous, verbally hostile and abusive to say the very least...Have a word later if you want to complain, but not just now – three day fast, chanting, dancing and what not.'

'I see,' I said, but didn't.

'Oh by the way, I shall be down soon, perhaps shortly to do your landing and it would be a very great help to me if I could plug my Hoover in that socket just through your door by the walnut veneer wardrobe – you know the one that I am referring to?'

'Erm, yes, please help yourself.' I hadn't so much as noticed any socket in the room, near, against or alongside any wardrobe or not. It was Mrs Aleppo's house and I was after all only a guest, passing through.

'Oh thank you so much. You are most helpful. I wish there were more people, kind and considerate like you in this world and we could get a damn sight more done in a day and that's the truth.'

'Does Mr Aleppo not help also?' I asked, somewhat rudely and very much out of character, but somehow I had to know more about this person. He was a mystery, plaguing my mind unduly no doubt, but I still wanted to know, something vital seemed to depend upon it, though it was a very unreasonable belief to hold at the time.

I wasn't answered as it was. Mrs Aleppo made some very dismissive clicking noise, bracing her tongue against the roof and palette of her mouth, before launching into some aria or other. I walked away. The vacuum cleaner rattled into service and for a while I forgot about the chanting man or Mr Aleppo. I had a little explaining to do, back in the bedroom it was required of me to mention something about my life in the sock.

Upon arriving back I found my girlfriend and Fertin in bed together. I wasn't so much angry as surprised.

'What the deuce is going on here?' I shouted and slammed the door shut.

'Don't be so damn Victorian. We're only chatting. And anyway, I'm a lesbian—'

'And I'm a gay blade.'

'I know that,' I said, kicking off my slippers and getting into bed. 'But, it's the principle of the thing that hurts. And anyway, how come, Eden Crow, you got in on his side? I mean, whose girlfriend are you?'

'Don't try to teach me my job. I'm a bloody professional, you know,' said Eden Crow, getting out of one side and marching around to my side. 'Budge up, Lard Arse.' Eden Crow got in, grabbed my arm and laid it over her shoulder and nestled into me. It wasn't erotic. It was homely, and for a while we all just lay half-slumped against the headboard taking it easy.

'It's not a bad old place,' I said after a while, just for something to say, though meaning it.

'Lived in worse,' said Fertin Squirtworthy.

'I live in worse,' said Eden Crow.

I raised my eyebrows, surprised at the disclosure, wondering whether it would be the right thing to do to ask my girlfriend to move in with me, but I didn't want to put pressure on her, certainly not so early in the relationship. I gave her arm a gentle squeeze, smiled faintly and lovingly down into her eyes and she wasn't impressed. Discouraged, my mind dwelt upon some of the places that I had lived in or on or at in the past. I suppose I fell into something of a brown study, hard to say, but Eden Crow broke my reverie.

'What you thinking?'

I came round, smiled again down at my girlfriend and decided not to lie, 'I was thinking of the time when I lived in a sock.'

'Oh aye,' said Fertin.

I was somewhat in the dark as to what he wished to convey by such an interjection.

Eden Crow scratched her pubis somewhat abstractedly, perhaps even absentmindedly, though it was good to know that she was becoming easier in my company. It was my girlfriend who bade me to go on, to explain something of what I had meant.

Signs and Portents in a Plate of Beans and Toast

'To fully understand why it was that I ran away to live for seven years or more in the bottom of a sock is not perhaps within my power to convey, but something of the dilemma that I faced can at least be transmitted without laboriously narrating every detail like some overblown melodrama or a mundane and mentally dulling soap-opera.'

Will you fucking be on with it, said the jester, wiping himself down on my best tea towel, his Qi-Gung exertions for the moment curtailed. I was pleased when my fellow bedmates bid him hush. Eden Crow found one of my slippers and flung it at the mischievous sprite, a palpable hit too as I recall. It is from this incident, more jocular than malicious, that I date the jester's open hostility and envy of my girlfriend, not that I discerned too much at the time, being too preoccupied with struggling to find a metaphor for all my dismal years of rearing under my mother and the step-dada.

'Beans and toast is the nearest that I can come to it. A simple basic meal that hints at the deeper unquietness that had settled into my home, marring my upbringing and making me the mockery of a man that I am and have been and shall remain, forever waiting to grow up, unable to shirk off the past whilst being bewildered by the present and pained by the future. I am aware that all of this may sound unduly pompous, but that's from the outside looking in; from the inside looking out all that I say or fail to say makes perfect sense to me, it only pains me that there are not words potent enough to reflect my all-sustaining unease.

'Beans and toast is a humble beginning, a poor meal to be having twice in the same day. My mother was a better and a more adventurous cook, her tastes moulded by her rather lavish upbringing at the house of my grandfather, whom I never met. But my mother was not cooking. It was the step-dada, a limited but, on the surface at least, not an unlikeable person upon chance acquaintance, who put beans on toast on the table twice that day. It was well for him and us I suppose that the larder was amply stocked with beans or otherwise it would have been poorer fare than it transpired.

'I digress, beans and toast it was and that was all – like it or lump it as is the expression. I suppose in a world of starving people where bairns, of equal age to both me and my sister as we then were, were doing without any nourishment whatsoever, it seems somewhat churlish to disparage the meal that had been given unto us. Indeed, I am not one to complain as a rule about my lot, but it was the relative injustice that still causes me to look back upon those dreary years with a great deal of heart-scalding regret.

'You may think too that it is wrong of me to bring this against the step-dada, seeing that in that household it was not his duty to be providing meals. By chance it was that he was cooking that day, my mother only just after arriving from the hospital to have her arm pinned and plated after been broken but two nights previously by the step-dada himself. It wasn't the step-dada's fault that he was so grievously ignorant of such basic culinary skills as knocking up a tatie-ash, toad in't hole, stew and dumplings or other such staples from the world of Yorkshire cuisine. All said at the end of the day, given his own rather traditional and narrow up-bringing, it was to be expected that the poor man managed only such a meagre meal at that time of re-adjustment and general unease.

'Sometimes, specially down there snided in the gap between big-toe and its nearest neighbour, lying there on my hammock listening to Radio 3 or Radio 4, I would shake my head in disbelief that it was a plate of beans and toast that first made me run away and chance my luck with the world. If I had known then what such ventures would bring, doubtless I would have remained at home despite the violence, terror and the spirit-crushing bleakness of it all. But run away I did.

'I told my buddy, the lad that sat next to me in those days. Paul Haw was his name, a great hulking ginger-haired youth, who had a grand sense of humour and many the good hour we spent at the back of the class chewing the fat, flicking ink at the two girls sat in front of us and making up strange rituals, such as the Golden Rule. I can clearly and distinctly remember that one of our Golden Rules, for over the years these tended to accrue indeed, sorry, there I go again rambling on without direction lost as I was lost in the sock, though scarcely a wrinkle, blade of hair or ragged nail I did not know as well as the back of my hand...Ah, that Golden Rule now, that I remember so well, childish yet elegantly cruel: Paul and I forbade each other to go to the toilet between breaks. Two other factors made the situation worse. Namely, firstly, that during dinner, what the Southern people or the well-to-do call lunch, we endeavoured to drink as much water as we could, limited only by the scowl of Mr Hagyard, who from beneath his bushy brows, would view with mounting annoyance our not infrequent trips to refill the water jug. Secondly, that once back at our desks we would persecute one another with fantastical images of waterfalls gushing endlessly over the edge of the world down into a huge latrine bowl or other images equally grotesque, such as a Jack Russell whose endless bladder could never be relieved and was responsible in days of yore for creating the River Calder merely by cocking his leg against an ancient mulberry tree. Diversions both childish and absorbing, rituals both pointless and loyally adhered to that for us made our long dull school hours pass to some effect; the humour of crossed legs and images of dripping taps was though, enough to cause us to be separated from one another as we approached our final year at primary school. Once apart, the Golden Rule, all our gloriously ridiculous rules, fell into disuse and neglect, robbed of value or relevance, as we made do with new diversions inspired by our newly acquired desk-mates. I was lucky. Paul was moved to a desk at the front, whilst I remained safely overlooked at the back of the class. Paul was sat next to a girl no one liked much, though I fain ken why as she seemed pleasant and amiable enough though she did look rather wan and on the undernourished side, whilst I was introduced to the sweet-natured company of a very pretty girl indeed whom I was too shy to tell that I loved her dearly, nearly as much as I had Sharon Drinkeld the lass from my very early youth when I would gauge strong affection by the central heating or up and down the universe.

'I remember too telling Paul that I planned to run away, but I knew he didn't really believe I would do it. He did though fully understand why it was that I wished to grab a stick, wrap a bundle upon the end of it and see the world. He said that I should go to the police, but instead it proved the case that the police visited me after I came back.

'And I did come back and I blush even now for my weakness and lack of resolve. Sometimes, swinging upon my hammock, mulling over these matters again, bitter with reproach, I would try to remind myself that I was but ten years old at the time, but age didn't then or now seem to be the relevant factor. What stands out and is with me always is that even at that age my spirit, my vigour to grasp life, to strike out and seize what walking, breathing, eating, loving and working had to offer me had been severely crushed and irreparably stunted. For the first time I was shewn to be a coward with no heart to make any mark on the world, not even later a gravestone when my thoughts did turn to self-slaughter. It is perhaps this belittling realisation that first drew me to seek the sanctuary of neglect down in the dark woollen walled caverns of the sock, safely out of harm's way, specially my own.

'My sister though had more reserves of spunk and get up and go and not shortly after the beans and toast affair and its naked injustice she did go and seek a fortune in the wider world. She travelled far, traversed strange towns and the alien cities of the south, recounting her woes whether real or imagined and finding listeners enough to empathise with her plight to offer board, lodgings and spare change no doubt. Over the years her discourse became so far-fetched and estranged from what was actually the case that she was even invited to speak at several charity events for the alleviation of such crimes against the person, as well as special guest appearances on the wireless and terrestrial television. Indeed, one day down in the sock collecting mushrooms I heard her myself on Radio 4's excellent *Woman's Hour* with her fantastical tales of our childhood, so grotesque in fact that I could no longer relate what was said to the events as I remembered them. But perhaps I was being too uncritical of the past, if not a little unkind to this poor deranged woman and her stories. There is always this possibility that I am forever prone to error, unable to find something indubitably true and beyond processes of doubt. Especially here, for two reasons in particular suggest this self-criticism: one, that she was far older than me; and for two, she did have a rather splendid ginger moustache. Thus perhaps, she was not my sister after all and I am in no position to verify the narrative regarding its accuracy or veracity.

'As for the other one, sister or brother…well that after all never came. I can remember my mother pulling my head to her swelling belly and bidding me feel the kick of the wee one inside. Nothing has ever seemed so magical as those moments of another living thing, living and growing from inside another living thing. It grieves me to this day the accident and I am sure that my mother never recovered. It wasn't just the physical damage caused when the step-dada threw her from the car, it was something else…It is something else too that I struggle to find the words to express: a hundred images fill my head – the mother hunched, shuffling around the house no longer caring how dirty or how dusty it had become, the way she hid from strangers, would refuse to answer the telephone or again being woken in the night by her sobbing… A policewoman came for a time to talk to her, a social worker and a doctor too, perhaps after I fled that other night, others called, but of this I cannot be sure, just conjecture – my mother needed help and, rather cowardly, I ran away rather than fail to give the succour and support that she craved.

'The only thing in my defence that I can say, is that she would then at oft times assure me that all would be well in the end, that there was a nest-egg maturing, that in time we'd all be okay and safe from harm. And, to be honest I never believed a word. My mother she was talking as if she was still gainfully employed, at the work that made the step-dada so jealous, being better paid than what he picked up on building sites, with a good pension and a career ladder to boot. My mother talked about the future like fools discussing a possible football pools' win, the lottery or premium bonds payouts. I left my mother promising, emptily promising, slouched in a worn chair as the dust settled more deeply day by day.

'The house and the way it fell into ruin too has had a lasting effect on me and how I related to my fellows. I would refuse to have birthday parties, because I did not want my classmates to see the squalor in which I lived. Later, there was a girl, young woman rather, whom I fiercely loved, but could never commit myself to, maugre all that we had in common. It wasn't her fault I suppose, for she had her own problems, but her two-up/two-down terrace was so untidy and badly maintained that it brought back those terrible dead, dull days of the past. Again, coward that I am, I just walked away, never explaining anything to this young woman whom I loved, that I could never make the necessary commitment to her, to us, to squalor...

'Morbidly sensitive, my favourite psychiatrist called me, or so I discovered when years later I obtained a copy of my medical records as was then my right. Dr A J P Khan probably underestimated just how sensitive I was. I tried to tell him the story of the beans and toast, but he never seemed to have the patience to listen carefully enough so that he could grasp to a nicety the difference between the two sets of plates. I can see the plates now: on one side the step-dada's and mother's and on the other my sister's and my own. The difference as I retell this tale sounds so slight, but the distinction was endemic and typified the underlying hypostasis of our family's power, economic and social structure. On one side there were these freshly toasted baps, lavished with a thick spread of butter, topped with beans overflowing to the plate. There was the other side where a slice of badly toasted, unbuttered cheap white bread lay alongside a spoonful of beans, all but burnt from the bottom of the pan. I try to talk this through with people from time to time, so as to explain something of why it was I came to live in a sock, but I am sure no one really understands, not even my sister, as she too had to lie about it all in order to make what happened understandable.'

I was about to continue with my story, but got no further than the beans on toast, for just before I came to describe my flight Mrs Aleppo came in to plug her ancient vacuum cleaner in the socket by the walnut veneered wardrobe.

Mrs Aleppo Takes Five

Plugged in and ready to go, Mrs Aleppo stood for a moment gazing curiously at the three of us tucked up in bed in various states of undress. She shook her head in some vague knowing manner, curiosity giving way to positive admiration.

'You young people, how so I envy you, so much more freer than my own youth, no inhibitions and no damn big deal guilt thing either. I wish I could have my youth again – didn't even get a damn orgasm thing till I was forty-four – hah.' Mrs Aleppo finished on a very breathy exhortation, a very strong 'ha' as voiced by the nose. It was an intriguing way of adding emphasis and I was not sure how she did it. I felt though, a little duty- bound to explain the true circumstances of our bed sharing before she re-commenced with her vacuuming and opera singing, but I was frustrated in acting upon this intention by my girlfriend setting the record straight first.

'Sorry to disappoint you, Mrs Aleppo, but we are in bed because of a sock and not sex,' said Eden Crow and I could not help but think there was the hint of some derision in her tone, certainly disbelief.

'Ah yes, I know all about those things,' said Mrs Aleppo, shaking her head from side to side knowingly.

'Really?' I asked or exclaimed, taken aback by Mrs Aleppo's casual, almost off-hand remark.

'Oh yes, my great great grandfather he ran a souk, a whole damn bazaar, before those bastard murdering Turks drove us out,' said Mrs Aleppo in a raw explosion of pique. Her vehemence was such that neither of us wished to correct her upon her mistake, besides it was obvious that she wished to say more, her face paling while her eyes seemed to flash darkly. 'We paid our damn taxes, we worked and traded hard with Turks, Ajerbaihanes, Ruskes, Tartars – the whole damn lot. We kept ourselves to ourselves and never caused trouble. Then they kill us, round us up and murder us, raped and robbed and only a few managing to flee to safety. It was hard times and my great grandfather made sure that his sons and daughters never forgot what happened to us, so that someone at least would remember our story.'

Mrs Aleppo took a duster from her apron pocket and dabbed her eyes. We looked away, shuffling uncomfortably, not really sure about any of this.

'I have never seen the homeland of my ancestors, it is not possible to go back…And anyway when I think of home I more often than not think of Delhi where my great grandfather finally arrived to become a member of the British Empire and to work on the Indian Railways. My greatgrandfather worked on the railways as did my own father too, then it seemed that we were no longer so welcome in that country also. There were us and there were the Anglo-Indians, we were the ones that did most of the railway work and we seemed a little superfluous in the New India of partition and distrust – we were hangers on from the last administration and it was time that we left.

'Clearly, I can remember arriving as a little girl in England, my Indian clothes and sandals so misplaced and so damn useless against the cold. I cried, wanting the sounds and smells of Delhi and all its crazy bastards: robber gangs, Hindu extremists, entrepreneurs and the occasional madman…Three years old, I saw a Jain monk out begging wearing no damn clothes whatsoever, four years old, out playing with some friends we saw this fellow, some Kaliwallah, pull a half-cremated body from a funeral pyre and eat it, but mostly we saw the new class aping the British, hard-hearted and practical and nothing mystical about them, not a damn, and it felt like time to move on again.

'My great grandfather lost his souk. I lost India. Now I live in this house. Now you live in this house. The whole world is changing, people always on the move. But it is good to remember – never forget what has been lost.'

Mrs Aleppo was lost in reveries and we were somewhat at a loss about what to do with the silence that followed. I hardly thought it appropriate to continue with my narration of my time living in the toe of the sock. Something more appropriate would have been to have talked more with Mrs Aleppo about her past as she seemed so overwhelmed by her memories. It was well though that I did not find some word or other to say upon such matters, for it was Mrs Aleppo herself who broke the silence and her resumption of conversation had nothing whatsoever to do with socks, souks or Indians.

'Ah, so you have a line, a real line telephone, bloody incredible, though at one time you know they were common enough.' Suddenly, Mrs Aleppo's voice dropped in volume, speaking barely above a whisper. 'You know, before Enabling Act and even for a few years after, phone-lines were so very common. True, the mobile phone started to be used a lot more frequently as time went on, but even then most people had two phones: a mobile for work and a phone-line for the home. No, it was the Porno Wars that made lines scarce. Porno Wars is such an unfair term I can tell you. True, the big Porn Barons funded the war, but it was the internet that challenged the government and tried to circulate information freely. It was a strange alliance: lefties, old commies, religious groups, greens, and anarchists having to do business with Porn Kings, just so they could keep alive debate, dissent and the vestiges of freedom. For a time they even began to have an effect, but then Charles the Fifth struck – no phone-lines, no internet connection, no lap-tops and, for certain, no freedom of information. It worked, everyone had their mobile and only the rich, the head of the military or the politically necessary had a phone-line.'

Mrs Aleppo walked over to the phone, gave it a quick dust and listened almost ecstatically to the buzz of the phone. She played at pressing a number, but placed down the receiver before a dial tone was heard. Without any dubitation whatsoever Mrs Aleppo was pleased with my phone-line.

'Ring someone if you like,' I offered, after all, as far as I knew I had no one to call.

'No, no, you rich men are so frivolous and what is more I have the whole damn house to finish hoovering, but thank you for your offer.' Mrs Aleppo left, soon the sounds of vacuuming and Wagner could be heard, a not disagreeable combination.

Fertin Squirtworthy was restless. He rose, saying that really he needed his own bed if he was to get a proper day's sleep. It was going to be a heavy night as some businessmen from north of the border were coming down for an illicit playboy weekend, indulging in the laxity and liberality of England. It was a hard life.

Nestling still below my oxter was Eden Crow. It felt good to feel her warmth, to smell her smell and for a moment there I really thought that she could be my girlfriend. She bent her head up towards me, nibbled my chin and briefly pressed her lips against my mouth. I wanted to kiss her, a deep, long lingering kiss, but so far that day I hadn't washed my teeth, morning breath is not such a thing as to be inflicting on a relative stranger, nor anyone else for that matter.

'Come on, lover boy, let's go for a long romantic walk by the river.'

'The river?'

'Aye, why not, we could have a coffee in the beer garden.'

'Erm…I had best check the old bank balance.'

'You, taking the piss?'

The Hole in the Wall Machine

Walking with Eden Crow brought a few surprises, like simulacra sentiments for example, ersatz feeling that does so often be put down and belittled without adequate reflection as to its utility. It was late morning, perhaps around eleven fifteen by the time that, washed and changed, I ventured forth to take a constitutional, that suggested stroll along the old towpath. The day had brightened and even I seemed to see the warm hues of early summer quite clearly and distinctly. I still felt like a stranger in that city at that time, for truth be told I had seldom explored my new environment, being content to remain at my lodgings and dispute with the jester as to what ought, if anything, to be written. At that moment we were at a deadlock and so perhaps might have remained if later events had not determined the outcome decisively.

But for the moment, quarrels with the jester seemed to belong to another age, for Eden Crow firmly took me by the hand and guided me to the nearest cashpoint machine. I had, while shaving, mentioned the fact again that I feared that my funds would not accommodate her plans for the afternoon, but she had only heaped more scorn on my remark. She considered me to be quite a parsimonious niggard or perhaps as some variety of fool to defer the walk by such a paltry subterfuge as my want of monies.

But her hand in mine was such a pleasant thing. Up until that moment I had never understood why seemingly intelligent men and women contracted liaisons with far younger people, mere girls and boys, when they must have known that they were only buying affection as such, that without wealth, status or power they would no more be a partner for these young beautiful people than some exotic ape. My comparison lacks something I fear, specially as it brings to mind something of my far away captivity. However, be that as it may, it did my soul good to walk down Kirkgate with a young beautiful lesbian warmly holding my arm.

But, for Eden Crow I suppose my joy, my delight in the verisimilitude of my emotional state was as nothing to her, except the possibility of the satisfaction of knowing that a job, her job, was being well done. She was so ruthlessly professional that over the time that I knew Eden Crow she did bring me some great ease and comfort. Though I could never forget that my girlfriend was state given, a symbol of ill-used hoarded capital, I was deeply grateful just the same. This never ceased to surprise me, perhaps I was just an organic automaton plugged into a few simple drives – this was what the Crions maintained and, though at the time that I lived in their charge I did so reject their opinions, later I must concede I found much latent truth in the holding of such a position.

Eden Crow, her strong, brown fingers delicately entwined around my own and the fast happy beat of my heart.

More surprising than the 'buzz' I gleaned from Eden Crow's embrace was the state of my balance as shewn by the hole in the wall machine. I was so staggered by the vastness of the sum that I had to check for myself inside the sub-branch of my bank that the account was in order. With great deference, I was asked to sit on the sub-manager's own chair while he rang my manager on his mobile. My manager was delighted to speak to me, though I feared that I was interrupting an important round of golf with some Caledonian oil sheikhs. Howsoever, I was assured that the read-out was indeed correct and that any time I wished to discuss my investment portfolio with him, he would only be too glad to accommodate me no matter what time of the day or night his services should be required. He also vented his condolences, but heaven knows why. I suppose I ought to have felt flattered by his attentions, but I could not help feeling downhearted and not a little weak. Eden Crow looked on, smugly sipping a pink gin proffered by the sub-manager still fawning over us, but I could not drink nor feel sated in any such degree, for I knew a terrible error had been made and that one day all would be found out and then…

It did not warrant speculation. I had heard reports of the debtors' prisons, forced labour and the like and darker rumours too of the debtors' hospitals where parts were taken and sold and the body maintained almost indefinitely producing blood, marrow and plasma products. The Crions had advised me never to leave and perhaps too that was something else about which they were correct.

Eden Crow finished her pink gin. She supervised me while I made out a withdrawal for what would have seemed to me at one time a ludicrously absurd amount of cash. But for the sobering reality of my new found wealth, I would have turned a few cartwheels upon the thick shag carpet, as I always had a talent for minor gymnastic feats when young. Anyway, we were going for a stroll along the river. Her strong brown fingers gripped my hand in a tight embrace as she led me along to where the path started by Ald King Olav's bridge. Strangely, for once I was reminded of my mother who would hold my hand in such a way when but a bairn and out walking amongst the traffic. It was at least or alas some sense of displaced comfort.

But by the start of the path I stopped.

The Sweet Shop that Time Forgot

Marshalls' Mint Imperials. Worstons' Traditional Cinder Toffee. Allsop's Pear Drops. Oughtershaw's Cough Candy Twist. Butterworth's Winter Nips. Oldroyd's Bonfire Toffee. Grimworth's Original Pontefract Cakes…

Like some starved urchin, I gazed with open longing and wonder at the displays of sweets before me. There were jars upon jars of brightly coloured 'spice' with names that echoed and resonated from my childhood. In those days I had been haunted both by the names and by the sweets, for a toffee was not simply a sticky lump found at the bottom of my pocket, but it was Hardy's Extra Hard sticky lump. The relationship between the brand name and the sweet seemed fast and necessary; the link itself wholesome and elemental. A winter nip was never just a winter nip, but a *Johnson's* Winter Nip, which was this particular nip in contradistinction to a *Butterworth's* Winter Nip, a horse of a different colour. The names were solid, stolid and thoroughly reliable. My home could contain my father or my mother and the step-dada. My home could be such a place to inspire dread, where doors were ripped from hinges and television sets thrown through windows, a place that both the social worker and the policeman frequented. My home could float above the earth on a cloud or swim beneath the grey great sea. My home, it was something or nothing. But those names were real and you asked for those names, you called out the little string of signs and symbols, phonemes and vibrations in the ether and you got your quarter, particular quarter, of goodies. Those names held me together by their soothfast and insistent elemental steadfastness.

There was something else I was going to say, but really, I do not wish to continually bewail my most unfortunate raising at the hands of mother and the step-dada. To be concise though, let me hereby point out that there was very little food in the house during my childhood, certainly my sister and I saw precious little of it. I can remember well the day that mother prepared tea for the cricket-team, the step-dada had been demoted to vice-captain that year, and the house was filled with plates of sandwiches, scotch-eggs, quiches, salads and the like – a veritable feast. Never had the sister or I seen such food and none of it was for us. We stole a plate and hid out the back, but we were found out and punished, beaten and sent to bed without any tea; we barely noticed the difference.

There is a smile about my face as I think about what has just been written. Explaining, trying to explain, renders what ought to be pathos into either the realms of the pathetic or something that panders to a very northern stereotype of hard times. Back there in my youth there was a rather rotund comedian, a Lancastrian I believe, who specialised in reciting tales of woe, normally directed at himself or less honestly at the 'wife' or 'mother-in-law'. All this in my youth I freely admit I found most amusing, but then less so as I grew more mature and more socially aware in my outlook, but what is strange is, as I attempt to say something very simple – I went to bed hungry, underfed and undernourished and was plagued in my dreams by sweets – I cannot help but slip into this dangerous cliché of 'life was tuff up North'. Even as I think of other stories such as my Uncle Tom's family was so poor that there was not money enough for new shoes, so once as a lad my Uncle Tom having out-grown his old pair was sent to school wearing his elder sister's cast-offs, that day all his mates ganged up on him, he fought everyone and the first thing he did on coming home was cut the pink bows and brass buckles off. Sorry, I digress in needless wordiness, but as I think of these stories and others, such as my father begging the butcher for dog bones to make a soup on for the family, I can only hear these stories in my head as said by this long dead comedian. Their power, their potency to relate the past has been drained by a long applause stretching back to the days of the music halls, where all such characters have been stripped and thereafter appropriately dressed as humorous caricatures.

Sorry, I did not really want to stray onto such matters after all,

all that I really have here is an aside. However, those dreams I had then seemed so hyper-real and sometimes several of the dreams would be repeated, becoming less de-familiar and almost quotidian. The commonest by far was when a young lady would invite me in to her shop and allow me my fill of chocolates and sweets, but I had to finish my selection before her father returned. I was filled with such joy, but also anguish as I had to choose between taking a large jar of Berston's Yorkshire Mixtures or Whartley's Limes and Lemons or Oughtershaw's Custard Apples. There I would be, perspiration dripping off me, fumbling, in a tizzy, almost having a duck fit, spoilt for choice and knowing any second my time would be up. I never did choose and I never did meet that kind lady's father, for always I woke up in a blind panic, sometimes having wet myself, but always with hot tears of frustration streaking my cheeks.

So, it was no surprise to me that I dallied so long by the shop window, gazing with longing and fondness at these old sweet jars. Eden Crow was bemusedly impatient and tolerant. She could see or sense that I was lost in some sort of reverie, shuffling along the lines, mouthing again never forgotten names. For a moment, I had a mad impulse to burst into the shop and grab a jar and run, run for old time's sake – one jar at least I must have been owed. Thankfully, I regained a little of my composure. Eden Crow squeezed my hand and asked if I wanted to go in.

Cling-ding…

Upon opening the door, setting a small bell to chime, I just stood there for a while savouring the past and the present, for if I closed my eyes I found myself back once more, a bairn in shorts entering Newton's Corner Shop and Beer Off with a stolen tenpence to buy a quarter of Rostons' Midget Gems – the ring of that bell, the slightly cloying smell of dust, polish and the vying scents of a thousand sweets. Gently, Eden Crow pushed me further inside, giving my upper arm a friendly squeeze. I smiled back a little foolishly and fondly inspected the jars displayed inside. A small, very attractive young woman came from a door from behind the counter, said a friendly salutation and then began to scrutinise me rather curiously. It wasn't an uncomfortable experience and, besides, I was too preoccupied perusing the shelves to take much notice, but Eden Crow certainly took note, commentating about this incident at length later as we lay in bed together.

'Marvellous! Where did you get such stock – worthy of a museum,' I asserted both enthusiastically and without my usual neurotic misgivings. The young woman tittered, almost girlishly, shuffling from foot to foot and she told me something of her enterprise. Later I was to know more, to discover just what these stacks of brightly coloured jars had cost her, but that first narration was an exquisite lucky dip into the one-pennorth jar – one small sweet taste.

'…Mother used to work for MacPherson's till she took bad. She was going to go back, as she recovered like, but then this Swiss firm took over…Firstly, they cut back on staff and, despite all the years that mother worked for MacPherson's, she was laid off – something of a bad risk, what with her dicky heart and that. Well, it was hard then, though I didn't know quite how hard. At first, all I missed was waiting on mother coming up the garden path with her work pinny concealing a handful of chows or chocolates. But it was hard and mother would at times take things bad, me promising her that one day when I grew up I would buy her her own factory to play in. Course, never managed that, but I had a bit of luck and anyway I managed to get the shop and stock it how I wanted and that…'

I knew even then that there was more, but I had no inkling not even the merest suggestion of the horror that hid behind the phrase, '…but I had a bit of luck…' She was a hero or heroine if you prefer, but we did not venture then into the darker side of that shop's acquisition. It was still all childhood and light, my eyes roving the shelves, spoilt for choice, unable to choose like the parable of the donkey who was placed before a bushel of hay and a bucket of water and who wanted both equally. But, I did manage to choose, to point to a jar before it was too late.

'Oo, please may I have a quarter of Headen's Peppermint Creams. I haven't had one of those in years. To be honest I never bought them after I ran away that time…' I said, faltering and blushing a little uncomfortably.

'Really,' said the young woman, smiling and measuring out a quarter on an old fashioned scale – imperial measurements.

'The young lady isn't interested in all that gumph,' said Eden Crow, rather maliciously. I couldn't understand what had come over her. She was so patronising, talking down to me as if I was some sort of idiot and she was my minder, like that job I once had working for the Brain Damage Trust. The girl though, took not the slightest bit of notice. She gave a quick twist of the paper bag and put Eden Crow in her place.

'Sorry, you were saying, peppermint creams – go on…'

This put me in a bit of a spot, but I thought there was just a chance of keeping everybody happy if I just cut the tale short – cut to the chase – as I think the Americans are supposed to say. I tried anyway.

'There is this dream that many people have had in one form or another, whereby they walk or drive home, but fail to find their house or flat. As a child I often had this dream that I would walk home but be unable to find my home, though the street and the corner house where we lived had been successfully negotiated. Sometimes this confusion was confounded by finding myself naked below the waist. But, though it seems strange to say, I was never troubled by being so lost.

'One day I walked home from school and just kept on walking, ignoring the turn down to my street and the house on the corner. I was running away armed only with a quarter of Headen's Peppermint Creams from Newton's Corner Shop and Beer Off. At first I was rather pleased with myself, my resolve never faltered as I trudged mile after mile, walking beyond the linear development of my village, finding the snicket down to the cart-tracks, over the fields to the magic wood, that dim smudge skirting the horizon.

'The wood wasn't magic. It was cold as I huddled beneath this gnarled and cracked ash. I lay against the bark, growing more apprehensive as the light failed, sucking slowly, savouring each mint. Within an hour, I was shrammed to the core, bones ached and my teeth chattered. I raked leaves together and tried to stack them round me, but the leaves blew away, save the ones that were wet, and I had to search again for something to stave off the cold. Luckily, I found some old fertiliser bags and like a primitive bivvy bag I stuck my legs and as much of my torso as I could inside, but even crouched down and doubled-bagged I was far from warm. I lay back against the tree, gazing upwards as the wind tossed the uppermost boughs, a chilling sight, not romantic – coldly indifferent. I lay back, looked and felt the cold earth take hold of my body. A part of me remained cold and incapable of being warmed for many years to come, only when I bedded down by the big toe, tucked up in the sock, did this core of cold dissipate and that portion of my body come alive once more.

'I failed of course. In came the dark and I grew frightened. Terror gripped me like a splinter of ice in my heart. I shuffled out of my bags and fled, stumbling in the dark back over the fields, hitting the cart track and then less hurriedly, but still in high panic, I made my way home.

'There was a light on in the kitchen. For a while I was unable to enter, knowing full well that I was in for it. I was cold, tearful and again scared, but this was a familiar fear and eventually I steeled myself and opened the back door.

'Nothing happened. My mother gave me a perfunctory nod and I kicked off my muddied shoes. No one had noticed my running away.

'The step-dada did notice the state of my shoes. This was unforgivable, ruining my best shoes and tramping mud into the house. I got a clout and then a few more clouts and then I screamed, "I ran away!" It stopped the clouting. I was terrified, this was it, now at last they were going to kill me. I had blown it. The step-dada merely said, 'Next time, don't come back,' but my mother was affronted, taking it personally and wanted me not only beaten, but officially chastised. She called the police.

'He was a young policeman, tall and slender like a willow tree with hard blue eyes. He talked and talked and jabbed his finger, while my mother suitably dabbed at her made-up eyes. This young man made me feel guilty for the way I had made my mother fret and worry. It was a farce, more so as two weeks later he was at our house again, helping to take away the step-dada who was just after breaking my mother's arm. Small world.

'Warm but awake I lay in my bed and dug from my soiled coat pocket my last peppermint cream. I didn't crunch it, but slowly let it dissolve – small frail circle of mint and I was asleep.'

I finished my tale much to the amusement of Eden Crow. I saw her mimic 'madman' by twirling a finger about her head, but the girl refused to be drawn into some sort of complicit dismissal of my story. She still looked at me intently, scrutinising my every feature. Then she did a very peculiar thing, she put her hand in the jar, drew out a peppermint and put it in her own mouth. I smiled. She laughed too, covering her mouth, only Eden Crow refused to join in our mirth. Sensing the increasing annoyance of my girlfriend I paid up and left the sweet shop, but not without promising to return.

'Oh yes, please do call again – bye!'

I closed the door, the bell merrily sounding our farewell as Eden Crow whispered to me, 'You made a right bloody fool of yourself there.'

Down by the Riverside

There is so much about this place where now I find myself living that I do not know. It's hard to get a fix on it all. I try to sort out and rationalise my thoughts, present them in a coherent order, whereby the syntax helps to clarify and orchestrate what it is that I feel needs to be said, but instead, I ramble. A hundred thoughts, a thousand possible ways of explaining myself all seem to cram into my head at once as I try to elucidate something about myself or where I live or the people that I have found to be in some way associated with my life. So little is happening, but so much demands to be said about this tiny section of life that is in a sense my life. What is worse is that I do not really want to write this story. I still entertain hopes of writing again of the Man. I see now clearly his stepping off on some platform of the central lowlands, being bewildered by the sheer number of people, the cityscape and the incessant traffic. A man lost, lost unto himself, but not despairing, savouring all that lies before, incomprehensible and simply given as it is. The Man is lost, but takes delight in lostness.

I knew that this town had a river, a reasonably famous river in fact as far as history is concerned. For example, the Vikings came up this river, braving the salt-spray of the whale-road, and took over the original settlement of Romano-Britons and Angles to create an important trading centre of the northern world. Another story of interest concerns a Saxon king who visited after England had been to some extent consolidated, and arrived by river. The people massed on the bridge to greet this king only for the bridge to break, throwing the spectators into the water, not a few drowning – so much for kings. So much too for my knowledge of this river, nothing more could I add to these mere anecdotes till Eden Crow took me by the hand and led me along the towpath. She had a rather baffling tale to tell me. At the time, I didn't know what to make of it or even if it was true, but assuredly it was a truth, for others later also affirmed something of the particulars of the events surrounding the ferryman.

We had stopped by some petty moorings. Eden Crow pulled at her bottom lip, looking deeply pensive, her gaze focussed upon the water, but her words were directed at me.

'You like stories, don't you? Something I noticed about you right from the start – stories, tales, tittle-tattle and the like…Well, don't you?'

'Oh, aye.'

'Aye, well, have you heard any of the tales about the ferryman who used to work here?'

'Ferryman! But, there's three bridges at least not counting the railway.'

'Happen. So you haven't heard aught?'

'Nay. No, don't think so.'

Eden Crow walked over to a bench. This bench had been erected to the memory of the boatman, put up by the council after his suicide as a commemoration of his life. It was some proof at least that some such ferryman had existed. It was a good solid job, sturdy and workmanlike. We sat on the bench, Eden Crow put her head on my shoulder and told me something of the mystery of the ferryman.

'I was only young at the time, but anyway we all thought he was mad, sometimes we even threw stones at him, but the tourists loved him, specially Americans, then this German gaje came along and stopped for a while, saying how the ferryman had discovered the 'way' and all that tosh. There were even a couple of appearances on television for foreign travel programmes and all the guides mentioned him.' Eden Crow raked her throat and spat into the water. 'We all thought it a load of bollox. I mean it's fucking stupid, innit? What's the point of getting into a leaky old rowing boat and being ferried across for a fiver or what have you, when you can cross over by the bridge and pay nowt; tourist crap.'

Eden Crow stopped talking a while. I offered her a peppermint cream, we stuffed them in our gobs and sucked on them for a while, happy just to let the river flow by. I did though want to hear more and instinctively knew that the story as yet wasn't over.

'Barking mad – he ended up barking mad. Now, there's two stories of what happened or, rather, he tells two different stories and there's other rumours besides. Anyway, one story goes something like how late one night this man stepped out of the mist and made him ferry him over the river. The man returns later with a dead man and they both go across the river, but on reaching the other side, the dead man kills the other man who falls back into the boat. The murderer runs off and the ferryman loses his boat.

'The second story has it that a ghost steps out of the mist and is ferried across. He comes back with someone else and the ghost takes the man across the river. On reaching the other side, the man runs off, then a river spirit enters the boat, lights two candles and drifts away downstream.

'Barking mad as I say. They took him away, going crazy, killed a pigeon and tried to shove it down his throat, trying to make himself immortal like Dracula… But the thing is, every time it's misty, oh, I forgot to say the river and whole vale were filled with mist, anyway, every time it's misty it's a bit creepy down here and some folk crack on that they've seen a ghost or two here-by. No one is too sure which ghost though, including the ghost of the ferryman, 'cos he topped his self one night in Bootham Car Park Hospital – hung himself by strips of bedding. What you reckon to that?'

'Great story.'

'It's not a story!' Eden Crow angrily took her head from my shoulder and stood up. She paced about, agitated. She was angry. She was going to say more, but suddenly she stopped, smiled and offered me her hand. She was such a professional was Eden Crow. We stood, popped another peppermint cream into our mouths and proceeded further down the towpath.

'Come on, lover boy, there's a great spot for lunch further down.'

We strolled arm in arm. The afternoon was bright, daffodil yellow sun and mute blue skies. I though saw only strange greens and smudge-browns in the flags of sedge by the river, but even that proved beautiful to me. I was in love. I couldn't stop thinking about the young girl in the sweet shop.

Stand and Deliver

Eden Crow said she saw a flash of grey squirrel skirting up the twisted trunk of a bank willow, but I knew whom I saw. I even heard his laughter too. But it was not funny. There was this dead man by his foldaway bicycle. There was blood, some seeping of stomach-fluids from where the arrows pinned his gut, his clothes lay rifled and a torn wallet lay cast upon the bank side.

'Come away, chuck,' said Eden Crow, pulling against me as I began to lower myself down to the corpse. 'You can't help him – don't get involved. Fucking anarchists again; the third this month and the police are eager to stick it on someone, before the whole fucking lot blows.'

I tried to pull against her, but Eden Crow easily managed to pull me up; my time away has stripped my frame of a third of its calcium content at least, besides I was never anyone's idea of a hunk even when in rude health. Also, the beatings of the step-dada have left a mark on me. I am an instinctual coward. Thank the sweet Lord God of Israel for Eden Crow. She took me by the hand, led me away to this beer-garden by the river's edge where we partook of a particularly fine Rhine wine and a robust lunch of lightly smoked eel and pickled herring in dill-cream sauce. The site was superb: a small roundhouse of a restaurant/café/beer-house that could not fail to remind me of the time I spent in Bremen amongst some very kind folk.

'Eden Crow.' I gazed into her warm brown eyes, flecked with green, it was a face that could inspire depravities as easily as tender love.

'What?'

I topped up her wine glass afore venturing my question, 'Whom do you consider to be the most hospitable people in Europe?'

'Irish – Scots – well, providing you're not English.'

'Not a chance, not even close. Their tourist smile is all pounds, shillings and pence. Try again.'

Eden Crow took a long sip from her drink, puzzled it over one more time and gave me an answer I could not refute.

'Well, I briefly shared digs with a Czech nanny and got invited back one Easter and they were lovely and kind to me, but I couldn't speak a damn word of Czech – drove you bloody crazy trying to match sounds to letters. But, they were a right good crack – generous to a fault, generous till you grew ashamed on your own folk. Any road, why do you ask?'

'Well, you could be right, as I haven't been there and just as long as you're not Roma, Sinte or Kallomanush... Anyway, to get back to what I was thinking about, there was a time when I worked in a hostel in Ireland – ran away from it all, not long before I found the way into the sock... So, oh yes, I met a lot of Germans and found them good company, wrote to a few. Then one time, just before I really lost my bearings, I scratched some money together and made my way out to Bremen. There was a place there, a maze of tiny streets, full of interesting shops, cafes, pubs and the like, bit like the Shambles, but much more of it and less like a museum... But, I've lost the thread again. No, what I wanted to say is that these people I stayed with took me to this place in the park. It was the last days of summer and this beer-garden wasn't long for opening further into the season, perhaps those first few crisp days of autumn. But nonetheless, we would go and chat, drink beers whilst eating good simple fare. Those afternoons were sweet as a nut. I tried to pay my way, but these people would not hear of me dipping my hand into my pocket. They put me up at various places, each one of which I was fed to my gills and more; drinking like a fish and loving every minute of it. I had run out of luck, love and the will to live, my life petering slowly to a dull dismal closure. But, these people turned it round. Their genuine generosity and heartfelt hospitality warmed me to the core. When I left, they cooked me this special meal of various sausages, kale and belly-pork all washed down with beer and schnapps and I savoured each bite. The Germans, Germany – there was this time when these names loomed darkly afore my mind, unable to forget the strain of Roma…Kallomanush, if you will, that is in me…but now I hear these names and can only think of those happy times and wish these honest, hard-working and big-hearted people luck. These people have done something that I have consistently failed to achieve, that is to say, to crawl out from beneath the collapsed weight of the past-'

Eden Crow silenced me then. She had drained her glass with a gulp. She leant across the table. Her fingers gripped my thinning hair. Strongly she pulled my head towards her. She kissed me full on the lips. She almost bruised my mouth with the insistence of that kiss. Finally, she broke off. I poured another glass of wine each.

'You really are a pretentious little fucker.'

I laughed, savoured the joke, washed my lips with another libation of chill Rhine wine pale as straw-gold.

Walking back from our meal we stopped to pause awhile by the cordoned off area separating the crime scene from the park and towpath walk. A team of investigators was busily combing the area for clues, while some sort of forensic expert made a cursory investigation of the body, as a detective stood nervously by pulling miserably upon the strands of an inadequate moustache.

The afternoon was balmy.

Again I paused by the gaily coloured jars of the sweet shop, but fought the temptation to go in. A small boy with red scuffed sandals pushed against me, pressing his nose against the windowpane, eyeing the sweets eagerly. I offered to buy him a quarter of what he liked, but he smiled sadly and ran off. Eden Crow tugged on my arm and we wandered back. It was upon our return that I discovered that my wallet had been mislaid. These shifts in time have made me forgetful.

Eden Crow was marvellous about it all. Like a busy busy bee she rang round, cancelling cards and contacting my various banks. She was though somewhat annoyed as she had banked upon me providing funds for a taxi fare home, but as it turned out this proved less troublesome than it might. A polite tattoo of a knock and my bank manager strode in, his face brimful with apologetic smiles, evincing obvious concern for my wellbeing. Not only had he brought round a new wallet, one generously stuffed with notes and new cards, including a double premium platinum card, but kindly he also offered to drive Eden Crow home. Eden Crow politely accepted his offer and they departed, seemingly little put out by my minor misfortune.

The excellent meal of which I had partaken was making me drowsy, imbibing at luncheon inevitably had this effect on me, but I fought it as long as I could. I needed to have words with the jester, before matters spiralled out of hand.

A Further Disclosure

Of course, I fell asleep. I wandered briefly around the flat, trying to hunt down my inheritance, lay back on the bed and scanned the ceiling. I once came in from a drink and found the jester hanging, quite literally hanging, from the light bulb. It wasn't a cry for help, it wasn't a bid to end it all, the jester was merely perfecting his act. This is not to say that the jester was playing some kind of prank: acting up, a mere playing at suicide – no, the jester takes his role very seriously. If he'd got it wrong, then it would have all been over for my diminutive companion. Even now I am not sure what I would have thought or felt about such an outcome ought it to have transpired. This too is far from an idle question. There was this some kind of an uncle to me who had cancer and hung himself. I did not know this man, though it is possible that as a child, a mere bairn, I may have been in this person's company, say at some family function, but perhaps given my rather fractured ties to kith and kin it equally well could be the case that we had never met. Howsoever, the salient point is that I had no real contact with this relation, but he committed suicide and his death to me was an inspiration. His choosing of death said something important and brave. It always annoyed me when at school amongst my fellows I would hear of a suicide being dismissed as the 'coward's way out' – rubbish. Speaking as such a person who has in the past attempted suicide with a marked lack of success, I find small comfort and little truth in such banalities. Nay, I envied my uncle's strength of character in choosing whilst being of sound mind, and not so sound body, self-slaughter. He knew what his life was worth, to what quality of life amounted, and his death cut the measurement to a nicety. For myself I have never been too sure of the sums or even how to set up the equation.

Perhaps this latter problem may be laid to blame at another's feet, though as I ponder over what I am about to say, again there is this irksome nag that I am being too precious, reading far too much significance into events that pander only to the mundane. Perhaps, such a charge can be levied at what I write, but it does not belittle my conviction to try to convey the very peculiar details of what in the end occurred, concerning what finally could be said of the sum total of all of my experiences to date. Howbeit, afore I stray once more, and leap onto the back of one of my favourite hobby-horses, it is incumbent upon me to say something of my suspicions regarding this failure of accounting.

There was a teacher at my infant school whom for the purposes of possible libel suits I shall re-christen Ms MacThomais. I can lay my hand on my heart and say without any shred of dubitation that all in her class were afeared of her. She had all the charm of a concentration camp sadist without any ideological substance to justify her persecutions. Before I go much further let it be said that I was far from a model pupil, slow, confused and depressed.

The last attribute may strike you as being something of an oddity, if not a little contrived. But, it is true, I swear, even at that age, even afore the step-dada knocked the heart out of me for living, there were times when I felt strangely ill at ease with the world, distanced, as if I did not exist, all lacked savour, life was a burden, worse than trying to tie one's shoelaces. I was no man at all at that game of tying the shoes. My mother sat me down in her parents' house and shouted and swore at me as I tied my laces and my psyche in knots. The more she shouted, the more I fumbled like a fool and the worse the whole matter became. My grandmother, a widow, whom I dearly loved and though I blush a little to say it, loved me to distraction, being her little favourite, well my grandmother, who died a most long and protracted painful death, she spoke up for me, 'leave the lad, alone – don't cry, my precious, I shall tie them for you.'

My mother of course forbade any such solution. At times, she was just a fucking bitch. My apologies. I hate such words and its usage always strikes me as being heavily sexist, almost woman-hating, which I hope I am not. But, some of the tricks, the life that person gave to me, still sets me quaking with rage and deep-seated hurt. Vile words come tumbling, spilling like arterial blood from my mouth. The taste in my mouth this sickening, clotted hate.

So, I was not a gifted child. I was in fact as I later learnt dyslexic and perhaps the other thing too – dispraxic – but of that I cannot really be so sure. Imagine that it was no surprise when I questioned my teacher's answer at maths, for indeed my questioning merely confirmed everyone's opinion of me that I was the classroom clown. The question that I asked then still ties my mind in knots and I am no nearer to its answering, despite learning several conceptual strategies of dealing with the speculative thirst for such epistemological certainty.

Again, I am suffocating this discourse with undue wordiness and the bairn still needs washing. To put things simply, it reduces to a question about bricks; building bricks, plastic, chunky and reasonably brightly coloured. I had three green bricks and two yellow and the question was what did they make when you added them together. Everyone knew it was five, even I knew that, but I wasn't happy about it. So, I did the logical thing and asked why it was, is and shall be the case that $3 + 2 = 5$. Of course, I did not put this so formally at the time, I just said, 'Why?'

The teacher was furious with me, called me all the names fit and suitable for a class of six year olds to hear whilst leaving it in no doubt whatsoever that I was a born fool. But I wasn't and I wanted to know, 'Why?' She took me through it again and again, even with different colours, but she never answered me. I could count bricks of infinite colours throughout infinity and still end up with the same answer and not know why. But, one thing I did know after being slapped and stood in a corner, I knew that Ms MacThomais did not know, 'Why?' either.

Since those times, I have always distrusted sums. I have never for one moment understood what is number, what it is that mathematicians, in particular, pure maths specialists, number theorists and the like, do. It frightens me. I think, perhaps people like these would have been better suited to the Crions' purposes – they wouldn't have made the arse of it that I did. They could have learnt and been exposed to such wonders too. I am afraid after rescuing me from that crevice they were very disappointed with their find. There was a time when I entertained fantasies that I would fall in love with a mathematician who could have explained to me throughout the drear nights of winter just what numbers, equations, relations, imaginary constructs were really about. I would have loved that, to have fallen in love with someone who finally understood something about the aesthetic mathematical niceties of the universe. It is over. I shall never understand. The best I can do now is sometimes just for the damn hell of it to sit down and give myself a page of real hard sums. Sometimes that can help and be a small comfort to me.

The Police are Called

Sirens woke me, but in all honesty I was somewhat awake sometime afore I heard the whine of emergency vehicles approaching. It was the jester, up to his usual tricks, sat atop my forehead letting his feet dangle over my eyes, drumming his heels against the lids from time to time, not harshly or even maliciously, just a little bored. Annoying as such a habit was, the jester did in a way have a point. My writing I had indeed neglected of late and I could not in all honesty remember the last time I met up with my fellows from the writers' club. Barely, could I recollect their names or faces; some indistinct sense perception lacking a frame of reference – can't be helped. My time spent away has conditioned me to accept that friends, acquaintances, no matter how close or necessary, are doomed to pass away. Certainly, that was the case with Grolk. None were closer than Grolk and myself, save perhaps gay couples in long term relationships. There was never any question of homosexuality neither latent nor manifest. It is hard for some people to accept such things now when they are related details of close male friendships. There is always the knowing glance, the nudge-nudge/wink-wink syndrome, which is a shame, for friendships can be a powerful source of joy and comfort in the world that does not need the added savour of any kind of sexual attraction. I remember from my reading of Kierkegaard, many years ago, that friendship to him was a source of anxiety directly pertaining to the nature of human existence. That poor lonely hunchback-hearted neurotic has ever been an inspiration to me, though I no longer have any such aspirations towards a life of faith. I do though feel sure that Kierkegaard would have fully comprehended the depth of my friendship with Grolk, and perhaps also, Kierkegaard would have achieved a better understanding of Grolk, for no matter the love I bore for him I found him to be a perplexing enigma, defying easy association or consideration. Though perhaps not…who can tell? Whenever I think upon those times playing travel chess upon the hump of the middle toe night after long night with Grolk, my thoughts twist and turn with myriad possibilities, perhapses and modalities. Sometimes I close my eyes and sense anew my surprise at finding another person traversing the hot, humid wilderness of the sock. Faint light filtered through the weft and weave of the wool, I glanced up from my humble meal to see staggering through the gloom a short, fat swarthy male whose hair was nothing but a wild, matted tangle, unkempt and untamed, impossible to determine in parts what was beard and what was the hair of the head. Never before nor since have I encountered someone so hirsute – Grolk seemed more ursine than human and this impression was not only gleaned from his hairiness, but also from his stumbling gait, as if the upright position was not entirely familiar or suited to his person. Grolk also had a habit of muttering lowly; his English masked by strange gutturals of his native tongue, not that he ever specified what was his mother tongue and I never had the audacity to ask, feeling that some hidden secret, some part of his tortured past would leak out into the present and spoil our special friendship, founded as it was upon mutual indifference. Grolk – I feel like growling when I recite his name. I feel like swaying like a bear. Mostly though, I feel like some gentle weeping and falling to my knees to offer a heartfelt prayer.

You on my case, was the first thing that the Grolk said to me. Of course, he could not accept my protestations that, far from being on his case, I had never been on anyone's case and would not dream of being so presumptuous as to enter such a relationship with a complete stranger. The Grolk did not like my answer, but more than this he resented the implication that he was unknown, that I had not recognised him – he, the great Grolk. It is fair to say that for quite some time I viewed my new-found companion as being something of a lunatic, suffering not only paranoia, but also such a person as entertained delusions of grandeur to no small degree. However, I was wrong on both counts, though I never discovered as to what particular degree of fame Grolk pertained. Certainly, I can say without any exaggeration that he was the greatest chess player that I had ever come across. In my youth I had avidly studied chess, considering it to be an avenue of pure escapism, where warfare could be conducted to the ultimate degree without any sad loss of life, injury or deep psychological damage. Such was my naivety, howbeit, for many years I entertained such beliefs and played and studied assiduously, meeting players from up and down the country and later touring the foreign circuits. During this time I myself never suffered any great harm, but it was plain upon first playing chess that Grolk had sustained great psychological damage by his utter and complete devotion to some chequered squares and curiously carved knickknacks. Grolk could be overwhelmingly generous in one game, playing a fast aggressive king's gambit, allowing me myriad possibilities for counterattacks, whilst the very next game, despite my losing, Grolk would give nothing away and I would struggle not to capitulate in less than a dozen moves. He was also a tyrant when it came to the post-mortem, endlessly going over alternatives, possibilities that left nothing unturned: strong, weak, interesting or suicidal moves. He was relentless. I would wish to be asleep, innocently dreaming, but long into the night, the gruff voice of Grolk would grind on, till I was near weeping with exhaustion. I suppose in his own way Grolk was alarmingly giving, giving me all that he had, all that he had left, but I failed to realise any of this till it was too late. Foresight is a perfect science. It is no science at all, nothing but an empty cliché. However, even resorting to such an empty phrase helps me to reconsider what happened, those long and protracted silences that welled up between us. His favourite place to indulge in his off moods was at the end of the second smallest toe, clinging to the rim of the nail, burying his head against the coarse wool sock, crying, hiding his tears, struggling to contain the shudders of remorse that shook his frame. There was nothing that I could do for him. Other glib phrases come to mind, for example, it is good to talk or a problem shared is a problem halved. I am no longer sure if such sayings are still current nor do I particularly care. They are no use. Talk never cured anyone least of all the Grolk with his fierce analytical mind and his naked contempt for fools. I did though try to get help, of that I am certain, though ultimately only I was rescued. But I found a way out. I left the Grolk, but my intentions were at least for a time honourable.

Under Siege

'Do please have a word with him,' Mrs Aleppo implored.

The siren but not quite the sirens woke me. The jester had a hand in the waking of me, and not just this too. Even then, afore I understood matters more thoroughly, I had this suspicion that the jester was responsible for many of those disturbing incidents. Nothing of course can be proved, but proof is not always the most damning factor. I can remember having been intrigued when young, by knowing that something is the case without the ability to prove what I contended does in fact appertain in the world. There was this really annoying little shit in my class who fancied himself as something of an armchair philosopher. He could not put together a conceptual argument to save his soul. He did though excel in filibustering and pointless gainsaying. His favourite ruse was to tag 'prove it' as a retort to anything that others ventured or suggested as being true. One occasion in particular infuriated me when he challenged my belief that the world was not flat, but rather like a lopsided egg by simply saying, 'Prove it!' Of course, I could prove no such thing, though for a while I vainly tried. Nothing could be substantiated, for no statement was impervious to his demand for me to prove the matter. I became quite mad, alarmingly so, venting my frustration and anger by a wild headbutting incident and kick to the knees. I hated myself, and though it sounds barely credible, my self-loathing afterwards was harder to deal with than being suspended from school and thereafter interviewed by a child psychiatrist. Years later I read with some interest Dr Khan's reports concerning those troublesome years, but I am not sure if anything ultimately depended upon his analysis. Neither am I convinced that his intervention then cured me of my violent outbursts. The simple fact of the matter was that I changed both then and since. I would cringe now if I had to walk into a room containing my former peers or meet with people from my comprehensive, for I would not only see my other self through their eyes, but in so doing would re-acquaint myself with the disturbed, alienated and dangerous creature that I was. To me that other person died long ago and I am not just being metaphorical here, for the time-shift, for when I was rescued from the sock and later returned to the old country, my time and this earth's time grew estranged. I can remember the Grolk trying to explain something about this phenomenon, but I didn't really understand it. A person in a fast spacecraft leaves earth. He travels for ten years, but upon his return he finds that he has been away from earth for twenty-six years… That was how the mighty-hearted Grolk would begin, thereafter he would explain in quite copious detail to me, the whys and wherefores of it all and I would have to confess my ignorance to his bewildered and agonised dismay. Indeed, once he became so vexed at my stupidity that he squeezed the queen's head and crown from the rest of the figure, then shattered the skull into fragments by grinding the head with his heel, muttering madly all the while. Thereafter, we had to play chess with a diminished set. The decapitated queen was like some Cain-like mark, a blemish of utter stupidity.

He cried then. For hours the Grolk was inconsolable and I did not have to be some sort of amateur psychiatrist to guess that deeper troubles were afflicting the Grolk than the violence done to the figurine. He never told me though, despite all my entreaties. Deep-seated unease and anxiety remained forever trapped inside and Grolk took his secrets to the grave. I do not think that it was a lack of trust that held Grolk back, after all he freely masturbated in front of me, no, I think that the problem was more organic, something structurally had gone wrong with so much of his mental faculties. I used to find him, gripping the nail's edge, screaming into the dark, 'why do I forget – why no memory?'

In the end you may believe that it was the blanks in Grolk's life that drove him to it…Perhaps, if he had just remembered a little of what he had done, then he could have found a way of coping. The not knowing was what brought him undone. But, then again, I never really understood the Grolk. It's impossible, certainly now, to say what happened, let alone venture an opinion as to why events unfolded as they did to the dismay and distress of two good friends. Aye, maybe that, maybe in the end that is all that I can say, that we were friends, at least for a time.

Hostage

'He's your friend. He needs your help. Talk to him.' Mrs Aleppo took me by the hand, pulling me out of bed and towards my open doorway. The jester was screeching harsh brays of laughter. There were sirens sounding all around. It was time to do something.

I still do not know if I did something or not. Weighing up the evidence it certainly seems the case that something was done. I could not do nothing. Yet, for all that I did, for all those weary weeks that I trekked back up the leg, reaching the mounds of the posterior, I would have been just as effective merely staying put. Intention...counts for nothing.

There was this time...actually, I believe that I am misrepresenting the facts once more...there were times when I asked hugely pompous and preposterous questions such as: 'What is my destiny?' or 'What does this age demand of me? or 'What role has history assigned for me to play?' I wince with shame now, but back then I took these questions very seriously indeed. I would brood, skulking away to my room or hiding in the cubby hole under the stairs, hoping never to be discovered – that dark, dank place was some refuge and comfort to me, when things were going awful hard with the step-dada and myself or even again mother and me were hardly...oh why bother going into all that now...Going away, travelling out of it and then in a sense coming back is what has done it to me. That going away and looking back watching the blue planet dwindle to a marble in mini-seconds then disappear has entirely knocked those kind of questions out of me. All I wish for now is some quiet time to put together something or other in a literary way, not so as to leave anything behind to history or to map my times or anything else like that, but merely for some benign kind of amusement. It doesn't seem too much to be asking for really, and the others of the group seem to be of a like mind, not that I can remember when it was that I last talked to them and as the days grow, loom and go I cannot really believe that these other writers exist, though the girl, I think there was such a person, woman really, whom I felt a little bit of affinity with, but then again this could be explained by my lack of a sexual life at all; this lack is something I wish to address, for it leads me so foolishly to lust after unattainable relationships. In some ways, this idea of a state registered girlfriend is no bad thing really when the only other option is to find someone to strike up a meaningful relationship with...but, I still have these wild hopes, even now I can but think of the beautiful seller of old fashioned sweets and the shy smile twittering at her lips as she dished out those peppermint creams, sneaking in at least one extra mint. This person I can be truly in lust with, example, while coming round from the drumming on my eyes by the jester, afore being dragged across the floor by Mrs Aleppo, I, in a semi-conscious state, was fully fantasising about making love to the sweet woman, stooping to my knees to declare my heart's desire. I knew I was dreaming, but I was anxious nonetheless. The jester was at waking me and I was afeared that the dream would end before receiving my reply. The fear is familiar. There is nothing new to add here.

Except, and this is the thing that keeps me thinking, as I climbed the shank, my heart beating fit to burst, intent on securing rescue, I picture myself...I saw myself, looking down on me or from the side, sometimes too in heroic close-up as I saved the Grolk...I saw myself through my unknown beloved's eyes. I was her hero and I let her down.

This is what really hurts, not my failing of the Grolk, that lone pervert, but cruelly disappointing a love unknown.

Endgame

'They're shooting! They're shooting!' Mrs Aleppo screamed, and for a while I just stood around waiting.

Truth to tell I do not know how long I waited. Those final leagues traversing the upper thigh, scaling the pockmarked face of the posterior really took it out of me. My breath came in huge racking sobs. I felt sick, dizzy and unable to go on. By a dark clump of hair I lay down and wept.

To be honest I no longer thought of Grolk then. I waited till the stars came out, gazed up in wonder, in some strange altered state of consciousness: wonder, surprise and deep seated fear – all contrived to distract all thoughts away from Grolk. I was free. I was going to die, out there in the cold, without shelter, without any hope. But, the main thing that I was free from was the onus of responsibility. I had scaled those heights in search of help. Assistance was still needed, craved almost, but now it was only a self-reflective reflex – I stood in need of being rescued.

Perhaps, I was dreaming. I was dreaming, away with the fairies, hallucinating without a shadow of dubition, but it was all so clear and real. What I took to be a shooting star fell towards me, burning brightly in the soft velvet night. I pinched myself, I made a wish, then jumped and leapt in wild exhilarated gyres, circling through the air. I was alive, never had I felt my own existence so immediately. Bright lights all around, a low insistent humming growing louder like thuds of blood in the head, dancing, jumping, shouting and I passed out.

Present and Correct

Eden Crow found me. She assured me that I was in a state of shock. There were these certain and soothfast indelible signs, but I was not so sure. However, Eden Crow is a professional of that I am mostly certain.

Carefully, she manhandled me outside where someone from the fire department ticked our names off on an electoral roll. I stood smiling, holding the hand of my state-registered girlfriend. A couple from one of the upper landings found themselves not on the list. This was rather unfortunate as they had only two minutes in which to gather up their belongings and vacate Mrs Aleppo's lodging house. This I felt was rather mean; they had nowhere else to go and what harm were they doing by staying there? Eden Crow said not to worry, that I was in shock, what with the shooting of my friend by the Police Special Arms Unit and Response Team. I cried then, for I realised that I had lost another companion in this life, even though I was not too sure concerning who had been killed.

'Don't tell me that…that the wee rent-boy died?' I said, forgetting the name of the prostitute with a collapsed arsehole.

'I won't then,' said Eden Crow, most definitely somewhat peevishly. I stood looking at my feet, shuffling in the back yard with the other guests waiting to be allowed back inside after the Scene of Crime Officers had finished. I was at a loss. Thankfully, Eden Crow relented and told me something of what was going on, 'That crazy fucker playing all them Indian chants kidnapped an American tourist, demanded the Black Hills back – they shot him dead five minutes ago.'

I felt sad, 'Sorry, I didn't know he was my friend.'

'Neither did I, that Aleppo woman said you were always knocking on his door – stupid cow.' Eden Crow spat on the cobbles, rubbed the phlegm into the dirt. Suddenly, she grabbed me, held me tightly to her breast. Her voice came out strained as if fighting off some great emotion, 'You could have been killed…shot…she wanted you to mediate…dead – where would I be then?'

I thought of Grolk as she held me in her arms and sobbed a little. She was right. There was nothing I could say.

Bathtime

Eden Crow assured me that I was traumatised. It could have been the case that I was in such a mental and physical state, certainly I never meant to have shat myself, most embarrassing, something that had never befallen me afore, though once when young I was sick in the bed after drinking two bottles of cider and downing several of my mother's distalagesics, yet another botched suicide attempt to chalk up along with the rest, but as for being in something of a trauma that was something I felt that I ought to gainsay, for after all I have always felt this way, or at least, I have felt this way after ceasing to love my mother up and down the central heating, so it seems somewhat incongruous to suggest that I was suddenly traumatised when I could not discern any qualitative difference atween my former or latter states of self-awareness, though I freely admit that it could be the case that self-awareness or indeed self-assessment of self-awareness is neither necessary nor sufficient for it to be a true statement that a given person is suffering a trauma. Either way I was most grateful to Eden Crow for bathing me.

Truth is it was a little embarrassing to be naked in front of one's girlfriend at such a time. She bade me bend over and touch the taps as she sprayed my arsehole and nether regions with a really quite powerful shower. In my time away it has been something that I have noticed from time to time, how far shower technology has progressed. In the old days of being stuck in digs the shower rarely worked well, dribbling either excessively hot or cold. Worse, they had been seldom clean; the whole area gunged up with scale, mashed-up dregs and spelks of soap and variously coloured pubic hair. Such places stank and it was impossible to have felt cleansed after endeavouring to shower in those supposed bathrooms.

Now though, I encounter showers everywhere that send all sorts of powerful jets of perfectly controllable spray over any desired area of the body. It is possible in certain showers to come out not only thoroughly cleansed but also to a degree massaged and stimulated by the hydro-dynamics of the bathroom's engineering.

The pinprick jets of hot water soon made short work of the shit stuck to my body hair and arse crevice. Eden Crow, after satisfying herself with her handiwork, bade me to take a bath too while she dealt with the soiled clothes.

It was while taking my bath that something strange befell me again. I lay back in the tub, soaping my arms or pugwashing, making sure all was clean in the plumbing department, when a small, brown man entered the bathroom too. He ignored my protestations that I was using the facilities and proceeded to strip quite naked and make full use of the latrine. He defecated protractedly and quite noisily, thereafter wiping his anus and washing his hands, finishing finally by resuming a clothed state. This I suppose was quite normal, but not his complete ignoring of me as he passed back out of the door.

However, what was most abnormal was that this small, brown man was almost quite hairless, as hairless as Gandhi, but unlike Gandhi or so I presume, this person had an unblemished stomach. The intruder had come equipped into the world seemingly without such a thing as a belly button.

Later, when I tried to convey all this to Eden Crow, she but dismissed it as mere fantasy, brought on, no doubt, by my earlier ordeal. This saddened me greatly. It is always such a cheap and superficially easy way to dismiss people and what they say, merely by subsuming the phenomenon under the heading of insanity. The weakest point with such an endeavour is to ask why must it be supposed that even if it is the case that a person is suffering from a mental illness, then, a priori, what is said has to be automatically dismissed as being not instantiated in the world. Of course, I did not try to explain my deep-rooted objection to Eden Crow. She had enough on her plate just then. And, after all, she had done a really splendid job of cleaning me up.

For the first time in many years, I felt really clean, shriven almost. When I walked back into my room Eden Crow had prepared for me a light tea upon a small tray, so that I could have some sustenance whilst being safely tucked up in bed. Eden Crow stroked my cheek almost lovingly. She wiped the dribble of gravy from my chin.

I said this small quiet thank you.

She left.

Visitors

I awoke. I did that. Gingerly, I reached down and gave my testicles something of a scratch, thereafter rearranging my willy so that it hung on the left – the sinister side, not that I am superstitious. I took the opportunity then to have a rather loud, joyous, if not to say raucous, long and heartfelt fart. Truly, something of a relief. I sniffed in bravely, snuck my nose under the covers and savoured not an unpleasant smell. Returning my head to the surface and opening my eyes for the first time since rousing myself from slumber, I was rather surprised to find that my room seemed swelled with people.

The jester was some sort of raving compere introducing everyone as if they were a variety act; apparently, I knew these people. To be honest, I am unsure as to proper names, but no matter, these visitors were writers. There was one fellow who insisted that he was Irish, and was writing a book in the style of Flann O' Brien – I believe his name to have been Patrick Thistle. There was another, a rather pretty woman, quite beautiful in fact with long luscious ebony hair that reminded me of Snow White when she trails her tresses from the tower of Babel and is rescued by a flying carpet; her long black hair covering the sky, creating night – the old tales you can't beat them, infinitely rich and unfathomable. Was she called Judy? She was, perhaps, but it doesn't really matter, for other than leaving me a bunch of seedless Israeli black grapes that glistened like burst Palestinian eyes, she does not really enter into any further relation to my own particular time line thereafter, or so I believe. Could be wrong here, but I am almost certain sure that there was another who wrote short fiction something akin to Raymond Carver, but he did not spend too much time around my bedside, as he kept creeping out for a smoke, seemed painfully shy and I am convinced that we had not met before, though he swore on oath that he was an acquaintance of mine of quite some standing, indeed, friendship is so fickle.

The most puzzling guest was this wee baldy fellow with smooth brown skin who popped in and talked furiously with the jester for more than a few seconds before leaving. This person I had known before, but had since forgotten. At least, this is my surmise, which well may be prone to irretrievable errors.

'When do you think you shall be well again – able to contribute to the mag?' It was the pretty woman and I wished that I could have answered her or even to be sure of her name. She clasped my hand in a manner that I am sure Eden Crow would have found irksome, trespassing no doubt upon her natural rights and expectations as my official girlfriend. She clasped my hand, brushed her lips against my lips and walked away.

'Be seeing you now,' said the sad wee Irish fart from Scunthorpe, backing quickly out of the door in obvious relief.

The other writer came back then, smiling, punching my shoulder, giving me a playful bear-hug, afore remembering to pocket his matches and go. I do hope that these people were indeed my friends whom I had known to some degree or otherwise the whole performance would have to be relegated as being somewhat arbitrary and pointless. A small kindness, a network of friends, or some charade to plague my remaining time – sadly, at that time I could not have cared too deeply which was the case, despite following Kierkegaard in believing in the importance of friendship as a factor of existence. I suppose I was contradicting myself again, but I no longer cared one way or the other. I dressed and left.

These visitors, they were unlike the other ones; the ones that rescued me from that old hairy arse and spirited me away through a wormhole to some other galaxy. Even though I was unsure about the nature of friendship and my relations with these erstwhile companions of the pen, they were in no way as foreign to my experience of what is instantiated in the world, as those other visitors from that far-away galaxy.

I have never been a fan of science fiction.

If I had been a fan of science fiction, perhaps, it would not have come as so much of a surprise to me to learn that these rescuers were so chemically alien to me. So much of our life here on earth is based on carbon and its subsequent relationship to oxygen, but on that far away planet, there were these sentient beings that had evolved from silicon-based primitive life-forms, which I found as fascinating as they found it irksome to keep me in a special ward that supported oxygen life-forms, such as the human being, the dodo and lesser red-striped pipperelle. They made such a fuss as they donned their gowns and masks and clonked about in their surgical clogs as they performed their various tests upon me, so much so, in fact, that I wondered why they bothered and even on certain occasions almost asked this very question, though, ultimately, I did not, fearing that such a request for enlightenment might be construed as being a little rude, granted that I was their guest; they who had so deftly rescued me in time too, so I remained mumchanced and in complete ignorance.

On leaving my room I found myself walking, quite by chance, though perhaps acting on some hidden whim or desire, to that sweet shop on the corner, the one that so reminded me of those dreams I had when but a bairn and living in fear and loathing of my life. Sweet shop, a grand place to find oneself walking to on a fine summer's day after illness, no doubt. I may also have been still a little traumatised, but it matters not in the long run I suppose, and after all, when all is said and done, who am I to judge.

I walked in. The shop-bell rang out. I waited, this warm and eager smile spreading about my face. She came.

The jester, he tells me that he is bored with all of this, that to him it is a waste, that no one is at all interested, that he once had high hopes of me, that I would become someone of importance, that I am throwing it all away, that can I not remember all those lonely nights of toil trying to put something together, those long nights when my whole head ached with ideas, and finally, that it is now too late. I ignored the jester. I stood by a jar of Harry Baggots' Witches' Fireballs.

'It's you again,' she said, and smiled, and a warm tingle spread about my body, bringing colour to my cheeks. In the past such a sensation would have left me tongue-tied and awkward, but now I savoured such elation and its hidden, underlying emotion. There was no point in pretending to myself; I was in love with this pretty young woman.

'Would you like a quarter of Baggots?' Her voice was thin and strained, a voice that had hungered and grown crippled with want. Her frame seemed thin and stretched, stunted through poor diet: such a face, such features now no longer so scarce – rickets found again in some of the drug-dealer estates across the river. There have been times when I have seen the hungry and homeless, the raped and the dispossessed on the news or covered by special in-depth documentaries and have just broken down and cried. I saw a woman once, mad and confused, baited by a crowd and not all of them bairns. I have seen small sparrow-thin children, begging and thieving and fending for themselves, and have wept, raged and folded inwards inside, incapable of doing anything but feel torn apart by the wretchedness of it all. It was such horrors that drew me to live in the sock, to avoid my fellow man, to shut out the world and its woes and there no doubt would I have remained, but for the coming of Grolk who brought his own peculiar brand of miseries with which to haunt our days lost in the darks folds of a 40% natural cotton and 60% polyester mix.

The girl took the jar from my hands and dished out a quarter. She passed them over to me and I paid. It all should have remained like that, but she told me in no uncertain terms that it was late and that she would be shutting the shop soon. I don't know why this news came as such a shock to me, perhaps I was thinking of that shop of long ago where the old man would stay open late in the night desperate to earn his pittance, to save up for his early retirement far away at some warden-run complex by the sea. Perhaps too, it called to mind that time was still flowing despite my best unintentional efforts to cheat on my own mortality. More probably, it was the thought that soon I would have to leave, to return to a place where tragedy had occurred that day or at least the day before. I felt the old unease, I savoured that ache in the heart that would trouble me when the going home bell would sound at the primary school there with the meaning that I must be a-going home to the house of mother and the step-dada. Some emotions, sensations, have a habit of lying dormant but of never truly leaving you. When at the boarding house there I do chance to hear arguments, possibly just the raising of voices through mirth and high spirits, my heart does beat all the more quickly, my body boils with sweat and fear is this sour queer taste on the tongue.

She rescued me.

'If you are not in a hurry you could stop for a bit of tea, if you like?'

I smiled, nodded and smiled. The beautiful thin girl shut and locked the door behind me, before leading me through the shop to the living quarters. Her mother eyed me suspiciously, but the girl did not care. She squeezed my hand, sat me by the fire and helped to lay the table for tea, setting an extra place for me.

A fine meal of boiled tripe and onions was made and my spirits lightened. I was served a slice of angel cake with a large mug of tea and I felt curiously that I belonged there living amidst such people. The old lady, the mother, took a chair by the fire and listened to a wireless while the two of us retired to the kitchen to fettle the pots. It was decided that I washed while the girl dried, seeing as I had no knowledge of where the dried items were to be put – small, rational practicalities. There was a quiet order to this household and the love the girl had for the mother was both obvious and heartfelt. We played several hands of cards, and dominoes too, for some hours afterwards. The old lady thereafter begged to be excused, ambling slowly up the small narrow stairs at the back to her room. The girl smiled at me then, bade me to sit by her on the settee, and I most gladly complied. We sat there holding hands, her pale, pinched face resting on my shoulder, her breath warm, softly blowing against my breast, neck and shoulder. I wanted to kiss her, take her in my hands and confess to her all my horrible truths, so that we could begin again, but it was she who first told to me the type of secret that people keep, twisted in the hidden spirals of the brain; taking off her clothes, removing her blouse, showing me the scars, showing me the crudely carved scrawl that spelt, 'Look no breasts,' this young girl explained to me a little of her past.

She told me of how for a time she was a demi-rep, a prison punk, earning, saving, keeping a roof above her and her mother's head, and hoping to put enough money by for a future. She told me how once a psychopath with money enough for privileges cruelly abused her, cut off her breasts and left her for dead. It was the compensation, the insurance money that had bought the shop. She was naked now, a broken little human, with a broken little story, lain curled up in the arms of a man who loved but couldn't help her. These were the stories that I gave much thought to when living away. It was these stories that first made me suspect that the Crions were right.

She wanted children.

Perhaps I could help.

But I had to tell her something of that other woman.

And she did not believe me.

A Chance Meeting

It was early summer, but the evening seemed suddenly tired with light, as if the sun had given up trying to illuminate the earth. No doubt I was wrong, that the evening was as well lit and clear as any other, but my time beneath another sun many light years away meant that I was more than prone to errors of perception, that I was again structuring the spectrum differently. Gloomy browns, sad sedge reds, wan leached yellows enwrapped the gloaming with colours both oppressive and sombre. I walked for a time, feeling unable to return, pondering much upon my reckless tendency towards total honesty.

I had tried to explain that the breeding programme had not been devised at my suggestion or invitation. That my co-operation, my acquiescence and compliance with the Crions' plans arose out of a mixture of fear, obligation and the desire to please, to fit in with this new environment. There are some things that cannot be explained, this I have often found, and the limits of credibility and credulity are forever strangely in flux. It is nothing to see a spaceship manned by Americans cruising space and meeting alien folk who also talk American English – all this is perfectly plausible and entertaining. But the facts of the matter, these are far, far different and infinitely stranger. What happens when a language is not some spoken sound, but a touch, or that language is a series of signs that have nothing to do with how they are voiced – few Crions, in fact, actually articulate any sounds whatsoever these days. They are superfluous, confusing and given to producing shadows of ambiguities. The highest language amongst the Crions is electronic impulses – there is no longer any need for signs – just interactive stimuli and response.

When they gave me a plant, their only carbon form of life, when they modified and re-modified genetic data, growing something to bridge the gap between plant and human, nothing was ever said or discussed or even in a sense considered. There was no gap for thought between the need to do and things done.

There was no way to voice my unease. I lay in a cell, and there, feet rooted in the soil, was a plant, firm to the touch, smooth and warm, with certain cells aping human breasts, with certain cells grown specially to resemble the outer lips of the labia; and the sensation derived from active intercourse was not unpleasant. This was an experiment. I performed as willingly or not as any pink-eyed white rat. That is all there was to it. When the results came in, I was released as was my wish at the time. There is nothing more I can say, but walking away from that sweet shop my heart felt unduly heavy, and the great truth of the Crions never seemed so certain.

'There you are.' It was Eden Crow.

I was not so pleased to see her and my feelings seemed to be mutually reciprocated, judging by the tone of displeasure in her voice. I could no longer care. I walked on.

'Where you going? Just where the hell do you think you are going – talk to me!'

There was nothing I could really say, nothing I wanted to say, in fact, I was sick and tired of words; what use were they to me? I breathed in. I breathed out. Food and water in. Piss and shit out. I tried to walk on, but Eden Crow grabbed the scruff of my coat and pinned me, quite expertly, against the wall of a public house. This, quite frankly, startled me. I was unsure too as to my rights and Eden Crow's rights in this situation. Given my upbringing I have always looked upon with deep revulsion and anger husbands or partners who beat up women, but, sadly, and this must be acknowledged, grabbed and pinned there by Eden Crow I felt for the first time like lashing out. To call it a pure gut reaction, a fight or flight mode of behaviour may go some way as to explain this urge, but such knowledge does nothing to alleviate my sense of self-disgust, if not despair. I started babbling uncontrollably:-

'...seen lots of things you never have, spent twenty-five light years cooked up in an oxygen tent, fucking a chlorophyll woman, till she budded up with a hundred brown foetuses, turning brown in the sun, ripening to fall and drop to the ground or disperse out among the stars and set to drift by the coming annual solar winds, raising comet dust across heaven…'

I was still rambling as Eden Crow carefully, firmly, but gently steered me into a public house, sat me at a table in some far-shaded corner and ordered me a port and lemon for my nerves. I was in a bad way. Tears fell and rolled down my cheeks. There was this sudden ache twisting in my breast.

'Don't worry, pet, we'll have a drink or two, then take a cab when things settle down. But don't fret, we'll be safe and snug in the old Hearty Choke.'

There was sawdust on the floor and I suppose spit too, certainly there was no want of dog-ends and I wondered briefly about the fire hazard potential of such a public place. Eden Crow did not like the bar, she opened the door to the lounge and bade me to enter, and, forthwith, I complied. I was feeling very obedient again, sometimes I think just blindly obeying is some help and not a little consolation. Perhaps, all would have been easier if I had learnt to obey; to be honest I do think I tried for a while, but those sort of career opportunities were no longer available when I finally fled the home. Suffice to say Eden Crow guided me to a corner where I dried my eyes whilst I perused the menu. I fancied a hot beef sandwich in rich mustard and onion gravy. Eden Crow thought about going vegetarian, but settled instead for a giant Yorkshire pudding containing a large and tightly curled Cumberland sausage, topped to the brim with onion and horseradish gravy, plus a side serving of Belgian chips, salad and a stotty. This food brought back memories; I felt an unreasonable pride in being brought up a northerner – pathetic. Such feelings the Crions most despised, failing to comprehend such subtle differences between hairless upright apes. Eden Crow ordered the food.

A small brown man in an ill-fitting suit came in, wrinkled his nose, before turning about heel and walking out. This man had been seen before; I believe I have written about him. I was hungry, that is certain.

There was a strange party at a nearby table. The old lady spoke a very antiquated northern English, a man in his late thirties sounded like a music hall comic while his parents said very little and footed the bill. I wondered if that is what families were now. I wondered a great deal, for Eden Crow seemed quite engrossed at the bar talking to the landlord, asking for news about a riot, or was it a beating, some altercation or disturbance that didn't seem really to trouble me at all.

There was a Black man with grizzled white hair and a very good suit and he ate alone this meal of fish and chips.

I suppose I am naturally curious, something too which the Crions could not appreciate but only question as to its inherent value. This was their only hypocrisy, for why then did they abduct me?

They did not abduct me.

I was rescued.

Without the Crions I would be dead.

This is something that I can only regret.

I am ungrateful.

Selfish.

I.

Don't Play the Joker

The jester came in, stood by the open gas fire and warmed his thin tiny arse. Eden Crow was back, she ignored him and I tried my best to achieve the same level of natural indifference.

'You must be starving! When was your last square meal? And why did you leave the hostel – were you not happy there? Mrs Aleppo is going frantic.'

'I was at a sweet shop.'

'Yes we know all about that little episode – proud of yourself are you?'

I realised with some pain that I was entering an argument with my girlfriend, maugre that she is in fact nothing but a surrogate, a substitute – one may even say, a placebo partner, but this row hurt all the same. I was tired of argument.

'Hey, Eden Crow, want to hear a joke?'

'Joke…what sort of joke?'

'Well, it's more what the Crions find amusing-'

'No.'

'They find it really amusing that our top scientists find it no contradiction at all to be both a top scientist and believe such tosh as is written in the Bi-'

'I said, "No". There is practically a civil war outside: guns, bombs, bows and arrows, and you, like a prat, have been missing in the thick of it for seven days…I'm off to see what's happened to the grub.'

Eden Crow noisily pushed back the chair and sauntered to the bar. I noticed the way the barman looked at her. Eden Crow could handle herself.

Let's leave, the jester was talking to me. Come on, charvo, let's nash.

I regretted not remaining to sample the sandwich. It was something that I was looking forward to, for Eden Crow was right about one thing, I was indeed famished. Still, it was nice to be out once more in the fresh air. There were fire engines everywhere, that and the wail of sirens. At first, I did not see many signs of trouble. Then the jester pointed him out, lain as he had fallen, two ambulance men stood watching over him, not wasting time on resuscitation. It was hopeless, obviously, but we strode over, feeling it my duty to pay my last respects.

'Looks like we could use the eyes, most of the major organs but the heart – have dissection ready.' An ambulance man switched off his mobile phone and I felt sick. The young, beautiful prostitute with the piles was dead and there was a price on his body.

'Leave him alone,' I said and was ignored. I repeated my warning this time screaming and waving the special card my personal bank manager had given me.

'Take it easy,' said the one with the mobile.

'Look,' said the other, 'What has a whore killing got to do with you?'

'He was my friend.'

'Well, your friend would be still alive if he hadn't stolen a pitch – he broke the rules, chum,' said the other, while the other walked away to mutter into his mobile phone.

'I've got a card. I've got millions in the bank. Can pay for everything – just leave him alone.'

'There, there old lad…' Something scratched my arm.

The jester laughs quietly to himself. A siren wails. Everything is going to be all right. There is a young man dead on the pavement. The jester hides in my top pocket. My Uncle Salty was a good man.

Endgame

Mrs Aleppo holds my hand. I am awake. Eden Crow has resigned. I do not know if this was voluntary or not. My friend Patrick Thistle called today. Already he is working on a new book; this one he thinks will be his big breakthrough – starts with a right frumth. I tried to tell him about the man, but he said it didn't sound like a promising idea. I told him what the Crions told me: no one cares about earth, the universe is alive with life and no one can be bothered with this world and its bald apes – we are not a promising idea. Patrick Thistle just shook his head, said he'd already told me that the SF idea was a dead end. He could be right, but I fell asleep for a while then too tired to discuss anything further. Patrick Thistle is a writer.

Something else, he came in today, that brownish looking man, said, 'Aha/Ahair' or something like. He tried to hold me, to caress me, he was crying. I could not bear this noise. I think I killed him. It doesn't though really seem to matter too much here, apparently I have been given a sweet allowance, every Sunday. This Sunday I think I shall start with some peppermint creams, something like this anyway. It has been a long time since I have seen the jester. I am worried. I don't know what Uncle Salty would say. I have squandered my inheritance. I was better off back in the sock before the Crions rescued me.

Part Three

The Truth

My name is David James Keogh. I have my birth certificate in front of me. It declares that I was born on the thirtieth of May in 1965 at the Maternity Home in Scunthorpe. My sex is said to be that of a boy. My father is stated as being one Michael James Keogh. The more astute of you may wonder if the name James is a family name, one particularly used as a second name – such a person would be correct to wonder over this, as it is in fact the case. My mother is said to be one Carol Ann Keogh formerly Guntrip of 8 Westerdale Road, Scunthorpe. It is quite an old name, Guntrip, and one that arouses a little mirth. I think it is a beautiful and interesting name, clearly marked as being of Norwegian or Danish extraction – Gunnar's Trap/Stair, perhaps. Scunthorpe itself is clearly marked as being a Danelaw placename – a thorpe being a Scandinavian word for something akin to a hamlet. As for Keogh, no, enough - I shall return to Keogh later as it has a direct input to the discussion at hand, namely, writing, but please pardon me while I continue to examine my birth certificate. My father's occupation is that of a Steel Works Labourer. My father talks a great deal about the hard times he had working at the mills or the 'Works' as they used to be called in Scunthorpe. My Auntie Doreen says that he was only there six months and for the most time worked at mopping out the latrine   hard times indeed. I also note that the registrar is a certain A. James of whom I know nothing, though strangely I find it rather pleasing that he too is a James. Names to me matter.

This brings me to my Uncle Salty. I did indeed have such an uncle, and the few times that I met him I liked him, further I believe he took to me too. He told me a bit of a dirty rhyme whilst I sat on his knee, great fumes of beer and smoke off the man. The rhyme wasn't really dirty except by infant school standards you must understand, entirely innocent if truth be told, but we shared this secret like the Crown Jewels and had a damn good laugh about it all. Uncle Salty was really called Joe and earned his nickname because he was always dry. He was a hard drinking miner and after he was pensioned off, he was a hard drinking pensioned miner who polished up his pit-boots till you could see your face in them good enough to take a cat-lick shave. Salty liked the ale, his mates and playing cards and such like down at the club. One day he walked in through the club doors, took bad and died. I did not go to his funeral. There are certain sections of the family I know not too well, for example, my cousin Adam is now a strapping lad of six foot or so, but the last I saw him was when he was nine and rather skinny. It is these gaps in family history that may salvage some of this nonsense for I cannot rule out a priori that what was posted to me was in fact authentic and not some elaborate piss-take, but more of that later.

Firstly, I must point out that my Great Uncle Salty was never called Walter and he never had such a thing as a jester. It is true to say that he did keep the papers for the study of a system that would reveal to him a soothfast way of winning the pools. Betimes, I entertain a vain fancy, wondering what he would be doing if he were still alive as regards the National Lottery. I can see him perhaps investing in a small PC and using something like Microsoft Excel programme to plot and predict the National Lottery results. This is an aside, barely worth further thought, save the mentioning of a small PC reminds me of the trouble that has befallen me regarding this project, or more specifically the trouble caused to me by the Internet.

I swore blind that I would never be connected to the Internet. I also swore blind that I would only use my computer for text, for my writing and not computer games, a vice I saw as being less socially acceptable than persistent masturbation in public places. (Within six months of buying my first PC I had up-graded and bought the whole anorak package, including some excellent games for wasting my life.) This though is getting off the point. The point is I linked up to the web, and how I do not know, but one day I found a rather large e-mail in my electronic pigeonhole from someone who purported to be my second cousin. This message if you haven't guessed was Part One. I read and was not impressed with what I read; neither the creative writing nor the letter from this long lost cousin excited my interest. Further disappointments were to ensue.

Several weeks later another large electronic package dropped in my lap – the second part. This was worse than the first, tiresomely written and so unstructured and idiosyncratic as to be unreadable. This second part was from a second lost cousin – what medication was this gaje on? I read, wished to send what I had read to the recycle bin, but did not. Something held me back.

I was at my Grandma's flat one time. On the wall, there is a montage of photographs of my distant kin. There is a picture of a young Uncle Joe, my Grandma's brother, and, maybe this is a vain fancy, but I thought that the auld charvo had a look of me or rather me him. Awful shy with the girls my Grandma says – he never married. Well, it's looking that I'll be left on the shelf myself and I have a wee Excel worksheet knocked up for plotting the lottery results, and lastly, as for the wee weakness, I'm a terrible man on the drink. Aye, there's a lot of me I think coming from the same stuff as made Salty. That night, after playing dominoes with my Grandma till ten past two in the morning, I dreamt about Great Uncle Joe, dreamt about Great Uncle George and his caravan and my Great Grandma looking at smuts in the fire blaze, making predictions and warning me against baiting her cat who was a bad 'un. The cousin thing, could all be an elaborate practical joke at my expense by friends of mine who ken a bit about me, but if it is not, if there is a chance that it is not, then I'll not erase what has been written and sent to me.

But why send it to me?

Sometime ago I won last place in a short story competition run by Stand magazine. This story I seem to remember got up a few folk's noses, which made me smile. Or, rather, it made Daithidh MacEochaidh smile. Daithidh MacEochaidh – what in hell's name is that?

It is Irish. I am an Englishman, a person who has spent most of his life in Yorkshire – more incongruity. To explain:-

I have spent some time in Donegal where I learnt a smattering of Gaedhilg Thir Chonaill. Later, I spent sometime in the Uists trying to learn a little Gaidhlig. In Ireland, in Gaelic speaking Ireland, I developed the habit of using a Gaelic translation of my name. Keogh is in fact a sad corruption of MacEochaidh, which roughly means, the son of the horse-rider. In Gaelic Scotland I continued with this practice. When I won last place I was living in An Tobha Mor – the result I was published under my Gaelic name. Thereafter, I have won a few more competitions, had poems published, done wee readings all under a name that few can pronounce; often I have had to introduce myself in Gaelic then read in broad Yorkshire. But what is the point of me telling you all this?

I think my very minor success or even lack of success on the writing front has been noted and talked about amongst family members, and as such, given the nature of tittle-tattle, distant branches have heard exaggerated rumours about my work. They think I am an author, a writer of repute – I am no such thing. But, this is not important, what is the case sometimes has less power to cause mischief than what people believe is true. I often think of the people in the Middle Ages being cupped and bled, a couple of pints a go, because after all what was six pints when it was believed a human body contained twenty-four good auld fashioned imperial pints?

I am straying off the point. Possibly, two distant cousins have sent me their work that distantly relates to my real Uncle Salty. Out of respect, I have tried to get it published. I do not like this work and I believe it to be unfinished and incomplete. Today, another e-mail arrived from cousin number one. He apologises for causing me so much trouble after arranging a publishing deal, but the end is all wrong. He now says that he has found the real ending which is jotted down in note form here:

Ron is on the ground, bleeding, dying. A policeman stands over him, bends down to try to staunch the blood, but it is of no use.

'Tell me who did it, son. The ambulance is coming, but it may not arrive in time. Tell me…You got insurance, son?'

Ron weakly shook his head.

'Tell me then, son, tell me quick. We'll claim on him or her or the company. It's your only chance, so tell.'

'No, officer. If I am going to die, telling you won't help. If I recover, then I'll deal with this myself, my own way.'

'No insurance?'

'Not a jot.'

The policeman rang through instructing the ambulance not to hurry. He leant down, whispered closely into Ron's ear. 'It's Arturo – Arturo did it?'

Ron laughed a bubble of blood. Still laughing he spoke one last time, '…I am Arturo. I am travelling.'

After reading this I have no doubt that other e-mails shall be forthcoming, in particular from cousin number two. The author of part one has already hinted as much in his last message, which contained this rather worrying question, had I been sent the journal yet, the journal written on the planet of the Crions? I haven't. I can hardly wait.

For me though, this book is finished. I can do no more with it, to be honest I wish to wash my hands of the affair completely. This at last is the truth.

Yours sincerely

Daithidh MacEochaidh